EIGH

THE LAND OF STORIES

WORLDS COLLIDE

THE LAND OF STORIES

WORLDS COLLIDE

CHRIS COLFER

ILLUSTRATED BY BRANDON DORMAN

LITTLE, BROWN BOOKS FOR YOUNG READERS
www.lbkids.co.uk

LITTLE, BROWN BOOKS FOR YOUNG READERS

First published in the US in 2017 by Little, Brown and Company
First published in Great Britain in 2017 by Hodder and Stoughton

1 3 5 7 9 10 8 6 4 2

A CIP catalogue record for this book
is available from the British Library.

ISBN 978-1-510-20134-7

Printed and bound in Great Britain by
Clays Ltd, St Ives plc

The paper and board used in this book are made from
wood from responsible sources.

Little, Brown Books for Young Readers
An imprint of
Hachette Children's Group
Part of Hodder and Stoughton
Carmelite House
50 Victoria Embankment
London EC4Y 0DZ

An Hachette UK Company
www.hachette.co.uk

www.hachettechildrens.co.uk

To Rob, Alla, and Alvina.
The Land of Stories would never
have happened without your
guidance, passion, and grammar lessons.

And to readers across the world.
I'll cherish the adventures we've shared
for the rest of my life.
Thanks for being my happily ever after.
Let's never grow up together.

"IF YOU WANT A HAPPY ENDING, THAT DEPENDS, OF COURSE, ON WHERE YOU STOP YOUR STORY."

—ORSON WELLES

A BIRTHDAY CELEBRATION

Bookworm Paradise had never been so crowded. Over a thousand guests were cramped inside the bookstore's event space, until there were no more open chairs and no standing room left. A small stage was flooded with light and set with two chairs and two microphones for the evening's program. It was difficult to see over the row of journalists and photographers crouched in front of the stage, but the attendees were assured the press would only be there for the first few minutes of the event.

The multigenerational crowd had come to the bookstore to see their favorite author in the flesh. The guests fidgeted as they stood and squirmed in their seats as they anxiously waited for him to make his first public appearance in years. Not only were they there to celebrate the writer's five-decades-long career, but the event was also marking a very special day in the author's life. A colorful banner painted by students from the local elementary school hung above the stage that said HAPPY 80TH BIRTHDAY, MR. BAILEY!

Just as the bookstore promised, at eight o'clock sharp a man in a chic suit stepped onstage and the evening's festivities began.

"Good evening, ladies and gentlemen, and welcome to Bookworm Paradise," the man said into a microphone. "I'm Gregory Quinn from the *New York Times Book Review* and I couldn't be more honored to be moderating tonight's event. We're all here to celebrate a man who has made the world a much more magical place, thanks to over a hundred published works of children's fiction."

The crowd cheered at the mention of Mr. Bailey's

accomplished career. All the author's books could be found in the audience as the guests held their favorite titles close to their hearts.

"As I look around the room, I'm very pleased to see such a diverse group of people," Mr. Quinn continued. "Mr. Bailey has always said his greatest accomplishment isn't the number of books he's written or the number of copies sold, but the rich diversity of his readership. I can't think of a better testament to his work than knowing it's enjoyed by families all over the world."

Many people in the audience placed a hand over their chests as they remembered the joy the author had brought them over the years. Some even became teary-eyed recalling what an impact Mr. Bailey's stories had had on their young lives. Luckily, they'd found his work when they needed a good story the most.

"It's hard to find someone who doesn't smile at the mention of his name," Mr. Quinn went on. "Mr. Bailey filled our childhoods with adventure and suspense, his characters taught us the difference between right and wrong, and his stories showed us that the imagination is the most powerful weapon in the world. You know someone is special when the whole world considers them family, so now, let's remind him just how special he is. Ladies and gentlemen, boys and girls, please give a warm welcome to the one and only *Mr. Conner Jonathan Bailey.*"

The seated guests leaped to their feet and the event space filled with thunderous applause. The photographers raised their cameras and covered the stage in quick pulsating flashes.

An adorable and skinny old man slowly made his way onto the stage and waved at the excited audience. He had big eyes the color of the sky and messy white hair that sat on his head like a fluffy cloud. He wore thick glasses, bright blue suspenders, and neon-red sneakers. From the way he dressed and the mischievous twinkle in his eyes, it was clear that Mr. Bailey was just as colorful as the characters in his books.

Mr. Quinn tried to help the author into his seat, but the old man waved the attempt off, insisting he didn't need assistance. Even after Mr. Bailey sat down, the crowd continued to shower him with their affectionate applause.

"Thank you, thank you, thank you," Mr. Bailey said into his microphone. "You're too kind, but it's probably best you stop clapping so we can get on with the show. I'm eighty years old—time is of the essence."

The crowd laughed and took their seats, each sitting a little more on edge than before.

"We can't thank you enough for joining us, Mr. Bailey," Mr. Quinn said.

"I'm delighted to have the opportunity," the author said. "And thank *you*, Mr. Quinn, for such a lovely introduction. I didn't realize you were talking about me until I heard my full name. After all those compliments, I was afraid the store had booked the wrong Mr. Bailey."

"The praise was all for you, sir," the moderator reassured him. "First things first: Happy birthday! It's such a privilege to celebrate this milestone with you."

"You've got to dig deep to find dirt older than me," Mr. Bailey joked. "It's funny, when I was young there was nothing I looked forward to more than my birthday. Nowadays, with every passing year, I feel more and more like an expired can of beans that God forgot to toss out."

"I don't believe that for a second," Mr. Quinn said. "Every time I hear your name mentioned, it's always followed with a comment about your impressive stamina. Do you have any secrets for staying in shape or how you keep your energy up?"

"As you get older, it's important to select the shape you most identify with, and as you can see, I've chosen a squash," Mr. Bailey teased. "When it comes to maintaining a good energy level, I simply make the most out of the four hours a day I'm awake."

A cheeky grin spread across the author's face, and the audience roared with laughter. They were pleased to hear him speak with the same trademark wit he wrote with.

"We're also joined tonight by Mr. Bailey's family," Mr. Quinn said, and gestured to the people sitting in the front row. "Thank you for sharing your father and grandfather with us. Mr. Bailey, would you like to introduce your children and grandchildren?"

"I'd be happy to," Mr. Bailey said. "That's my older daughter, Elizabeth, her husband, Ben, and their daughter, Charlie. Next we have my son, Matthew, his husband, Henry, and their boys, Ayden and Grayson. Last but certainly not least, my daughter Carrie, her husband, Scott, and their children, Brighton, Sammy, and Levi. As you can see, they're all adopted—a bunch that good-looking couldn't possibly share my DNA."

The audience chuckled and gave the author's family a warm round of applause, forcing them to stand and wave bashfully.

"We were very saddened to hear of your wife's passing earlier this year," Mr. Quinn said. "As most of our audience knows, Mr. Bailey's wife, Breanne Campbell-Bailey, was also an accomplished writer and served as a United States senator for twenty-four years until her retirement."

"Would you believe we were middle school sweethearts?" Mr. Bailey said with a smile. "As far as I'm concerned, I was the first and only mistake she ever made."

"How long were you married?" Mr. Quinn asked.

"Fifty-two years," Mr. Bailey said. "She insisted on finishing her master's degree before marriage and publishing her fifth book before starting a family."

"I'm not surprised," Mr. Quinn said. "The late senator was a major advocate for women's rights."

"Yes, but I must clarify, Bree was never *late* for anything," the author said with a laugh. "She did absolutely everything on her own time, and her death was no exception. But in my family we don't say *died* or *passed away*, we say *returned to magic*—it suits her much better. Before she returned to magic, my wife hid thousands of notes in our home for me to find after she was gone. Not a day goes by I don't discover a Post-it reminding me to take my medicine or eat breakfast."

"Magic indeed," Mr. Quinn said. "You were both born and raised in Willow Crest, California. Is that correct?"

"That's right," Mr. Bailey said with a nod. "And what a different world it was. Paper came from trees, cars ran on gasoline, and caffeine was legal. It was practically the Dark Ages."

"Can you remember the first person who inspired you to write?" the moderator asked.

"It was my sixth-grade teacher, Mrs. Peters," the author said. "At first we didn't see eye-to-eye; she thought her classroom was a place for education, I thought it was a great place for naps. A year later she became principal of the middle school and read some short stories I had written for my English class. Mrs. Peters saw potential in my writing and planted the seeds in my head. I'll always be so grateful to her. I dedicated one of my books to her—but I can't recall which one."

"It's *Fairytaletopia 4: The Literary Journey!*" shouted an excited little girl in the back row.

"Oh yes, that's the one," Mr. Bailey said, and scratched his head. "You'll have to be patient with me; my memory has been on vacation since my early seventies. These days I'll pick up a book and read the whole thing without realizing I wrote it."

"Speaking of which, let's talk about your remarkable writing career," Mr. Quinn said. "As I said before, you've published more than a hundred books over the course of five decades. Among those are the Starboardia sagas, the Adventures of Blimp Boy mysteries, the Galaxy Queen chronicles, the Ziblings graphic novels, and most notably, the Fairytaletopia series."

The crowd cheered the loudest at the mention of Mr. Bailey's fantasy series, Fairytaletopia. The author's six-book franchise was the most successful and acclaimed publication of his career. The series had been translated into fifty languages, was sold in over a hundred countries, and had helped improve children's literacy around the world. The Fairytaletopia books had also been adapted into several major motion pictures, a dozen television shows, and countless items of tacky merchandise.

"Although the majority of your work has been bestsellers and critical hits, you're most known for writing Fairytaletopia," Mr. Quinn said. "What is the special ingredient that makes that series so beloved?"

"That's an easy answer. It was written by a child," Mr. Bailey confessed. "Not many people know this, but I finished the first draft of *Fairytaletopia: The Wishing Charm* when I was about thirteen years old. I was very embarrassed about writing, so I kept it a secret; I didn't even show it to my family. Later, in my twenties, after a few mild literary successes, I came across a dusty old manuscript in my mother's attic. I brushed it off, fixed some typos, and had it published. Had I known what a hit it would be I would have pursued it much sooner."

"How interesting," Mr. Quinn said. "So you're saying the series is successful with children because it was conceived by one."

"Precisely," Mr. Bailey said. "Children will always be drawn to stories written in their own language. And as children's authors, it's our job never to lose touch with that language."

"You've had plenty of opportunities to write for adults, but you've always stayed in the realm of middle grade. Why do you enjoy writing for children?"

"I suppose I just like children more than I like

adults," the author said with a shameless shrug. "No matter how much the world evolves, the children of the world will never change. Every child is born with the same need for love, respect, and understanding. They're unified by the same fears, compassion, and convictions. They're tormented by an endless curiosity, a thirst for knowledge, and a desire for adventure. The greatest tragedy in life is how soon children get robbed of these qualities. We could accomplish great things if we held on to such a fresh point of view. Think about how wonderful this world could be if we all saw it through the eyes of a child."

"What would your advice be for aspiring authors?" Mr. Quinn asked.

It was a very important question to the author, and he went silent for a moment while he thought of a worthy answer.

"Always let the world inspire and influence you, but never let it discourage you. In fact, the more the world discourages you, the more it needs you. As writers we have the profound privilege and responsibility to create a new world when the current one takes a turn for the worse. Storytellers are more than just entertainers; we're the shepherds of ideology, the street pavers of progress, and the scientists of the soul.

If it weren't for people like us, who imagine a better world and are brave enough to question and stand up to the authorities that suppress them...well, we'd still be living in the Dark Ages I was born into."

It became so quiet the crowd could hear the ticking of a clock. At first the author was afraid he had said something to upset the audience, but once they'd had a few seconds to process his words, the event space erupted into another thunderous round of applause.

"I'm afraid to follow that answer with another question, so why don't we open the questions to our audience members?" Mr. Quinn proposed.

Nearly all the hands in the room shot up at once. Mr. Bailey chuckled at the sight, tickled by how many people wanted to ask a question of an old geezer like him.

"Let's start with the woman in the brown shirt," Mr. Quinn said.

"The Starboardia series is much darker than most of your work, especially the history about American slavery. Were you worried that might be too much for your younger audience?"

"Not once," Mr. Bailey said. "I will never sugarcoat

history so that certain people sleep better at night. The more we shed light on the problems of the world, past and present, the easier it will be to fix them."

"Now let's go to the boy in the front," Mr. Quinn said.

"How many of your characters are based on yourself?"

"All of them—especially the villains," Mr. Bailey said with a wink.

"Now we'll go to the young man in the middle," Mr. Quinn said.

"What inspired you to write the Fairytaletopia series?"

The mischievous twinkle in the author's eye grew so bright, it practically shined like a searchlight.

"Would you believe me if I told you it was all auto-biographical?" he said.

The crowd giggled, and Mr. Bailey's children collectively sighed at their father's remark—not *this* again. However, Mr. Bailey's twinkle never faded. He looked around the room as if he was disappointed the audience wasn't taking the answer as seriously as the others.

"It's true," he said with conviction. "This world is

full of magic if you choose to see it, but it's a choice I can't make for you."

The comment inspired a little girl in the third row to stand on her seat and wave her hand energetically in the air. Whatever her question was, she was more desperate to ask it than anyone else in the room.

"Yes, the young lady wearing pigtails," Mr. Quinn said.

"Hello, Mr. Bailey," she said. "My name is Annie and I love your books. I've read all six Fairytaletopia books a dozen times each."

"I appreciate that more than words could describe," the author said. "What's your question?"

"Well, it has to do with what you just said, about Fairytaletopia being true," she said. "Everyone knows Fairytaletopia is about a pair of twins who travel into the fairy-tale world, but I bet a lot of people don't know you're a twin yourself. I looked you up online and saw you have a sister named Alex. So I assume you based Alec and Connie Baxter from Fairytaletopia on you and your sister."

The question took Mr. Bailey off guard. His readers were usually so invested in the worlds he wrote about that they rarely asked him questions about his personal life, especially ones about his family.

"That is both creepy and correct, Annie," Mr. Bailey said. "I'd say you have what it takes to be a private investigator some—"

"That's not my question," the girl said. "According to my research, Alex Bailey attended school in Willow Crest until the seventh grade, but then she vanishes from all public records. I've looked everywhere but can't find a single document about where she went or what became of her after that. So I guess my question is less about the books and more about your sister. Whatever happened to Alex?"

The world-renowned author went dead silent and the twinkle faded from his eye. He was shocked, not because of the question, but because he couldn't remember the answer. He searched every corner of his patchy memory, but he couldn't recall where his sister was or the last time he had spoken to her. The only memories coming to mind were from when Alex was a teenager, but he refused to believe that was the last time he'd seen her. He was certain he'd had some communication with Alex since then. She couldn't just have disappeared, as the girl in pigtails claimed...or could she?

"I...I..." Mr. Bailey mumbled as he tried to focus.

It was obvious something was wrong, and the crowd began to shift in their seats. When the author realized his audience was growing uncomfortable, he laughed at their reactions like he was only playing a joke on them.

"Well, it's a simple answer," he said. "What happened to Connie at the end of Fairytaletopia?"

He phrased the question like he was playing a trivia game with the young girl—but secretly, the author couldn't remember the conclusion of his beloved series, either. Trying to recall the whereabouts of his sister made him realize how much information was missing from his memory.

"She and Alec both had a happily ever after," Annie said.

"Did they?" the author asked. "I mean, *of course* they did! Then *that's* your answer."

"But, Mr. Bailey—"

"Well, this has been a wonderful evening, but I have to cut it short," the author said. "I would love to stay and answer all your questions, but my four hours of consciousness are almost up."

The author yawned and stretched like he was tired, but it wasn't a convincing performance. In truth, the mental void had terrified him, and he didn't know how much longer he could keep his fear from surfacing. Mr. Bailey always made jokes about his fading memory, but it wasn't until tonight that he'd realized it wasn't a laughing matter.

Later that evening, once his children had dropped him off at home and made sure he was settled, Mr. Bailey searched his house for any clues he could find leading to his sister's location, but he found nothing— not even a photograph. His children already treated him like a toddler, so he was afraid to ask one of them what had happened to her. For peace of mind, he had to find her on his own.

The author could envision every detail of his sister's face. Her pale skin, her rosy cheeks, her pale blue eyes, the freckles on the bridge of her nose, and her long strawberry-blonde hair were instantly accessible every time he closed his eyes and thought of her. However, this was how Alex had looked in her youth. She most certainly would have been an old woman by now—so why couldn't he picture it?

"Oh, Alex, where did you go?" he said to himself.

Mr. Bailey knew only one thing could jump-start his memory. He locked himself in his study and searched his bookshelves until he found copies of the Fairytaletopia series. Just as he'd told the audience at the bookstore, all six books were based on true events he and his sister had experienced when they were much younger. If he couldn't recall the information on his own, perhaps one of his stories would trigger the memories for him.

Mr. Bailey eagerly pulled the first Fairytaletopia book off the shelf, but remembering the events that inspired each book wasn't as easy as he thought it would be.

"Think, old man, think!" he said. "*Fairytaletopia: The Wishing Charm* was about our first trip to the fairy-tale world. . . . We were collecting something. . . . There were things we needed to get back home. . . . *Oh, I know—the Wishing Spell!* Our dad's journal helped us navigate and find all the items! We were chased by the Big Bad Wolf Pack and barely survived our encounter with the Evil Queen! That's also the year we met Froggy, Red, Jack, and Goldilocks!"

The old man was so excited to retrieve these memories that he jumped in the air and his back cracked, reminding him he was too old to be doing such movements. He put the first book in his series aside and moved on to the sequel.

"*Fairytaletopia 2: The Evil Fairy's Revenge,*" he read. "What on earth was that about? *Wait, that was the year the Enchantress returned!* We flew all over the fairy-tale world in a flying ship called the *Granny*! Alex defeated the Enchantress by taking away her pride! Boy, was she brilliant for doing that. That was the same year we met Mother Goose and Mom married Bob."

The second remembrance gave him a boost of confidence, and he eagerly moved on to the third book in the series.

"*Fairytaletopia 3: The Long-Lost Army,*" he read. "*That must be based on the Grande Armée that tried conquering the fairy-tale world!* The soldiers were trapped in a portal for over two hundred years, thanks to Mother Goose and the Brothers Grimm! Our uncle joined them and found a dragon egg! He raised the beast and our grandmother slayed it right before she returned to magic! Wow, I can't believe our mother let us out of the house after that one."

As he moved on to the fourth and fifth books, the memories began to flow so freely he had trouble keeping up with them. It was like a tropical rainstorm had formed in the middle of a terrible drought.

"*Fairytaletopia 4: The Literary Journey* was when Alex and I chased Uncle Lloyd through the worlds of classic literature! We would have stopped him sooner if he hadn't separated us into Camelot and Robin Hood. *Fairytaletopia 5: A Storyteller's Quest* was when we traveled into my short stories! We accidentally went inside Bree's writing, and our uncle Lloyd was trapped in the Cemetery of the Undead! We rushed back to the hospital to tell Alex what had happened, but when we arrived, she was gone...."

The author pulled the sixth and final book in his series off his shelf and stared down at the cover.

"*Fairytaletopia 6: The Great New York Adventure,*" he read.

Unfortunately, the title didn't trigger a memory like the rest of the books had. Mr. Bailey tried as hard as he could to remember what the book was about and the events that had inspired it, but he drew a blank at every turn. The answer might have escaped him completely, but he knew that the information he craved was somewhere inside the book. Even if he had misled his readers to a false happy ending, he was certain he could read between the lines and discover the truth.

So the beloved children's book author took a deep breath, opened his own book to the very first page, and began reading, hoping with all his heart that the story would remind him where his sister had gone all those years ago....

CHAPTER ONE

DISTRESS CALL FROM THE PUBLIC LIBRARY

I t was a typical afternoon at the main branch of the New York Public Library. The marble halls of the world-famous structure echoed with the footsteps of obnoxious tourists, restless college students, and noisy groups of elementary school students on field trips. Tour guides shared little-known facts about the library's expansive history and refrained from rolling their eyes at questions about the movies that had been filmed there. Librarians gave directions to the renowned reading rooms on the upper floors and reminded the guests that library books weren't allowed in the bathrooms.

There was absolutely nothing to suggest that anything strange or peculiar might occur later that evening, but strange and peculiar events rarely give any warning before they happen.

Security guard Rudy Lewis began his four-PM-to-midnight shift by patrolling the library's entrance on Fifth Avenue. He yelled at teenagers for climbing Patience and Fortitude, the iconic lion statues that flanked the library's sprawling front steps. He kindly asked the homeless people sleeping beside the fountains to continue their naps at the shelter down the street, and once they obliged, he went *back* to the statues to yell at a new gang of teenagers for climbing them. Once the library closed and was cleared out, Rudy spent the rest of his shift patrolling the interior.

For hours and hours Rudy walked up and down the vacant halls of the four-level structure, inspecting its various forums, galleries, studies, and stairwells. Five minutes before the end of his shift, he was positive there wasn't another soul in the library and was eager to hand his duties off to the next security guard.

But as he made his final inspection of the third floor, Rudy discovered he was mistaken.

At the end of a long, dark hallway, the security guard found a young woman standing alone. She wore a sparkling white dress and had strawberry-blonde hair, and her head was bowed as if she had fallen asleep standing up. At first, the sight of the young woman startled Rudy. He had walked past this part of the library a dozen times and hadn't seen anyone before now. It was like the young woman had appeared out of thin air.

"Excuse me," he said. "What are you doing?"

The young woman didn't respond.

"Hey, I'm talking to you," Rudy said.

The angry security guard shined his flashlight on the young woman to get her attention, but she didn't move. Once she was illuminated, Rudy could see that she was trembling and her skin was as pale as a ghost's. For a split second, he worried that she *was* a ghost. His co-workers had always warned him that the library was haunted, but until now, he'd had no reason to believe them.

"The library's closed." Rudy's voice cracked as he spoke. "Unless you're an employee, you're trespassing on city property."

Still the young woman neither looked up nor said a word. Her silence was making Rudy paranoid. The longer he stood in her presence, the creepier the young woman became. The fate of every security guard in every horror film flashed before Rudy's eyes, but he mustered the courage to approach the strange young woman.

"I'm gonna call the police if you don't say something!"

Suddenly, the young woman gasped and jerked her head up, causing Rudy to jump. She frantically looked around in a panic as if waking from a bad dream.

"Where am I?" she panted.

"You're at the library," Rudy said, but that only confused her more.

"The library? *Which* library?"

"The New York Public Library at Fifth Avenue and East Forty-Second Street," Rudy said.

"Oh no!" the young woman cried. "You have to get out of here! Something terrible is about to happen!"

"What are you talking about? How did you even get in here?"

"I don't know what she has planned, but you've got to go before she makes me hurt you!" the young woman pleaded. *"Please, you have to listen to me! I can't control it!"*

Tears spilled out of her blue eyes and rolled down her face.

"Who are you talking about?" Rudy asked. "No one is in here but me and you."

"The witch who cursed me! She put me under some kind of spell that makes me do things—awful things!"

"Lady, you're clearly on a lot of drugs," Rudy said. "I'm taking you outside and calling the cops."

"You have to get my brother! He's the only one who can help! His name is Conner Bailey—he should be at Saint Andrew's Children's Hospital in Willow Crest—"

"Yeah, yeah, yeah," Rudy said, and grabbed her arm. "This city is full of places that help people like you, but you can't stay here."

The security guard tried to escort her to the exit, but the young woman wouldn't budge. He pulled on her arm with all his might, but she stayed exactly where she was, as if she were glued to the floor.

"It's too late!" the young woman said. "The spell—I feel it coming! The witch must be close! *Please, you have to run!*"

To the security guard's horror, the young woman's eyes rolled back and began to glow. Her hair rose above her head and floated in the air like a slow-flickering fire. In all his years in security, Rudy had never seen anything like this before.

"What the heck is happening to you?"

The young woman placed a palm on his chest, and a bright blast erupted from her hand, knocking him all the way down the hall. As Rudy lay on the floor, his whole body tingled as if he had just been electrocuted. His vision was blurry and fading fast. With all his remaining strength and in the few moments of consciousness he had left, Rudy reached for his radio and held it against his mouth.

"Police..." he wheezed. *"We need police at the library...NOW!"*

Within minutes, Fifth Avenue was illuminated by red and blue lights as two police cars sped toward the library. A policeman emerged from the first vehicle and a policewoman from the second. The officers hurried up the front steps with their guns raised.

"I just got the call. What's the situation?" the policewoman asked.

"We don't know," said the policeman. "A distress call came from somewhere inside the library. Approach with caution."

"Oh my God." The policewoman gasped. *"Look!"*

The officer pointed to the library's entrance as the large doors slowly opened on their own. A moment later the young woman in the white dress levitated through the doorway and landed at the top of the library's front steps. Even in New York City, the police weren't accustomed to seeing someone with glowing eyes and floating hair flying out of a building. Once the initial shock faded, the officers knelt behind a lion statue and aimed their weapons at her.

"Hands up!" the policeman ordered.

The young woman didn't follow his instructions. Instead, she pointed at the statues and two powerful bolts of lightning struck the lions. The police dived to the ground to avoid getting hit.

"What was that?" the policeman asked.

"Lightning!" said the policewoman. "But I don't understand. There aren't any clouds in the sky!"

Once the officers helped each other to their feet,

they jerked their heads toward a strange cracking noise coming from the statues. They watched in astonishment as the stone lions stood up from their perches, leaped into the air, and landed on the steps in front of the young woman, blocking the officers from coming any closer. The statues roared so loudly, they set off all the car alarms within a block.

"Holy crap," the policeman said. "*The statues are alive!* How is this possible?"

The policewoman clicked the radio on her shoulder. "Officer Sanchez to Dispatch," she said. "The library is under attack, I repeat, the library is under attack! We need all available units to join us immediately!"

"Copy, Officer Sanchez," a voice responded over the radio. "All available units have been notified. Are you able to identify who or what is behind the attack?"

Still in disbelief, the policewoman hesitated to respond.

"It's *magic*," she said breathlessly. "*The library is being attacked by magic!*"

CHAPTER TWO

ACCIDENTAL YET UNEXPLAINABLE

The Willow Crest Fire Department had never seen an incident like the one at Saint Andrew's Children's Hospital. The fire-fighters were called in the middle of the night to view the damage from a reported explosion, but when they arrived, they had no idea what they were looking at. There weren't any flames to extinguish, there was hardly any debris to clear, and the remaining walls of the hospital weren't blackened or singed by the alleged blast. As far as they could tell, the women's bathroom hadn't *exploded* as much as it had *vanished*.

"It's not damaged, it's just *missing*," one firefighter said to another. "If there had been an explosion, this place would be covered in bits of porcelain, but there's not a piece of the bathroom anywhere."

"The hospital staff swears a fully functional bathroom was right here just a few hours ago," the second firefighter said. "If it wasn't an explosion, what could have removed it so quickly?"

The firefighters asked around the hospital, but no one had witnessed the phenomenon, further complicating the strange situation. They checked the grounds surrounding the hospital in case the bathroom had been detached by some type of tractor, but there were no tracks on the ground.

"What should I put on the report?" the first firefighter asked the second. "The hospital's insurance company is going to need something from us, but I can't exactly say the bathroom got up and walked away."

"Write *accidental yet unexplainable*," the second firefighter said. "I think this case is above our pay grade. They're going to need an investigation to get to the bottom of this—a *thorough* investigation."

With no further assessments to make, the firefighters taped off the area and gave the hospital manager the contact information for a destruction investigator who lived in the next town. The specialist wasn't available for another week, so the missing bathroom remained a giant and mysterious hole until his arrival.

The scene was completely untouched until midnight on the eve of the inspector's visit. A fifteen-year-old young man stepped over the yellow tape and had a seat in the doorway that led to nowhere. His eyes were baggy, his heart was heavy, and he hunched as if the weight of the world rested on his shoulders. Deep in thought, he gazed through the large hole at the buildings of downtown Willow Crest in the distance.

The young man had hoped that if he returned to the missing bathroom, it might provide answers to the questions haunting him. Unfortunately, all the answers had disappeared with the bathroom.

"Hey, Conner!"

A sixteen-year-old young woman suddenly peeked into the hospital from outside, almost giving Conner a heart attack. She wore a purple beanie and had blonde hair with a streak of pink and blue at the front.

"Bree!" Conner said. "What are you doing here? I thought you were grounded for running away."

"Oh, I *am*," Bree said. "I'm not allowed to leave the house until college. I've never seen my parents so furious. As far as they know, I just snuck off to visit family in Connecticut. I can't imagine how they'd react if they knew we flew to Germany and back."

"What if you get caught sneaking out?" Conner asked.

"Don't worry, I won't," Bree said. "I've been sneaking out of the house since I was eight. I put a wax head on my pillow and leave a cassette playing of someone snoring in case my parents check my bedroom."

"That's both impressive and scary," Conner said.

Bree shrugged. "It's just like Laurel Thatcher Ulrich said. *'Well-behaved women seldom make history.'*"

She climbed into the hospital, carefully stepping on the remaining floorboards so she didn't fall into the basement below, and had a seat next to Conner in the doorway.

"You weren't home, so I figured I'd find you here," she said.

"I wanted to take one last look at the damage before the inspector starts digging around tomorrow," he said. "You know, just in case there was something we missed."

"Any luck finding Alex?"

"Not at all," Conner said with a sigh. "It's been a week since she disappeared and we haven't found a single clue to where she went. My mom and step-dad have looked all over town, but there's no sign of her. Jack, Red, and Lester are searching the fairy-tale world as we speak, but so far they haven't returned with anything."

"It's so bizarre," Bree said. "I barely know her, but it seems so out of character for her to run off like that. Has she done anything like this before?"

Conner's knee-jerk reaction was to defend his sister's reputation, but the more he thought about it, the more he remembered it wasn't entirely unlike her to go missing.

"Sort of," he recalled. "Alex went through this weird phase not too long ago. She would get over-whelmed about something and lose control of her powers. But the circumstances were so different—she was really stressed out and easy to provoke."

"What was she stressed out about?"

"It was back when we were searching the fairy-tale world for our uncle Lloyd," he explained. "All her hunches about him were right, but no one wanted to believe her. The Fairy Council thought she was becoming reckless, so they ordered her to stop looking for him. Alex got so upset, she disappeared into a ball of flames, but she resurfaced a couple of days later."

"Oh," Bree said. "So maybe it *isn't* out of character."

"Disappearing, maybe, but she's not the type who abandons her friends in their hour of need," Conner said. "Things were finally looking up for a change. We had *just* recruited all the characters from my stories. We were *finally* ready to fight the Literary Army in the fairy-tale world. So why would she vanish now? It makes no sense."

"The detective in me wants to believe your uncle had something to do with it, especially if he was the reason behind her previous outbursts," Bree said. "But Emmerich and I were with him the entire time he was in the Otherworld. Alex never laid eyes on him. If she was provoked, it was by someone else."

Conner nodded. "And that's what I've been trying to figure out."

Alex's behavior puzzled them as much as the vanished bathroom puzzled the fire department, and just like the firefighters, they knew they were missing a piece of the story. Unfortunately, there was no specialist *they* could call to help them solve Alex's disappearance.

"How are all the characters doing?" Bree asked.

"They're a little stir-crazy from being cooped up in the commissary," Conner said. "We have to let them outside for fresh air in shifts so no one around here gets suspicious. Bob has been teaching the Merry Men and the Lost Boys how to play football at the park to burn off some energy. My mom has rewrapped all the mummies with fresh bandages, so the commissary smells a lot better. The Cyborgs have blown every fuse in the hospital from using the outlets too much. The Ziblings have been patrolling downtown at night to get their hero fix, so the city's crime rate has gone down. And the Starboardia pirates found a television and have been watching *I Love Lucy* reruns non-stop—it annoys everyone else, but at least it keeps them occupied."

"I'm glad everyone's hanging in there," Bree said. "I can't imagine what it's like for you. Being in the Cemetery of the Undead for a couple of hours was surreal enough for me, but you've been surrounded by your creations for days. It's got to feel like a trippy family reunion."

"Once you've seen your elderly grandmother slay a dragon, everything else pales in comparison." Conner laughed. "Speaking of family reunions, did Cornelia and Emmerich get to Germany safely? It was so kind of her to offer him a ride home."

"Thankfully," Bree said. "Cornelia said Emmerich and Frau Himmelsbach were very happy to be reunited. They're also moving to Australia to get as far away from Neuschwanstein Castle as possible. Wanda and Frenda had been stranded in Bavaria since your uncle Lloyd kidnapped us, so Cornelia picked them up and they flew back to Connecticut yesterday."

"I was amazed at how well Cornelia handled it all," Conner said. "Usually people freak out when they learn about other dimensions, but she barely flinched."

Bree forced a smile and nodded—she hadn't been completely honest with Conner. He knew Bree was in Connecticut when she learned Emmerich had been kidnapped, he knew Cornelia had generously offered to fly Bree to Germany so they could help Emmerich's mother look for him, and he knew they happened to be in Neuschwanstein Castle when Uncle Lloyd brought Emmerich back to the Otherworld. However, Conner had been so overwhelmed by Alex's disappearance, Bree thought it was best to leave out the other details.

She never mentioned *why* she had gone to visit her family in Connecticut—that she'd discovered they were part of a secret league known as the Sisters Grimm, or their extensive history of tracking portals into the fairy-tale world. Bree hoped a better time would present itself to fill Conner in, but the longer Alex was gone, the more inappropriate it became.

"At Cornelia's age, there's not a whole lot that shocks her," Bree said. "In fact, when you get a minute, I'd love to tell you more about my trip to her—"

Bree was interrupted by the sound of footsteps coming from the hallway behind them. A moment later, Trollbella appeared in the doorway of the missing bathroom. The young troll queen immediately crossed her arms and scowled at the sight of Bree and Conner in the same location.

"Well, you can lead a horse to water, but you can't keep her away from your man," Trollbella quipped.

Conner rolled his eyes. "What do you want, Trollbella?"

"I came to let you know that Beansprout, the Frog Mistress, and Plucky McGee have returned," she said.

"Who?" Bree asked.

"She means that Jack, Red, and Lester are back from the fairy-tale world," Conner said, and quickly jumped to his feet. "Maybe they know something about Alex! Trollbella, will you let my mom and Bob know? They're working a night shift on the third floor."

"I am *not* your errand girl, Butterboy," Trollbella said. "There'll be no more favors between us until you're ready to commit."

"Fine," Conner said. "*Bree*, will you please get my mom and Bob—"

"*Fine*, I'll fetch my Butter-in-laws," Trollbella said. "But please stop begging—I hate seeing how vulnerable you've become without me."

Conner and Bree ran down the hall toward the commissary as Trollbella fetched Charlotte and Bob. They found all their friends from Oz, Neverland, the Sherwood Forest, *The Land of Stories*, and Conner's short stories "The Adventures of Blimp Boy," "The Ziblings," and "Galaxy Queen" huddled around Jack and Red. The only ones who weren't paying attention to their arrival were the pirates from "Starboardia," who never looked away from the television.

"Are they *still* watching that ditzy woman?" Red asked. "The Otherworld may be advanced, but it sure leads to some awful habits."

"Well?" Conner asked, getting straight to the point. "Did you find my sister?"

Jack slowly shook his head. "No," he said. "We looked at all the places we thought she would be—the ruins of the Fairy Palace, the Giant's Castle in the sky, the clock tower of the Charming Palace—but we didn't find a trace of her."

The news was so disappointing, Conner had to sit down. If Alex wasn't in the fairy-tale world, he didn't know where else to look. His train of thought shifted from thinking of places she might be to worrying she'd never be found.

"I'm sorry you didn't find Alex, but I'm so glad you're back," Goldilocks told Jack as she cradled their newborn son. "It's a miracle you weren't spotted, even at Lester's heights."

Jack went to his wife's side and kissed Hero on the forehead. Red gave Goldilocks a large hug from behind, as if the sentiment were meant for her.

"Goldilocks, you're back on your feet!" Red

pointed out. "Is it safe for you to be walking again so soon after giving birth?"

"Red, I had a baby, not a whale," Goldilocks said. "How is the fairy-tale world? Are the conditions any better?"

"It's exactly as we left it," Jack told the room. "The citizens from all the kingdoms are still being held in Swan Lake, if they're not building monuments to the emperors. The Literary Army is lined up on the lawns of the Northern Palace, but all they do is march all day—as if they're waiting for something to happen."

"It sounds like they're preparing for battle," Goldilocks said. "They couldn't be expecting us, could they?"

"I imagine it's just a scare tactic to keep the citizens from rebelling," Jack said. "They still haven't discovered the royal families in the abandoned mine, so I doubt they've caught wind of us. How could they?"

"And the others in the mine? Are they still... *made of stone*?" Goldilocks asked.

"Unfortunately so," Jack said. "Same goes for the Fairy Council."

"Oh, it was a terrible sight!" Red said, and

shuddered at the thought. "All their faces were frozen in the most unattractive expressions of terror. If someone turns me into stone, I hope they have the decency to tell me something amusing beforehand."

"What about the creature that did it?" the Tin Woodman asked. "Was there any sign of who or what it is?"

"They wouldn't be here if they had seen it," Blubo said, and recalled the terrifying moments he had spent in its presence. "All it took was one glance, and *boom!* Everyone went stiff as a rock. I wouldn't be here if my eyes hadn't been closed."

Commander Newters gulped fearfully and turned to Conner. "There are creatures that turn others into stone in the Land of Stories?" he asked.

"It didn't come from the fairy-tale world," Conner said. "It must have been a character my uncle recruited using the Portal Potion—I just don't know which story it's from."

"Does it have to be from literature?" Beau Rogers asked. "If I didn't know any better, I'd say you were talking about Medusa from Greek mythology."

"What's a Medusa?" Peter Pan asked.

"She's a *horrible* monster," Beau Rogers animatedly replied. "Legend says she has a long, scaly body, fangs, and snakes for hair! Just one gaze into her red eyes will turn you into a statue!"

The Lost Boys covered their eyes, ears, and mouths at the young archaeologist's frightening description. The Blissworm clapped its tiny hands together, anxious to meet her.

"DON'T WORRY, LADS," Robin Hood said. "I'VE COURTED MANY A MAIDEN WHO TURNED OUT TO BE FAR WORSE. WITH JUST A FEW VERSES OF A ROMANTIC POEM, SHE WILL BE PUTTY IN MY HANDS."

The Prince of Thieves didn't make anyone feel better about the situation, especially Conner. He got to his feet and started pacing around the room. A very difficult decision had to be made, and Conner couldn't delay it a moment longer.

"We can't waste any more time," he said. "Tomorrow we're going to fight the Literary Army and reclaim the fairy-tale world. I never thought we'd have to do it without my sister, but we can't let the people suffer any longer."

"Poor Alex," Red said. "There have been many times I've disappeared for some me time, but I always return after a couple of hours. I hope she'll resurface in time to help us. She put so much work into recruiting our army—it'd be a shame if she missed the war completely."

Suddenly, Goldilocks's face lit up with an idea. Red's nonsense always had a funny way of putting things into perspective for her.

"Hold your horses," Goldilocks said.

"Which horses?" the Tin Woodman asked.

"No, it's a figure of speech," Goldilocks said, and got back to her point. "We've been looking at the Literary Army and at Alex's disappearance like they're separate situations, but what if they're more related than we think? After all, we're *at war*—a war Alex is a key player in. It's very possible someone is using Alex to sabotage us. Perhaps it's time we stop asking *where Alex went* and start asking *who took her*."

Of all the directions Conner's mind had gone in the last week, this was a conclusion he'd never come to. His sister was so powerful and strong-minded; it was hard to imagine that someone could abduct her from the hospital without anyone noticing, especially someone from the Literary Army.

"They couldn't have taken Alex," Conner said. "Even if the Literary Army knew we existed, they have no way of accessing the Otherworld. Besides, I think one of us would have noticed a card soldier or flying monkey walking around."

"I didn't say it was the Literary Army," Goldilocks said. "In times of conflict, there's always the enemy *you know* and the enemy *you don't*. The Literary Army may be who we're up against, but who's the third party we're forgetting to consider? Who else would benefit if either of our armies was defeated?"

The whole commissary went quiet as all the characters thought it over. It was highly likely that they were leaving someone out of their equation, but who could it be? Who or what was just as invested in the upcoming war as they were? Who at that very moment was also assembling in secret and forming plans to dominate the fairy-tale world?

The answer hit Bree like a bolt of lightning. The realization made her gasp so loudly, all the characters jumped.

"I know!" she exclaimed. "We're forgetting about *the witches*! We know they have access to the Otherworld because one of them kidnapped Emmerich using the portal at Neuschwanstein Castle!"

"I think you're onto something!" Jack said. "Conner, do you remember the night we followed the Masked Man to the Witches' Brew? The witches were meeting because they were afraid they'd get blamed for the missing children—they were paranoid a witch hunt was coming. It's very likely they began plotting to take over the fairy-tale world as a way to protect themselves."

"Then the Masked Man invaded with the Literary Army," Goldilocks said. "The witches probably kidnapped Emmerich so they would have leverage against your uncle, so maybe they plan to use Alex as leverage against *us*!"

"Of course the witches are up to some vile scheme," Red said. "I mean, *they're witches*—hello! I wouldn't be surprised if that goat who took Charlie had something to do with it! The Lost Boys and I found the missing children in *her* basement—Morina probably kidnapped them to purposely stir up paranoia in the witch community so they had a *reason* to plot a take-over! I bet *she's* behind the whole thing!"

Everyone froze and looked at Red in shock. If she was correct, it was a little unsettling how easy it was for her to figure out Morina's intentions.

"Don't look at me like that," Red said. "It takes a conniving genius to know a conniving genius. Obviously, there's a type of woman Charlie's attracted to."

"But how could the witches know we're planning to

defeat the Literary Army? How do they know *we're* a threat?" Conner asked.

Bree looked at him like the answer was obvious.

"Conner, they figured out Emmerich was your cousin before you or your uncle did," she reminded him. "I'm sure it wouldn't be hard for a witch to look into a crystal ball and figure out what we're doing with a bunch of interdimensional beings inside a children's hospital!"

Unfortunately, it made sense. A witch could easily have crossed into the Otherworld and snuck into the hospital without being detected. They could have used magic to overpower Alex and take her back to the fairy-tale world as a hostage. Conner had prayed for a clear answer all week, but he'd never guessed how much it would complicate matters.

"Let's lay everything out on the table before we go any further," he said.

"Which table?" the Tin Woodman asked.

"*Also* a figure of speech," Conner said. "Not only do we have to liberate the fairy-tale world from the scariest villains in literature and slay a mythological creature before it turns us all into stone, but we also have to defeat an evil coven of witches before they use my sister against us."

All the characters in the commissary shared glances with wide, timid eyes. The Blissworm cheered—it couldn't wait for the battles to begin.

"I know what you're thinking," Conner said. "This is a much different fight than you signed up for. If the witches are involved, then we're easily outnumbered, especially if they have my sister. I was confident we could defeat the Literary Army, but I'm not sure we can win the war."

Conner rubbed his hands together, desperately trying to think of a way to get the odds back in their favor. Jack had a seat beside him and placed a hand on his friend's shoulder.

"For once, I'm with the Blissworm," Jack said. "We've seen a lot of scary situations over the years, but we've always gotten through them together. Yes, there were many times when a little of your sister's magic went a long way, but we would never have pulled through if it weren't for *both* of you. Now look around, Conner—you're surrounded by an army from *your* imagination! That means there's a piece of you inside each and every one of them, and even if it's just a fraction of your bravery, your aptitude, or even your wit—I know those bastards won't stand a chance against us."

It was the exact pep talk Conner needed to hear, and it also inspired all the characters in the commissary. Jack's words even made the pirates of "Starboardia" look up from the television for the first time in days.

"It'll be dangerous," Conner said.

"We love danger!" the Lost Boys shouted.

"Some of us may get hurt," Conner added.

"Speak for yourself," the Cyborg Queen said. "I can adjust *feelings* in Settings."

"And regardless of what happens, at the end of the day, we'll all be heroes!" Bolt said, and flipped through the air.

Conner couldn't help but smile at his characters' willingness to help him. He'd never thought his own creations could inspire him so much.

"All right, all right," he said. "It's going to be a challenge, but we can do this. Tomorrow morning we're going to go into the fairy-tale world and we're gonna kick some Literary-Mythological-Witchy butt!"

All the characters cheered. The Blissworm was happy they were finally on the same page.

"DID YOU HEAR THAT, MEN?" Robin Hood said. "WE'RE ON THE EVE OF WAR! WE SHALL FOLLOW THE SORCERER VALIANTLY INTO

BATTLE AND WILL BE SHOWERED WITH RICHES AFTER OUR VICTORY!"

"Robin, no one is getting paid," Conner said.

"OH," Robin Hood said. "THEN WE SHALL BE SHOWERED WITH COMPLIMENTS FOR OUR GOOD INTENTIONS! AFTER ALL, PRAISE IS THE CURRENCY OF THE BRAVE!"

Suddenly, the doors opened and Bob and Charlotte rushed into the commissary. They were flushed and out of breath, as if they'd run the whole way there. A moment later, Trollbella entered behind them—they had moved so fast, she couldn't keep up.

"Mom, I've got good news and bad news," Conner said. "The bad news is Jack and Red didn't find Alex, but the good news is—"

"We know where your sister is!" Charlotte panted.

Conner couldn't believe his ears. "You *what*?"

"Turn on the news!" Bob told the pirates. *"Channel Four! Hurry!"*

"But Ricky just let Lucy perform in his club!" Auburn Sally said.

"CHANGE THE CHANNEL!" the entire room yelled in unison.

The pirates reluctantly changed the channel, and everyone gathered around the television to watch the news. A reporter appeared on the screen, broadcasting live from somewhere in New York City.

"I'm standing on the corner of Thirty-Ninth Street and Fifth Avenue in Manhattan, where police have stopped all vehicles and pedestrians from going any farther," the reporter said. "The NYPD are preventing everyone from entering a two-block radius around the main branch of the New York Public Library. Police officials have yet to say the reason for such precautions, but one thing is certain, *something dangerous is happening at the library.*"

The news station played shaky footage from a helicopter flying over the library. It was difficult to see anything except the red and blue police lights surrounding the building on all sides.

"This isn't the first peculiar incident in the area this week," the reporter continued. "As I mentioned earlier, just a few days ago the wreckage of a bathroom mysteriously appeared in the middle of Bryant Park, just behind the library. The dumpers have yet to be identified."

"Did she just say they discovered a *bathroom*?" Conner asked.

"We rushed here as soon as we heard!" Charlotte said.

"We've just learned police have begun evacuating all the residences in the area as well," the reporter said. "As I said, very little information is being shared at this time, but according to eyewitness reports, the iconic lion statues at the library's entrance have been vandalized."

The helicopter footage showed a close-up of the library's sprawling front steps. Once the camera refocused, everyone could see that the lion statues were absent from their perches. Instead, they could be seen standing right in front of the library's entrance, as if the beasts were guarding the front doors. For a split second, it almost looked like the statues were *moving*.

"Did you just see that?" the reporter asked. "It appears the statues are being manipulated somehow. The one on the right looks like it's *growling* at the approaching police—*Oh my, the lion statue has just knocked the officer to the ground! The police are retreating! I've never seen anything like this! If I didn't know any better, I'd say we were witnessing magic!*"

Conner went pale and looked at his friends in disbelief.

"Oh my God . . ." he said. *"We've got to get to New York City!"*

CHAPTER THREE

THE FROG IN THE MIRROR

Froggy hadn't seen sunlight in weeks. All he had to look at, day and night, was the macabre sight of Morina's basement. The missing children from the Corner Kingdom and Charming Kingdom still lay peacefully in their beds as the witch's horrible spell drained them of their life force. The children's youth and their vitality were magically transferred into potion bottles at the foot of their beds, which Morina usually sold to customers in her shop upstairs. Luckily, the witch hadn't returned in days to switch out the bottles, giving her captives more time before they were drained completely.

The longer Froggy was forced to witness the dark magic, the more it angered him. He desperately wanted to free the children from the witch's cruel spell, but he couldn't even free himself. No matter how hard he hit or kicked the plate of glass between them, it never budged. Unfortunately, neither he nor the children could be saved without magic powerful enough to counteract the witch's enchantments— and Froggy wasn't convinced such magic existed anymore.

If there had been any passing observers, Froggy would have appeared as a reflection without a source. Inside the mirror, he was completely alone in a pitch-black world, and the view of Morina's basement hovered in the air like a window without walls.

Regardless of how far he traveled in each direction, there was absolutely nothing but darkness for miles around. As he searched the strange world, he'd often wander so far from the basement that it would shrink to just a speck of light behind him. As much as it pained him to watch the cursed children, Froggy was afraid to lose sight of it completely. Morina's basement was his only source of stimulation, and he worried he might go mad without it.

Life inside the mirror was affecting his mind enough already. The longer he was imprisoned, the faster time went. A simple daydream could cost him a few hours if he wasn't careful, and if he fell asleep, a day or two would pass by before he'd wake up. It also became increasingly difficult for him to remember where he was, how he had gotten there, and most concerning, *who he was.* Each passing moment felt less and less like reality and more like a bad dream.

"Get a grip on yourself!" he said. "Your name is Charles Carlton Charming. You were born twenty-five years ago in the Charming Kingdom. You were the fourth son of King Chester and Queen Clarice. Your brothers' names are Chance, Chase, and Chandler. Your mother passed away when you were a boy and your father died shortly after Chance married Cinderella. You have two nieces named Hope and Ash and have always wanted a big family of your own."

Froggy held his head and paced in a circle as he recalled the information. Whenever he felt his sanity start to slip, he found that reciting facts was the quickest way to restore it, but it became harder each day.

"When you were a teenager, you made the mistake of courting a witch named Morina. You discovered she practiced dark magic, so you called off the engagement. It enraged her so that she cursed you and made you look like a frog. It made you ashamed of your appearance, and you lived in seclusion for years. You built a home underground, where you read thousands of books and drank lily pad tea. Then one day, you found twelve-year-old twins in the forest and they changed your life forever!"

The memory of meeting Alex and Conner in the Dwarf Forests made him laugh. Had he known then about all the trouble they'd get him into, he probably would have run screaming in the opposite direction. But now, he was thankful for every second of life he had to claim.

"The twins are the ones who nicknamed you Froggy. Thanks to them, you're friends with Jack and Goldilocks, you're engaged to Red Riding Hood, and you were recently elected King of the Center Kingdom! You managed to create a wonderful life despite Morina's spell! She couldn't stand how happy you became, so she cursed you into this blasted mirror! But you can't let her magic get the best of you—you can't let yourself fade away!"

This wasn't Froggy's first exposure to mirror entrapment, so he knew what to expect. A few years earlier, he'd witnessed the Evil Queen using the legendary Wishing Spell to free the man trapped in her magic mirror. Tragically, by the time the man was rescued, all his memories, his personality traits, and his physical features had melted away. Without a doubt, Froggy knew the same effects had begun creeping over him.

"You can't let the darkness consume you," Froggy told himself. "There is too much you'll miss out on if you give in to it! You have to find a way out of this prison so you can have a future with the people you love! You must hold on to your identity so you don't suffer the same fate as the man from the Evil Queen's magic mirror! You must fight off this horrible curse so Morina doesn't win!"

Froggy had no idea *how* to free himself from the mirror, but he knew he'd never find an answer by lingering around Morina's basement for eternity. So, putting one webbed foot in front of the other, Froggy journeyed into the great shadowy world surrounding him until Morina's basement disappeared from sight.

He wandered aimlessly through the darkness for what felt like hours, but he never found anything.

It was so dark, he couldn't see his hands or feet, let alone something he might collide with. With every step, he worried he had made a grave mistake by leaving the basement and feared the oblivion would drive him insane.

"Please, let me find something that proves I'm not alone," he prayed aloud. "I just need something—*anything*—that can guide me to help!"

Suddenly, a speck of light appeared in the distance ahead. It was only the size of a pinhole but seemed as bright as the sun against the darkness. The discovery filled Froggy's stomach with butterflies—maybe he wasn't alone after all! He ran toward the light as fast as he could, and it grew into the shape of a tall rectangle—perhaps it was a door! As Froggy neared the anomaly, he realized it was another plate of glass, and his spirits sank. Had he walked through the darkness in a giant circle? Was the view of Morina's basement the only thing that existed in the dark world?

Froggy's heart skipped a beat when he noticed that the glass plate was much taller and wider than the plate he was used to. Perhaps he had found something new! He peered into the glass and found, not the missing children as expected, but a massive great hall with pale brick walls, green curtains, and silver chandeliers.

"My word—*it's a palace!*" Froggy exclaimed happily. "Wait a moment, I recognize this place! I've been here many times before—it's the entrance hall of the Northern Palace! *This must be the view from another mirror!* The darkness must somehow connect the two mirrors."

Suddenly, hundreds of other square and rectangular plates of glass appeared all around him like floating windows. The bizarre phenomenon startled Froggy so much, he croaked—it'd been a while since he'd been excited by anything. He looked through the glass plates and saw into sitting rooms, drawing rooms, bedchambers, and hallways—all locations he recognized as well.

"I can see through all the mirrors in the Northern Palace!" Froggy said. "This must be how the man in the Evil Queen's magic mirror was such a capable spy! He was using the darkness as a path between mirrors!"

The discovery made Froggy's heart flutter. Perhaps the more he learned about the strange dark world, the closer he was to finding a way out of it. He desperately searched all the mirrors for someone to communicate with, but oddly, he couldn't find a single soul in the palace.

"That's peculiar," he said. "I've visited Chandler and Snow White a number of times and their home has never been this empty."

Finally, Froggy peered through a small circular mirror and found a cook in the palace's kitchen. She looked exhausted and was placing a bottle of wine and three glasses on a serving tray. The cook must have felt Froggy's eyes, because she stopped what she was doing and looked up before he could say anything.

"Hello!" he said happily.

"AAAAAAAAAHHHHHHHH!" the cook screamed.

She dropped the tray and glass shattered across the kitchen floor. Her reaction was so dramatic it scared Froggy, and he impulsively ducked out of sight. He wasn't really surprised by the cook's response, though—his appearance usually gave people a fright. He couldn't imagine how alarming it'd be to see an enormous frog in a mirror when they weren't expecting it.

"WHAT'S GOING ON IN THERE?" yelled a gruff voice.

Froggy peeked through the mirror again and saw

a soldier storm into the kitchen, but he was unlike any man Froggy had ever seen. The soldier was seven feet tall and had an unusually flat, square body. The number three was displayed on the upper right and lower left corners of his armor, and three symbols shaped like clovers were set in a line down the middle.

"Forgive me, sir!" the cook pleaded. "I was fetching wine for the emperors and thought I saw something in the mirror!"

The soldier glanced at the mirror, but Froggy ducked out of sight before he could be spotted again.

"Stupid woman," the soldier said. "Quit this foolishness and get back to work! Any more nonsense and you'll be thrown in the dungeon!"

"Yes, sir," the cook said with a bow. "It won't happen again, sir."

The cook quickly swept up the mess, placed three new glasses and a new bottle of wine on her tray, and hurried out of the kitchen.

"I don't understand," Froggy thought aloud. "Who are these *emperors*? What happened to Chandler and Snow White? And where are all the servants and guards who used to work here?"

Froggy followed the cook from mirror to mirror

as she traveled through the palace. She entered the spacious dining hall, and Froggy appeared in the mirror above a large fireplace. He had been inside the Northern Palace's dining hall many times before, but he barely recognized it anymore.

All the portraits of the White Dynasty had been removed and replaced with paintings of a red-faced queen, an old hag wearing an eye patch, and a pirate with a hook. The three people pictured in the paintings sat around the table, enjoying a feast that could have fed hundreds. Froggy thought they were unattractive in their portraits, but they were even more hideous in the flesh. The barbaric way they scarfed down their food was equally unpleasant to witness.

"Your wine, my emperors," the cook said, and bowed to the table.

"IT'S ABOUT TIME!" the queen yelled, and hit the table with a clenched fist. "How dare you keep your emperors waiting! Do it again and you'll lose your head!"

"My deepest apologies," the cook said.

The cook trembled in the emperors' presence and could barely keep her hands still enough to pour wine into their glasses. When she was finished pouring, she bowed and rushed out of the room. The pirate and the queen raised their glasses before taking the first sip, but the hag didn't join them.

"None for me," she growled. "I'm not much of a drinker."

"To *us*," the pirate toasted. "May the three great emperors continue their mighty reign as the conquerors of the new world!"

"Hear, hear," the queen said. "And may our upcoming invasion go as smoothly as the last!"

The pirate and the queen clinked their glasses together and drank the wine in one gulp. The hag wasn't in the mood to celebrate and angrily threw a half-eaten lamb shank across the room.

"How much longer will we have to wait?" she moaned. "It's been weeks since we heard from the witch! How cruel of her to tease us with such a conquest, then force us to stay put! Our army is ready—why can't we invade the new world *now*?"

"The *new world*?" Froggy whispered to himself. "What are they talking about?"

"I agree with Westie!" the queen said. "It's impossible to enjoy the luxuries of this world when we know there are far greater pleasures in the other.

What is taking the witch so long to contact us? I'm starting to doubt her competence!"

The pirate chuckled at their annoyance and twirled his moustache with his hook.

"Ladies, your eagerness is sabotaging your judgment," he said. "Remember what the witch said: As soon as the portal opens, she will lead the other witches into the new world first. Once they've weakened the new world's defenses, and the new world's defenses have weakened them, she'll send for us. *We'll charge through the portal and claim the new world for ourselves!* It's a guaranteed victory if we stick to the plan. Patience is a virtue—"

"PATIENCE IS FOR PEASANTS!" the queen yelled. *"Instant gratification is the only gratification for the powerful!"*

"Allow me to finish my sentence," the pirate said. "Patience is a virtue *we'll never need again*! The final days leading up to the invasion will be the last time we *wait* or *want* for anything. As soon as we conquer the new world, we'll have a whole planet to ourselves and billions of slaves to serve us!"

"I will rule the land!" the queen declared.

"I will rule the skies!" the hag announced.

"I shall rule the seas!" the pirate professed. "And that silly witch is in for a rude awakening if she actually believes we plan on sharing any of it with her!"

The emperors roared with devilish laughter like a pack of evil hyenas. Once the amusement wore off, the queen yawned so wide, a watermelon could have fit inside her massive mouth.

"Universal domination is exhausting," she said. "We'd better start conserving our energy before the invasion."

"Oh what sweet dreams await us tonight!" the pirate said with a sinister grin.

The emperors stood up from the table and left the dining hall for bed. Once the room was empty, Froggy started pacing behind the mirror, and a thousand questions raced through his mind.

Suddenly, Froggy spotted something moving out of the corner of his eye. Until this moment, he'd thought the object in the middle of the dining table was a flickering candle. After taking a closer look, he realized it was a small and shimmering pixie stuck inside a tiny jar. The emperors had been using her as a centerpiece.

"Excuse me, young lady in the jar?" Froggy asked. "Can you hear me?"

The pixie looked around the dining room in a daze. Obviously, she could hear just fine, but she couldn't see who was speaking to her.

"I'm over here! In the mirror above the fireplace!"

The pixie looked up and stared at Froggy like he was the most unusual thing she had ever seen.

"How did you get in there?" she asked.

"I could ask you the same question," Froggy replied.

The pixie lowered her head sadly. "I've been trapped in here for weeks," she said. "At first the captain was using me as a hostage, but now he's using me as decoration—*it's so degrading!* No matter how hard I try, I can't escape! The jar is shut too tight!"

"Then you and I are kindred spirits," Froggy said. "What's your name?"

"Tinker Bell," the pixie said.

The name sounded familiar, but Froggy couldn't remember where he had heard it before.

"Forgive me, but I'm rather confused," he said. "Who were those awful people eating dinner? And where did they come from?"

"Well, they're all from different places," Tinker Bell said. "The Queen of Hearts is from a place called Wonderland, the Wicked Witch of the West is from the Land of Oz, and Captain Hook and I are from Neverland."

It suddenly clicked where Froggy had heard the names before. With every piece of knowledge he obtained, reality became much more difficult to comprehend.

"Wait a moment," he said in shock. "I know those names—you're characters from the books in my library! The late Fairy Godmother gave me those stories as a gift! How on earth did you get into *this* world?"

"I'm still trying to figure out where I am!" Tinker Bell said. "One night I was flying through London with my friend Peter, and the next thing I knew, some guy called the Masked Man was kidnapping me!"

"The *Masked Man*? But how did *he* get into your story?"

"He was using some kind of potion to travel into a bunch of stories," the pixie said. "He was recruiting characters into something called *a literary army*. The Masked Man used me to enlist Captain Hook and the pirates from the *Jolly Roger*. Once he had the Wicked Witch, the Queen of Hearts, and their armies of card soldiers, Winkies, and flying monkeys, they invaded this world! All the kings and queens were dethroned and sentenced to be beheaded!"

Froggy gulped, fearing the worst for his family.

"And what happened to the royal families? Did they lose their heads?"

"No, luckily they all got away!" Tinker Bell said. "The queen, the captain, and the Wicked Witch blamed the Masked Man for their escape—they were so angry, they had him dropped from the sky!"

"Do you know where the royal families went?"

"Nobody does," Tinker Bell said. "After the Masked Man was killed, a witch approached the emperors with an offer to conquer a new world—one much bigger than this one. They've been so excited about it, they stopped looking for the royal families. The witch and the new world are all they can talk about!"

"Did this witch or this world have a name?"

"I think they mentioned it once or twice," the pixie said, and struggled to recall it. "I believe the witch's name was Morgana—no, it was *Morina*! And the world she was planning to invade didn't have a name, but she called it *the Otherworld*."

Froggy went pale green and felt sick to his

stomach. His escape from the mirrors would have to wait—clearly, there were much bigger problems at stake.

"Oh dear," he gasped. "The witches and the Literary Army are going to invade the twins' world! I have to find Alex and Conner—I have to warn them!"

CHAPTER FOUR

A SUBCONSCIOUS SURPRISE

Arthur was having the most interesting dream. He started it as a small ant crawling on the ground. Blades of grass towered over him like trees, and patches of dirt stretched into the horizon like enormous canyons. It was a very unique perspective, but Arthur figured he wouldn't get very far at an ant's pace. So the future king of England grew long legs and began hopping across the lawn as a grasshopper.

He landed on the roots of an evergreen tree and marveled at all the branches stretching into the air. Arthur wanted to climb to the branches, but he knew it was an ambitious journey to make as a grasshopper. So he grew four claws and a furry tail and scurried up the tree as a squirrel. Once he reached the very top of the tree, Arthur stared in awe at all the fluffy clouds in the sky. He desperately wanted to fly through the clouds above, so his tiny arms grew into a pair of magnificent wings, and he soared into the sky as an eagle.

Without a doubt, Arthur's dream had been inspired by Merlin's theatrical teaching methods. Recently, the wizard had been transforming the young squire into a variety of creatures to teach him lessons about greatness and gratitude.

"Oppression is a sport for the small-minded. *Empathy* is the path to true power," Merlin lectured. "A great leader respects all walks of life; otherwise, life will walk all over them."

"Ain't that the truth," Mother Goose agreed. "It's just like I told my friends during the Boston Tea Party: Tyranny is a revolution's welcome mat."

Arthur was reminded of his elders' wise words as he flew above the land they were training him to rule one day. The flight made him very thirsty, and he descended toward a small lake. As soon as his claws touched the ground, they transformed into hooves, and Arthur galloped the rest of the way to the water as a horse.

When he arrived at the lake, Arthur found a young woman standing alone on the shore. She wore a white dress and had long strawberry-blonde hair, and stood with her back facing him. Arthur transformed back into his human self upon seeing the young woman. At first, he worried she might be one of the Mists of Avalon that Merlin was always warning him about, but there was something very familiar about her. Eventually, the young woman heard him approaching and turned around.

"Alex," Arthur said with a big smile. "It's so good to see you."

"Arthur?" she said. "Is that you?"

Alex was much more surprised to see him than he was to see her. In fact, Arthur wasn't rattled in the slightest; Alex made regular appearances in his dreams.

"Of course it's me," Arthur said. "Who else would it be?"

Alex looked around the lake, completely disoriented; she seemed to be afraid of her surroundings.

"Where am I?"

"You're in my dream," Arthur said. "I know it's a dream because it's the only place I get to see you. And now that I know I'm dreaming, I imagine I'll be waking up soon."

Whenever Arthur realized he was dreaming, he immediately returned to consciousness. He could feel his mind's clarity returning by the second, but oddly, this time he didn't wake up.

"I must be more tired than I thought," he said. "I'm grateful for every extra second I get to spend with you, even if it isn't the real you."

For the first time, Arthur noticed that Alex looked very different than she normally did when he dreamed about her. Her face was much paler, her eyes were red like she had been crying, and she blinked frantically like something deeply troubling was on her mind.

"This is so strange," she said. "I thought this was *my* dream, but maybe I've stumbled into yours."

"So I'm dreaming of *you* dreaming of *me*?" Arthur asked. "Well, I'm afraid to look up what this means in Merlin's dream dictionary—"

"No, I mean *we're both asleep*," Alex said. "Just a minute ago, I was dreaming of my hometown, and then I suddenly found myself at this lake. I think we're communicating in our sleep."

"So it's really you?" he asked softly.

"Yeah," she said. "It's really me."

Arthur didn't know which possibility was more overwhelming: that he and Alex were connecting subconsciously, or that he was standing in front of the real Alex and not a figment of his imagination.

"But how is this possible?"

"I don't know," Alex said, and struggled to think of an explanation. "When my brother and I were little kids, we used to see each other in our dreams all the time. We would wake up the next day and recite everything we had done and everything we'd said. No one believed us, so we stopped mentioning it— we figured it was just a twin thing other people didn't understand. I was hoping it still worked and tried contacting him now. But it looks like my dreams led me to yours."

The two shared a small but very telling smile.

"If this is real, it's no mystery why it's happening," Arthur said. "We probably spend so much time thinking about each other, our subconscious minds are trying to tell us something."

"Arthur, please don't start this again; it was hard

enough the first time," Alex said. "We both agreed that living separate lives was the responsible thing to do. You have a destiny to fulfill, and you can't jeopardize it by running off with the first girl you met in the woods."

"I'm not jeopardizing anything," he said with a playful grin. "I plan on fulfilling everything on my destiny to-do list. I'm going to pull the sword from the stone, I'm going to start Camelot, I'm going to form the Knights of the Round Table, and I'm even going to find the Holy Grail. Once I'm done, I'm going to find *you*, and you won't have any more excuses to keep us apart."

"Arthur, I may not be around by the time you do it all," she said quietly.

"Of course you'll be around," Arthur said with a laugh. "I've been training twice as hard with Merlin and Mother Goose so I can finish much faster than the legend predicts. It may have taken another King Arthur a few decades to complete his legacy, but I know it'll only take me a couple of years because I've got you to inspire me."

Arthur's devotion brought tears to Alex's eyes, but not in a good way.

"No," she said, and shook her head. "Even if you

finish it earlier than expected, you have to stay in Camelot. You'll throw your life away if you do it all for me."

"You can't throw a life away if it's already fulfilled!"

"You're not listening! I'm trying to tell you it'll be a complete waste! If you rush through your legacy you might get hurt!"

"On the contrary, I'll be even more careful knowing you're at the finish line—"

"Arthur, I'm trying to tell you I won't be alive much longer!"

Once this heavy confession was made, Alex covered her face and began to sob. Her words made Arthur freeze where he stood. He prayed she was being sarcastic or overreacting, but if the tears streaming down her face were any indication, Alex was telling the truth.

"Alex, please tell me that's a joke," he said.

"I wish it were!" she cried. "I would love to live happily ever after with you, Arthur, but it's not meant to be."

"But why? Are you sick?"

"I've been cursed by a very powerful witch. She has me under a spell that controls my every waking moment. So far, she's made me do a lot of terrible things to innocent people. I don't know what she has planned next, but I know something horrible is coming—thousands of people are going to get hurt! The witch puts me to sleep when she isn't using me. That's why I was trying to contact my brother in my dreams. He's got to find a way to stop me—*no matter what it takes!*"

"Alex, don't be ridiculous," Arthur said. "There's got to be another way to free you from the witch's curse besides killing you."

"I'm afraid there isn't," she said. "This curse is unlike any dark magic I've seen or heard of. It fills me with so much anger, it blinds me—I'm barely aware of the damage I'm causing! I get trapped inside my head with feelings of self-doubt, self-hatred, and regret. All I can think about are my mistakes, my flaws, and how undeserving I am of love and happiness! The more my misery grows, the more powerful I become—and the more powerful I become, the stronger the curse gets. The voices in my head have to be stopped, and there's only one way to put a creature out of its misery!"

Arthur couldn't believe he was hearing such things. Their shared dream had quickly escalated into a nightmare.

"I refuse to believe that," he said. "There must be something Merlin and Mother Goose can do to help you—there must be something *I* can do to save you!"

A thick layer of mist suddenly rose off the lake and blew toward them. The mist formed the shape of a large hand, wrapped its fingers around Alex's body, and started pulling her toward the lake.

"What's happening?" Arthur shouted.

"The witch must be waking me up!" Alex said.

Arthur grabbed Alex's arm, but he was no match for the giant misty hand.

"Alex, you need to listen to me!" he said. "We're going to save you from this! We're going to find you and free you from this curse, I promise! You just have to stay strong—don't give up yet!"

Alex stared up at Arthur with eyes full of tears and fears, but very little hope.

"Good-bye, Arthur."

Alex was pulled from Arthur's grip and dragged underwater, and she disappeared from sight.

"AAALLLEEEXXX!"

Arthur rapidly awoke from the nightmare. He was sweating profusely, and his eyes darted all around his room as he remembered where he was. His heart was beating so hard, he could hear it over the sound of

Merlin and Mother Goose snoring in the next room. Arthur had never been so affected by a dream in his life, so he knew it hadn't been a normal dream. *Alex was in trouble and she needed help.*

The squire leaped out of bed and stormed into Merlin and Mother Goose's room. His elders awoke in a terrible fright and sat straight up like they had been electrocuted.

"Arthur? What is it, my boy?" Merlin asked, and reached for his glasses.

"Where's the fire?" Mother Goose said, and reached for her flask.

"Forgive the intrusion, but something terrible has happened!" Arthur announced.

"Have the Saxons invaded?" Merlin asked.

"Are parachute pants back in style?" Mother Goose asked.

"No, it's *Alex*," Arthur said. "She's been cursed by a terrible witch! We need to go to the Otherworld immediately and rescue her!"

"How do you know all this?" the wizard asked.

"Alex and I were communicating with each other in our sleep! She was trying to contact her brother but found me instead. She told me she's been cursed and is being forced to do terrible things! Then a hand made of mist rose out of a lake and dragged her under the surface!"

Arthur explained himself so quickly, he had to catch his breath afterward. Merlin and Mother Goose looked at each other with sleepy, uneasy eyes—but they weren't concerned about Alex.

"Artie, have you been drinking my bubbly?" Mother Goose asked.

"You have to listen to me!" he pleaded. "Alex is in trouble, and she thinks the only way to stop the curse is if someone kills her! We've got to do something before she gets hurt!"

"It sounds like you just had a terrible nightmare," Merlin said.

"It wasn't just a nightmare. It was the real Alex!" Arthur said. "I swear I'm not overreacting!"

His elders still weren't convinced.

"It's not uncommon for dreams to feel very realistic when they're about the people we love," the wizard said. "Why don't you fetch my dream dictionary, and we can get to the bottom of what Alex actually represented in the dream."

Arthur grunted loudly and paced in a circle. No matter what he said, Merlin and Mother Goose only saw him as a love-struck teenager. Arthur desperately needed their trust, but they would never take him seriously unless he proved himself trustworthy. A transformation was needed to gain their respect, and luckily, Arthur knew just the thing to do it.

The squire raced out of Merlin's cottage and ran into the woods. It was raining and still dark outside, but Arthur persisted. He wasn't wearing any shoes and was barely clothed, but he was numb to everything except his fiery determination. Finally, he arrived at his destination and entered the clearing where the great sword lay in the stone.

Arthur was destined to remove the sword once his training was complete and he was ready to be crowned King of England—but given the circumstances, he hoped his desire to save Alex would somehow expedite his destiny. Arthur might not have been in any danger, but if Alex was in trouble, then his whole world was at stake.

So the young squire wrapped his hands around the sword's handle and pulled on it with all his might. His fingernails bled and blisters covered his palms, but Arthur kept pulling, as if his life depended on it. . . .

CHAPTER FIVE

TURBULENCE AHEAD

As soon as Conner had an inkling of his sister's whereabouts, he rushed to the nearest computer and bought the five remaining tickets on the next flight to New York City. He used Bob's credit card without asking, but Bob couldn't care less. All that mattered to anyone was finding Alex and bringing her home. Liberating the fairy-tale world would have to wait until they figured out what was happening in Manhattan.

At five o'clock the next morning, without any sleep whatsoever, Conner, Bree, Jack, Goldilocks, Red, and Charlotte piled into Charlotte's SUV and headed to Willow Crest International Airport. Conner had no idea what to expect once they got to New York, but he knew it'd be easier to handle it with his friends at his side. They left the hospital in such a hurry no one had a chance to pack, but knowing what his friends usually carried on their persons, Conner managed to grab a duffel bag before they left the hospital so Jack's and Goldilocks's more *questionable* belongings could be stowed.

When they arrived, Conner ran into the airport to check their bag while his friends waited outside. They stood on the curb by Charlotte's car and took in their first sights of the Otherworld beyond the halls of Saint Andrew's Children's Hospital.

"So this is what they call an *air port*," Jack said as he cradled Hero. "What exactly is a *port of air*?"

"It's where you board planes that take you to other locations," Bree explained.

"Like a stable?" Goldilocks asked.

"Yes, but with *much* bigger horses."

Jack and Goldilocks nodded and looked around in awe, but Red wasn't as impressed.

"It's rather *colorless* in the Otherworld, isn't it?" she remarked. "If you ask me, the whole *gray and glass* thing is a bit overdone."

As soon as he finished inside, Conner emerged through the airport's automatic doors and joined his friends at the curb.

"The bag's been checked under my name," he said. "Apparently it's completely legal to travel with a sword and an axe as long as they're checked. That's America for you."

"What is *checked*?" Jack asked.

"It means they'll stow our luggage under the plane before we leave, and then when we arrive, it'll come out on a conveyor at the baggage claim."

Conner's friends from the fairy-tale world stared at him like he was speaking in tongues.

"We have absolutely no idea what any of that means, but we'll take your word for it," Goldilocks said.

"Does everyone have their tickets and IDs?" Conner asked the group.

Bree, Jack, Goldilocks, and Red held up the tickets they had printed at the hospital and the identification cards they'd been assigned. Unfortunately, traveling with friends from another dimension meant that airport security would be a challenge. If they'd had more time Conner could have come up with better IDs that resembled his friends more, but given their time crunch, they had to work with what they had.

"Will someone notice these aren't our *actual* identities?" Jack asked.

"I'm praying the TSA officer won't notice," Conner said. "We'll get into serious trouble if we're caught, so if anyone asks, Jack is Dr. Robert Gordon, Goldilocks is Charlotte Gordon, and Red is Bree's cousin, Amanda Campbell."

"Bree, would you happen to have a more *attractive* relative I could impersonate?" Red asked.

"Sorry, that's all I've got," Bree said. "Amanda's ID has gotten me into dozens of concerts I was too young for. I hope it brings you the same luck."

Conner nervously eyed the airport. "We're going to need more than luck to pull this off," he said.

"Conner, this is too risky," Charlotte said from inside the car. "Why don't Bob and I just come with you?"

"I need you guys to keep an eye on the characters from my short stories," he said. "Besides, the five of us have a long history of magical dilemmas. We'll know what to do if things get out of hand. We'll call you if we need backup."

Charlotte closed her eyes and let out a long sigh. She knew Conner and his friends were more than capable of handling themselves, but it didn't make it any easier knowing that her son might be walking into danger.

"Please be safe," she said. "If you find your sister, let us know as soon as possible."

"We will," Conner said. "I promise."

Conner hugged his mother through the car window and led his friends into the airport. At first glance, Jack, Goldilocks, and Red were completely overwhelmed. Travelers brushed and bumped into them from all directions. Everywhere they looked was another flashing screen that displayed departure times and announced delays. The commotion was too much for Hero, and he began to fuss.

"Here, give him to me," Goldilocks said, and took the newborn from Jack. "There, there, no need to cry. Who's Mama's good boy? *Who's Mama's good boy?*"

It tickled everyone to watch Goldilocks interact with her son. Ever since Hero had been born, Goldilocks had been a different person altogether. The infamous fugitive and swashbuckling swordswoman was now the queen of baby talk and changing diapers at record-breaking speed. However, motherhood hadn't softened Goldilocks one bit. On the contrary, being a mother had made her tougher than ever— especially when someone came between her and her child.

"Goldie, are you sure taking Hero to New York is a good idea?" Red asked. "Babies need lots of attention, you know."

"We're still taking *you*, aren't we?" Goldilocks snapped.

Red raised her hands defensively. "I'm just suggesting you leave him with Charlotte while we're gone. Caring for an infant *and* searching for a friend is quite a handful."

"Absolutely not," Goldilocks said. "I refuse to be one of those women who puts her entire life on hold because she's a mother. I'm more than capable of fulfilling my responsibilities to my child without abandoning my friends."

"Sorry I asked," Red said. "Personally, I would have hired a nanny before purchasing a cradle."

Conner guided his friends through the crowded airport to the long security line. He stood on his toes to see over all the heads and took a good look at the TSA officer working the front. The officer was an older man who scowled at all the travelers as if a piece of sour candy were stuck in his mouth. He thoroughly checked every person's ID and ticket before allowing them to pass.

"Oh crap, he's good at his job!" Conner bemoaned. "Bree and I will be fine with our student IDs, but I don't know how to sneak you guys past him. It would be so much easier if Alex were here. She could just zap him with a magic spell and be done with it."

"Looks like we'll have to zap him with a bit of *your* magic instead," Jack said.

Conner sighed. "Jack, I appreciate the sentiment, but this is not the time for another pep talk."

"I'm being serious! We don't have your sister's talents, so you have to use your own. Imagine this was one of your stories and your characters were in this exact predicament. What would you have them do or say to get past the officer?"

Conner scratched his chin and walked in a circle as he thought about it. He appreciated the encouragement, but the consequences of failure were more severe than his friends could imagine. It took creativity just to survive the Otherworld—he would need a stroke of genius to manipulate it.

"I've got an idea," he said. "If the officer notices your IDs are fake, you'll need to *distract* him. Say something completely unexpected that'll make him forget what he's thinking about."

"Oh, I know!" Red said. "I'll say I'm a queen in another dimension!"

"That'll only make things worse," Conner said. "I've got a line for each of you—but you have to say it exactly as I tell you."

He whispered the diversions into his friends' ears and hoped they would do the trick.

"We shouldn't stand together in line," Bree said. "If he notices the IDs are fake, it'll look less suspicious if we're spaced out."

"Great idea," Conner said. "All right, here goes nothing!"

Conner and Bree entered the line first. Once five passengers had lined up behind them, Jack followed. Goldilocks waited for six passengers to line up behind her husband, then joined the line with Hero. Red was a little confused about how a line worked. She let over a dozen people cut in front of her before realizing she was supposed to wait behind them and follow them to the officer.

Finally, after forty very anxious minutes, Conner

and Bree reached the front and presented their tickets and identification to the TSA officer. He read their boarding passes and looked them up and down with the same scowl he had worn all morning.

"Are you two together?" the officer asked.

"What?" Conner asked in shock. "No, we're just friends—well, at least I think. We haven't had a chance to figure it out."

"Sir, I'm asking if you're *traveling* together," the officer said, and scowled even harder. "The airline is not concerned with your relationship status."

Conner blushed so hard, he was afraid his cheeks would melt off his face. Obviously, his anxiety was getting the best of him. If Bree hadn't been equally anxious she would have burst out laughing.

"Yes, we're traveling together," she said.

The TSA officer looked them up and down one last time and initialed their tickets.

"Go ahead," he said. "Next!"

Conner and Bree walked past the officer and joined a smaller line for the metal detector. They took their time putting their shoes and belts into bins so they could keep an eye on their friends. After a few moments, Jack was next in line and handed his ticket and identification to the TSA officer.

"Good morning," Jack said cheerfully. "I'm going to New York."

The TSA officer read Jack's documents before looking at him. As the officer's gaze moved upward, Jack repeated Conner's suggested line before the officer could notice that the ID wasn't legitimate.

"Hair plugs," Jack announced.

"Excuse me?" the officer asked.

"Hair plugs," Jack repeated. "I'm sure you're wondering how I got my hair back. I see you're follicle-challenged yourself, so I'm happy to pass along my doctor's information if you're interested in getting plugs. Technically he's not a *real* doctor—and he works out of a kitchen in Chinatown—but as you can see, his work is wonderful!"

The TSA officer was so offended, his mouth fell open. He shook his head as he initialed Jack's ticket and handed the documents back to Jack without giving the ID a second glance.

"I'm not interested in *hair plugs*," the officer growled. "Get out of here."

"Suit yourself," Jack said.

Conner and Bree were relieved when Jack joined them in the line for the metal detector, but their mission was far from over. Before they knew it,

Goldilocks and Hero were stepping up to the TSA officer's stand. The officer looked back and forth between Goldilocks and Charlotte's ID and meticulously studied both faces.

"Ma'am, have you recently lost weight?" he asked.

"Obviously," Goldilocks said, and nodded to Hero.

The TSA officer wasn't convinced. He knew something was different, he just couldn't put his finger on it.

"Did you also change your facial structure?" he pressed further.

Goldilocks glared at him with a scowl that rivaled his own.

"You'd be *amazed* how much a body can change after giving birth. Shall I give you the details?"

The TSA officer looked like he was going to be sick. He quickly initialed the ticket before she had the chance to elaborate.

"Have a nice flight," he said without looking Goldilocks in the eye.

With Conner, Bree, Jack, and Goldilocks successfully past the officer, the only one left was Red. They tried to stay close in case they needed to intervene, but they were herded toward the metal detector by other TSA officers. Soon they were out of earshot and prayed Red could handle it herself.

Red sauntered up to the TSA officer and presented her ticket and Amanda Campbell's ID with a large smile. The officer scanned her documents, initialed her ticket, and handed them back without a problem. Conner was shocked it had gone so smoothly, but then the officer said something that absolutely infuriated Red. She stomped her foot and pointed dramatically at him.

"HOW DARE YOU, SIR!" she yelled loudly enough for the whole airport to hear. *"THAT IS THE BIGGEST INSULT I'VE EVER RECEIVED IN MY LIFE!"*

The officer's scowl shifted to a look of terror. Red stormed past him and joined her friends at the metal detector.

"What the heck just happened?" Conner asked. "What did he say to you?"

Red held up the ID of Amanda Campbell. "He said *this* was a good picture of me!" she grumbled.

The metal detector was a very foreign concept to Conner's friends, so it required a great deal of supervision and reassurance. Conner had to promise Jack he would get his boots back after they were scanned,

Bree had to stop Goldilocks from putting Hero into one of the bins, and Red had to be scanned by hand because she refused to part with her jewelry—but once they were through the detector and had gathered their things, they had *officially* snuck through airport security.

"I can't believe we just pulled that off," Conner said. "I don't think I've breathed since we joined the security line."

"I wasn't worried for a second," Jack said. "But then again, I have a lot more faith in you."

They turned a corner, and Jack, Goldilocks, and Red froze. The sight of all the stores, coffee shops, bars, and restaurants throughout the terminal was almost too much to bear.

"Oh my, it's like a little kingdom!" Red said.

"What's that heavenly aroma?" Goldilocks asked.

"That's called *coffee*," Bree said. "It's a really big deal in the Otherworld."

"What's that place with all the moving pictures of men on grassy fields?" Jack asked.

"That's called a sports bar," Conner informed. "It's where people go to watch other people play games."

"What about that shiny room with all the small

bottles and portraits of beautiful but bored women?" Red asked.

"That's a perfume store," Bree said.

Red was amazed such a place existed. "They let *commoners* wear perfume in this world? Oh, this I've got to see!"

The young queen dashed for the perfume store before Bree could grab her. Since they had some time to kill before their flight boarded, Conner thought it was perfectly fine to let his friends explore the Otherworld amenities in the airport. He took Goldilocks to the coffee shop and ordered her a vanilla latte. While Goldilocks enjoyed her latte, Conner took Jack to the sports bar. He did his best to describe the rules of the football and baseball games being broadcast, but Jack was convinced he was making it up as he went along. Bree had the exhausting task of supervising Red as she bounced from shop to shop. It was like watching a hyper toddler in a toy store.

At six-thirty, fifteen minutes before boarding, the gang regrouped at Gate 26 and took seats. Red proudly showed off all the purchases inside her enormous shopping bags.

"I must say, what this world lacks in color, it makes up for in merchandise! I found this exquisite leather bag made from an animal called a faux. I got this delicious bottle of perfume called Febreze. I bought this handy hand mirror with little electric torches around the frame. And lastly, I couldn't walk away from this colorful pamphlet called *Glamorous Magazine*. Look, it has an article inside titled 'How to Steal Your Man Back from His Ex.' I hope it mentions something about magic mirrors."

"How did you pay for all this?" Conner asked.

"Pay?" Red said, as if it were a word from another language.

"She didn't—*I* did," Bree said. "She would have gotten arrested for shoplifting if I hadn't had my emergency credit card on me. It's maxed out, so the next emergency is on someone else."

"Don't worry, I got gifts for all of you," Red announced. "Conner, I got you this shirt that says 'I Do My Own Stunts'—classy, right? Jack, I got you this 'World's Greatest Grandfather' hat—sorry, they were out of 'father.' I got this adorable stuffed frog in a suit for Hero so he'll always know what his uncle Charlie looks like. And Goldilocks, I got you this convenient little contraption called a BabyBjörn—why carry your child when you can wear him?"

"Thanks, Red! That's so kind of you! Your thoughtfulness always surprises me!"

For whatever reason, Goldilocks was speaking much faster than she usually did, and her left eye started to twitch.

"Good heavens, Goldie. What happened to you?" Red asked.

"It's called caffeine!" Goldilocks said. *"I had a latte! A vanilla latte, to be exact! It's a brilliant beverage! I was so tired a few moments ago, but now I feel invincible! I could fight a whole army with my bare hands! Actually, I'm going to get some more!"*

Jack gently placed a hand on his wife's shoulder. "Sweetheart, maybe take it easy on the caffeine. People are starting to stare."

"Attention, all passengers on Flight 219 to John F. Kennedy International Airport, it is now time to board the aircraft," said a voice over the intercom. "Please line up with your boarding passes readily available."

Conner, his friends, and all the other passengers formed a line at the gate. They had their tickets scanned, then proceeded down the long Jetway and boarded the plane. Their flight was filled with businesspeople, families on vacation, and a troop of Boy Scouts.

"Follow me and I'll show you to our seats," Conner instructed. "We're in the back because we booked our tickets so late. Bree and I are in seats 38A and 38B, Jack and Goldilocks are behind us in seats 39A and 39B, and Red is in 40A—wait, *where's Red?*"

Conner searched the cabin, but Red was nowhere to be found. The corner of her new purse caught his eye, and he saw that she'd seated herself in the first-class cabin. He tried waving to get her attention, but Red was already enjoying a moist towel and reading her copy of *Glamorous Magazine.*

"Ma'am, is this your seat?" a flight attendant asked her.

"No, but it'll do just fine," Red said, and went back to her magazine.

The flight attendant pulled the boarding pass out of Red's hand and read her seat number.

"I'm sorry, this cabin is reserved for first class only. You need to sit in your assigned seat."

"Assigned?" Red asked like she had never heard the word before. "Which seat is that?"

The flight attendant pointed to the back of the plane where Red's friends were.

"I'm supposed to sit *back there*?" Red said in disbelief. "I thought those were for elves! No human being can feasibly fit in such a small space!"

"Welcome to commercial travel," the flight attendant said. "Now, either move to your seat or I'll have you escorted off the plane."

Red gave the flight attendant an impressively dirty look. As the young queen walked through the economy cabin, she held her nose like she was walking through a field of manure. She squeezed into seat 40A behind Jack and Goldilocks. Luckily, no one was sitting in 40B beside her, because her dress took up both seats.

As the last passengers boarded the aircraft, the constant slamming of the overhead bins started to hurt Hero's ears. The infant began to cry, and everyone in the cabin glared in Jack and Goldilocks's direction.

"Everyone is looking at us like we've personally offended them," Jack remarked.

"It's because you brought a baby on a plane," Bree said. "They're worried he's going to cry the whole way to New York."

Goldilocks was *not* going to put up with this. She

passed Hero to Jack and stood in the aisle where all the passengers could see her.

"Now, wait just one Hickory Dickory second," she called out. *"I don't care if you have to listen to my baby cry! Eight days ago I experienced the worst pain humanly possible by pushing him out of my body! It's something all mothers must endure for the survival of our species! It's natural, it's brave, it's beautiful, and I will NOT be disrespected for it! Now, I suggest you all wipe those foul looks off your faces or YOU'LL be the ones crying all the way to New York!"*

"I'd listen to my wife if I were you," Jack added. "She's on *caffeine.*"

All the passengers quickly diverted their gazes elsewhere. Bree tried to start a round of applause for Goldilocks, but no one joined her.

Once his friends had stopped causing problems and settled into their seats, Conner was able to take his first deep breath of the day. He looked around the plane and saw a Boy Scout sitting across the aisle. He was cute and chubby and obviously took the Boy Scouts very seriously, because his whole uniform was covered in pins and badges. The boy eagerly stared down at a map of New York City and was so giddy, he could barely sit still.

"Hi!" the Scout said when he noticed Conner. "My name's Oliver. What's yours?"

"I'm Conner. Are you excited about New York?"

"I've never been so excited in my whole life!" Oliver exclaimed. "This is actually my first time on a plane! New experiences don't make me nervous, though. *This* badge is for bravery."

"Are you doing anything special in New York?" Conner asked.

"I'm going for the big Boy and Girl Scouts of America Camp-Out!" Oliver said happily. "This year they're having it tonight in Central Park! Normally the city doesn't allow campers in the park, but they're making an exception for us. My family doesn't have much money, so I had to sell a thousand pounds of popcorn to pay for the trip. I sold more than any other Scout in the Western Region! That's what *this* badge is for."

"Congratulations," Conner said. "That's a lot of popcorn."

"How about you? What are you going to New York for?"

"Um...visiting family. At least, I hope. It's kind of a surprise trip."

"Neat," Oliver said. "Well, it's been nice talking

to you, but I'd better get back to my map. I'm trying to memorize it before we land. I'm really good at navigation, that's what *this* badge is for."

"Good luck," Conner said. "Have fun camping."

The Boy Scout smiled so hard, dimples appeared in his cheeks. He looked back down and became lost in his map of New York City again. Oliver's excitement reminded Conner of Alex on their first trip to the fairy-tale world. He remembered how she'd hogged their map of the kingdoms and how they'd fought over directions. The memory made Conner smile for the first time all week, but it was odd to think of a time when the Land of Stories didn't feel like home.

"Ladies and gentlemen, please lend us your eyes and ears as we go over our safety demonstration," said a voice from the speakers.

The flight attendants stood in the aisles and gave instructions on how to buckle the seat belts and wear the safety vests, and pointed to the emergency exits. A cartoon showed the passengers how to properly put on the oxygen masks and evacuate the plane in the event of an emergency. By the time the safety demonstration was done, the plane had departed the gate and was cruising toward the runway.

Red reached over Jack's and Goldilocks's seats and tapped Bree and Conner on the shoulders.

"Sorry, those yellow vests were so ugly, I zoned out," she said. "Could you repeat those bits about *cabin pressure* and *water landings?*"

"If the cabin loses oxygen, masks will drop down from the ceiling so we can breathe." Bree filled her in. "And in the event of a water landing, the bottom of the plane will turn into a flotation device."

"But that's absurd," Red said. "Why would we end up in water? Can't the driver just steer around it?"

Suddenly, the plane rocketed down the runway. The force slammed Red into her seat and she screamed.

"WHAT'S HAPPENING?" she shouted.

"Relax, we're just taking off," Bree said.

"TAKING OFF *WHAT*?"

"Into the air."

Bree thought it was obvious, but judging from the horrified look on Red's face, it wasn't.

"THIS THING GOES INTO THE AIR?" she asked in a panic.

"Yeah, that's why it's called a *flight.*"

"I WISH SOMEONE HAD SHARED THAT

MINOR DETAIL BEFORE WE BOARDED! IS IT TOO LATE TO GET OFF?"

"Yes!" the whole cabin said in unison.

As the jet launched into the air, Conner closed his eyes. The subtle movements of the plane quickly rocked him to sleep. Unfortunately, it wasn't a peaceful rest.

Conner saw flashes of his sister in his dreams.... He couldn't understand her completely, but she was desperately trying to communicate with him.... She was trying to warn him that something terrible was going to happen.... He needed to stop it before all was lost.... He asked her to repeat herself, but it became harder and harder to hear her.... As if a dying strobe light were illuminating them, Conner could see less and less of her.... A dark, smoky cloud suddenly wrapped around Alex.... It pulled her away from him like a giant hand.... She was screaming, but there was nothing he could do to help....

"Alex!" Conner cried, and awoke with a jolt.

"Are you okay?" Bree asked him.

"Sorry, bad dream. How long was I out?"

"For about an hour. You've been twitching since takeoff but I didn't have the heart to wake you up. I can't imagine how exhausted you are."

"I suppose shaky sleep is better than no sleep at all," he said. "You've been up as long as I have. Did you manage to nap at all?"

"I tried but *no bueno*," she said. "There's just too much on my mind."

Conner nodded. "I hear you," he said. "Gosh, I would give anything to think about something besides my sister. I'm even starting to worry about her in my dreams. I just had a nightmare where she tried to warn me about something, but I couldn't understand her. I'm sure it's just the stress talking."

He turned to Bree, hoping to find some reassurance in her eyes, but she had none to spare.

"Conner, there's something I need to tell you," she said. "I was trying to be considerate and didn't want to overwhelm you, but I can't keep it to myself anymore."

Although he had no idea what she was talking about, Conner's whole body went tense. Bree was always so calm and cool about everything; she wouldn't be so worked up if it weren't serious.

"You can tell me," he said. "I doubt there's much that'll trouble me more than I already am troubled."

"All right," Bree said, and took a deep breath. "I wasn't completely honest about my trip to

Connecticut. I was visiting family, that part is true, but I lied about the *reason* I went."

Conner gulped. "Was it another guy?"

This was the last question Bree expected to come out of his mouth.

"No, it's nothing like that," she said, and went straight to her point. "When Emmerich and I came back from the fairy-tale world, after the Grande Armée was defeated, I kept thinking about the portal in Neuschwanstein Castle. The more I thought about its history, the less sense it made."

"It was a pretty complicated story," Conner said, remembering. "In the early 1800s, the Grande Armée forced the Brothers Grimm to lead them to the fairy-tale world. The brothers took them to Neuschwanstein Castle and activated the portal with the magic panpipe, and the Grande Armée went inside it. What the Armée didn't know was that Mother Goose had bewitched the portal so anyone without magic blood would be trapped inside it for two hundred years."

"Exactly," Bree said. "So what I couldn't stop asking myself was how Emmerich and I got through the portal without being trapped."

Conner's life had been so complicated since

the Grande Armée invaded the fairy-tale world, he'd never had a chance to think about the portal at Neuschwanstein Castle—but Bree was absolutely right! She and Emmerich *should* have been trapped for two centuries just like the Grande Armée. There was only one reason why they weren't.

"You have *magic* in your blood!" Conner exclaimed. "Emmerich's my cousin, so that's where his magic came from, but what about *yours*?"

His heart skipped a beat as he thought of one possibility.

"Oh no—we aren't related, too, are we?" he asked.

"Um…no," Bree said. "You're forgetting the grossest part about the story. In order for the Brothers Grimm to activate the portal at Neuschwanstein Castle, they *also* needed magic in their blood. Mother Goose transferred some of her blood into theirs so they could use the panpipe to trap the Armée. And that magic was passed down from generation to generation of the Grimm family."

"Holy DNA test," Conner said. *"You're a descendant of the Brothers Grimm!"*

Bree nodded. "As you can imagine, I was really eager to prove it. That's why I ran away to my cousin

Cornelia's house in Connecticut. I needed to confirm my family's heritage."

"So that's why Cornelia was so calm about everything she saw at the hospital! Your family has known about magic and the fairy-tale world for longer than my sister and I have!"

"They know about a lot more than that," Bree confessed. "Cornelia, Frenda, and Wanda are part of a secret group called the Sisters Grimm. My fifth-great-grandmother, Maria Grimm, founded the group in 1852. Knowing that the fairy-tale world existed, the women in my family began investigating some magical incidents happening around the world."

"Magical incidents?" Conner asked. "Like what?"

"There have been hundreds of things they've covered up over the years! Mermaid skeletons washing ashore in North America, pixies being photographed in Europe, trolls found wandering the deserts of Australia—you name it! The Sisters Grimm realized creatures from the fairy-tale world were crossing into the Otherworld, but they didn't understand *how*. Your grandmother and the fairies were in charge of all the portals, so how were the creatures getting through without their help?"

"Magic?"

"No—*science!*" Bree said. "The Sisters Grimm discovered that the fairy-tale world is just an alternative dimension of the Otherworld. They're like race cars on the same track. However, the Otherworld used to move at a much faster speed than the fairy-tale world. So every so often, the worlds would briefly overlap—or rather, *collide*. Each time the worlds collided, unbeknownst to the fairies, a portal between worlds would briefly appear. Over the centuries, thousands of magical creatures have accidentally stumbled through a portal and wound up in the Otherworld. But about sixteen years ago, the worlds stopped colliding and the portals stopped appearing altogether."

"Why? What happened?"

Bree laughed. "Do you really have to ask?"

"Wait—it's because me and my sister were born!" Conner exclaimed. "We are children of both worlds, and our birth magically set the Otherworld and the fairy-tale world on similar speeds."

"Right!" Bree said. "And race cars moving at similar speeds take a lot longer to overlap."

"So, how long until the worlds collide again?"

"The Sisters Grimm predict it's very soon.

They're also worried that when it happens again, the overlap may be permanent. It won't be a portal that appears, but a *bridge* that connects the worlds forever."

"Do they know *where* the bridge will appear?" Conner asked.

"They've scientifically mapped everything out," Bree said. "Judging by all the locations of past portals, they're expecting the bridge to appear in the middle of New York City."

"New York City!" Conner said. "What are the chances?"

"I don't think it's a coincidence, Conner," Bree said. "This is a huge interdimensional phenomenon! The Sisters Grimm can't be the only ones who know about it. And if they were able to discover it using *science*, I imagine someone else has discovered it using *magic*. If your sister was kidnapped by a witch, there's a reason she took her to New York City, and I'd bet serious money it has something to do with the worlds colliding."

Conner was pushed back into his seat again, only this time it wasn't from the force of the aircraft, but from fear. Apparently he was wrong—something *could* trouble him more than he already was troubled.

"Attention, ladies and gentlemen," a flight attendant said over the speakers. "The captain has turned on the seat belt sign, as he expects turbulence ahead. We ask that you stay in your seats, because things are about to get very bumpy."

Conner sighed. "She can say that again."

CHAPTER SIX

PRISONERS OF THE MIRROR

Froggy frantically searched every mirror in the Northern Palace for someone who could help him contact Alex and Conner. He figured the twins were most likely in hiding with the royal families, so if he found a person who knew *where* they were hiding, he could send them a message and warn them about the Literary Army's plans to invade the Otherworld.

The more he searched, the more doubtful his

mission became. Each room in the palace was either empty or occupied by the Queen of Hearts' card soldiers, the Wicked Witch's flying monkeys, or one of Captain Hook's pirates. Occasionally Froggy would spot a servant in the palace, but they were never far from the despicable emperors or their loathsome henchmen. When the servants weren't forced to serve, they were locked away in the dungeon, where there were no mirrors for Froggy to communicate through.

Even if Froggy *could* find someone willing to help, it was very unlikely they'd know how to reach the twins. Still, he continued his exhausting pursuit regardless of its improbability. Soon he learned that help wasn't as impossible as he'd thought—*he was just searching the wrong side of the mirrors.*

"Hello."

A soft voice made Froggy jump. His eyes darted back and forth between the palace mirrors as he searched for the source, but he couldn't find where the voice was coming from.

"I'm not in the palace, silly," it laughed. "I'm right behind you."

Froggy looked over his shoulder and jumped when he discovered he wasn't alone in the mirror dimension. Walking toward him out of the darkness was a young girl. She had long raven hair and pale white skin and didn't look a day over eight years old. Froggy had become so used to isolation, it took him a moment to realize the girl wasn't a hallucination.

"Oh my word," he said in disbelief. "You're a... a...*person*!"

The little girl giggled. "Of course I'm a person. What else would I be?"

"Forgive me for being overwhelmed," Froggy apologized. "I'm just so relieved to see someone else. I didn't realize there were *others* trapped in mirrors."

"Oh, there are hundreds of people trapped in mirrors," she said. "I find dozens of them each day."

Froggy searched the darkness around him but didn't find a single soul besides the young girl.

"But where are they?" he asked. "I've been in this world for weeks and I haven't seen anyone but you."

The little girl smiled at Froggy like he was an amusing cartoon.

"You don't have to be trapped *inside* a mirror to be trapped *in* the mirror," she said. "Think about all the people who stare at their reflections and dislike what they see. Think about all the people who base their happiness solely on what they look like. Think about all the people who don't enjoy life because they don't enjoy their appearance. If you ask me, the mirror imprisons us all."

Froggy went silent for a few moments. He hadn't expected such insight to come from someone so young.

"When you put it that way, I suppose this is the second time I've been trapped in a mirror," he said.

"When was the first?" she asked.

"A long time ago, when I was cursed to look like a frog," he explained. "I was so ashamed of how I looked, I spent years hiding from the rest of the world. I let my fear of what others might think of me dictate my whole life. Fortunately, I overcame my fears before it was too late."

"What changed your mind?"

"I found the greatest love and friendship of my life while I felt the ugliest," he said with a smile. "If that doesn't prove how little appearance matters, I don't know what else would."

The little girl sighed and shook her head.

"That's lucky," she said. "It takes most people their whole lives to learn that lesson. Every day I watch more and more people stare at themselves with such deep sadness in their eyes. I try to give them compliments and tell them it's the inside that counts, but they're always so frightened to see a little girl appear, they don't listen to a word I say."

The girl was one of the most peculiar children Froggy had ever met. She spoke so elegantly and moved around the mirrors so freely, it made him question whether she was really a little girl at all.

"What's your name?" he asked.

The girl thought about it, but nothing seemed to come to mind.

"I don't remember," she said. "I'm sure I had one once, I just can't recall what it was."

"That doesn't surprise me," Froggy said. "Memory loss is a side effect of living in this dimension. The longer we stay inside it, the more we fade into nothing but reflections. How long have you been trapped?"

The girl thought even harder but still couldn't find the answer.

"I don't remember that, either," she said with a laugh.

"Doesn't that concern you?"

"It did once, but I forgot why," she said. "Actually,

I find forgetfulness very pleasant. A memory is nice for people with good memories, but amnesia can be quite comforting to others."

"You must have lived a rather tragic life to believe that," Froggy said.

"I suppose I did," she said, pondering. "I miss having dreams, but at least I don't live with nightmares anymore. Perhaps you'll enjoy forgetting, too."

The little girl's bizarre outlook made Froggy even more anxious. He didn't know how much longer he would have his own memory, but she was proof it was only a matter of time before his mind was wiped clean.

"I wish forgetfulness were all I was concerned about," he said. "I'm in desperate need to find someone who can give my friends a warning. Their home is about to be invaded by a terrible army, and I need to contact them before it's too late. Have you ever communicated with someone in the palace without scaring them off?"

The little girl thought about it, and to the amazement of both of them, she had an answer.

"I've been able to communicate with lots of people in the past without frightening them," she recalled. "However, I don't believe I've ever talked to someone in *this* palace."

"You mean, you've traveled to *other* palaces?" Froggy asked.

"Well, of course! I've traveled all over the kingdoms. Haven't you?"

"No," he said. "Besides a witch's basement, the mirrors in the Northern Palace are all I've been able to find in this world."

"You can travel to any mirror you'd like," the little girl explained. "All you have to do is visualize *where* you want to go, and the mirror dimension will take you there. It's as simple as that."

Suddenly, all of Froggy's time in the mirror dimension began to make sense. Had he realized what he wanted to find before he'd started searching, the Northern Palace would have appeared much sooner than it had. Knowing that all the mirrors throughout the kingdoms were available to him gave him his first rush of hope in weeks. If the Bailey twins were near a mirror, he could deliver a warning himself—he just needed to figure out *where* they were hiding.

Froggy closed his eyes, and the first location that came to his mind was the castle in the Center Kingdom. He visualized the castle's hallways, the sitting rooms, the dining rooms, and the spacious library Red had built for him.

"You did it!" the little girl cheered. "Look over there! You made more mirrors appear!"

Froggy opened his eyes and looked where she was pointing. In the distance amid the darkness was a cluster of twinkling lights, as if a small patch of a starry night sky had manifested. The little girl grabbed Froggy's hand and pulled him toward the lights.

"We'll search these mirrors first, and if we don't find your friends there, we'll search every mirror in the kingdoms until we do!" she said.

"You don't mind helping me look for them?" Froggy asked.

"Not at all," the little girl said. "It's been ages since I had an actual activity. By the way, I forgot to ask—what's *your* name?"

Froggy opened his mouth to respond, but nothing came out. He thought he was just experiencing a mental hiccup of sorts, but his silence continued. No matter how hard he thought about it, Froggy couldn't recall his name.

"I...I...I can't remember," he admitted. "But that doesn't matter now—all that matters is finding my friends and warning them."

The little girl shrugged and started to skip as she

pulled him toward the newly materialized mirrors. Froggy was glad she was escorting him; otherwise he would have frozen with panic after forgetting his own name. Wherever the Bailey twins were, he prayed they'd find them quickly. Froggy had to warn them about the Literary Army while he still knew there was something to warn them about.

CHAPTER SEVEN

PIZZA BAGELS AND BARRICADES

In Midtown Manhattan, on the corner of Fifth Avenue and Thirty-Fourth Street, was a famous bistro called Cheesy Street. The café was a tourist hotspot and sold all the food New York City was famous for. Visitors and locals alike journeyed to Cheesy Street for their renowned pizza, bagels, cheesecake, pastrami, and clam chowder. The staff had seen their fair share of eccentric customers over the years, but nothing like the party of twelve who joined them for lunch today.

Mindy, Cindy, Lindy, and Wendy (known in their community as the Book Huggers) shared a plate of Cheesy Street's signature pizza bagels. The girls stared down at the cheesy hybrid on their plates in total silence, with blank expressions. Sitting across from them were all four pairs of the Book Huggers' parents. They eyed their daughters with great caution and concern, as if the girls were explosives with faulty wiring.

"I'm so glad we decided to go on this trip," Mindy's mom said. "It was very last-minute, but sometimes a spontaneous trip is exactly what you need to *clear your head.* Isn't it?"

The Book Huggers didn't respond or look up from their plates.

"I think we picked the perfect place to visit," Cindy's dad said. "Isn't New York an amazing city? There are so many things to do and see here. What's been your favorite attraction so far?"

Once again, the Book Huggers didn't say a word or move a muscle.

"I loved Central Park," Lindy's mom said. "I also liked the Empire State Building, visiting Ellis Island, our tour of the United Nations, and of course, last night's performance of *The Phantom of the Opera*."

"I imagine everyone leaves New York feeling influenced or inspired in some way," Wendy's dad said. "It really makes you think how many *different* people there are in this world. It reminds you how many *different* interests there are to devote your time and energy to. It sure makes Willow Crest and everyone who lives there seem rather dull. *Wouldn't you agree?*"

The Book Huggers nodded in perfect unison without looking up. It was rather creepy, but their parents were thankful for any response they could get.

"Let's address the elephant in the room, and I'm not talking about Cheesy Street's mascot," Mindy's other mom said. "We know the last week has been really challenging for you. Recovering from a psychotic breakdown requires profound strength. *Hallucination* and *obsession* are very difficult things to recognize and admit to, but we couldn't be prouder of you girls for taking the proper steps to treat yourselves. Dr. Jackson was very confident that all you needed was a little time, a little love, and some pleasant distractions, and you'd be good as new. Hopefully this spontaneous trip will be just what the doctor ordered."

Finally, the Book Huggers looked up from their plates and smiled at their parents. The trip itself wasn't enough to take the Bailey twins off their minds, but the compassion coming from their parents warmed their hearts.

"Thank you," Mindy said. "And even though we've been quiet all week, we really appreciate you taking us on this trip."

"Yeah, this week has been awesome," Cindy said. "It was really nice of you guys to all take time off from work to treat us like this."

"Whatever we may be going through, we're lucky to have parents like you to go through it with," Lindy added.

Wendy pointed to her heart and then pointed to their parents—implying that their compassion was fully reciprocated. The Book Huggers' parents were so relieved to finally hear their children speak, tears came to their eyes.

"Fantastic," Cindy's mom said. "I'm so glad we're all on the same page. Now, let's make the most of our last day in the city. I say we take a helicopter tour after lunch, but first, let's order some dessert!"

The party of twelve happily looked over the dessert menu. Their concentration was momentarily interrupted by a procession of four police cars speeding down the street with their sirens blaring.

"Wow, whatever is happening at the library must be serious," Lindy's dad said. "We've seen dozens of police cars headed that way, and I heard they evacuated all the buildings in a two-block radius."

"When we were shopping on Fifth Avenue earlier, we asked an officer what was going on," Wendy's mom said. "They told us it was a big gas leak but nothing they couldn't handle. The evacuation is just a precaution."

The Book Huggers looked out the window behind their parents to watch the police cars racing down Fifth Avenue, but their hearts stopped at another alarming sight on Thirty-Fourth Street. Through the front window of a taxi van waiting for the cops to pass, they saw a very familiar freckled face.

"Conner!" the Book Huggers collectively gasped.

Their parents quickly snapped their heads back toward their daughters and stared at them as if they were explosives whose fuses had now been lit.

"What did you say, girls?" Mindy's mom asked.

"Cobbler," Cindy's dad suggested. "I think they said they want the *cobbler.* Isn't that right?"

"No, Dad!" Cindy said. "Look behind you! It isn't a hallucination this time! Conner Bailey is in a taxi outside Cheesy Street!"

The Book Huggers' parents quickly turned to the window, but thanks to some unknown force in the universe that constantly made them the punch line of a big cosmic joke, Conner bent down a second before they would have seen him. The only person the Book Huggers' parents saw inside the taxi was its Middle Eastern driver. The taxi had continued down the street before Conner resurfaced.

"NOOOO!" Mindy screamed. "He was right there—*right there!*"

"I saw him, too, I swear it!" Lindy protested. "Conner Bailey was just outside the window!"

"But why would he be here?" Cindy asked. "Of all the restaurants in New York City, why would he be outside ours?"

"There's only one explanation!" Mindy announced. "We've been right the whole time! Something otherworldly is going on with the Bailey twins! It started in school, it spread to the hospital, and now it's in *New York City!*"

Wendy made two fists and slammed them on the

table, as if to say *"THERE IS A VAST CONSPIRACY AGAINST US AND WE MUST GET TO THE BOTTOM OF IT!"*

The Book Huggers burst into tears. Their parents exchanged exasperated looks and sighed—apparently New York City wasn't the pleasant distraction they'd hoped it would be. Even though everyone in Cheesy Street was already looking at their table, Lindy's mom raised a hand to get the waiter's attention.

"Check, please!" she said.

After a turbulent flight and a rough landing at John F. Kennedy International Airport, Conner and his friends hopped into a taxi van for another bumpy ride into Manhattan. As if the driver were being paid per pothole, the taxi rattled and shook as it traveled down the highway toward Midtown.

Goldilocks had a difficult time holding on to Hero, so she put him in the BabyBjörn Red had purchased. The newborn wasn't bothered by the rocky ride at all. After nine months in Goldilocks's womb, Hero was used to such commotion and found it quite comforting. The rougher things became, the easier it was for him to sleep.

Conner sat in the front passenger seat and changed the driver's radio to the local news to hear if there had been any developments since the night before. According to the news, a massive gas leak was responsible for all the barricades and evacuations in the area surrounding the New York Public Library. However, to Conner's surprise, nothing was mentioned about the lively lion statues they had seen on television.

"I don't understand," he said. "There was footage of the statues swiping at police officers! We can't be the only ones who saw it."

"They're probably covering it up to prevent hysteria," Bree said. "It's just like the 1947 UFO crash in Roswell, New Mexico. Newspapers reported that wreckage of a flying saucer had been discovered, and then the following day, the army ordered the press to retract the story and say it was just a weather balloon."

Conner gulped at the thought of Alex being turned into another weather balloon. He was so worried about his sister, he barely noticed the Queens neighborhoods zipping past his window or the Manhattan skyline in the distance ahead. The taxi entered the Queens-Midtown Tunnel, which stretched underneath the

East River, and reemerged in the middle of Manhattan. Conner and his friends stared at the city in awe as their taxi zigzagged between the crowded sidewalks and towering skyscrapers. The hustling metropolis was such a spectacular sight, it almost took Conner's mind off Alex.

"The whole city feels like it's buzzing," Goldilocks noted. "They must sell a lot of caffeine here."

"The buildings stand higher than beanstalks!" Jack said. "Conner, why didn't you tell us New York City was so . . . *tall*?"

"Actually, I'm just as amazed as you are," Conner said. "I've written about cities like this, but I've never been able to describe the feeling it gives you at first sight. Now I know it's because it *can't* be described in words."

Red grunted—forever unimpressed with the Otherworld.

"Sure, it's *big*—but why does everything need to be so boxy?" she asked. "Is it too much to ask for a tower, or a dome, or a sensible spiral? I feel like a mouse in a shoe-box closet."

They drove through a wide intersection, and the glistening roof of the Chrysler Building came into view. Red squealed and pressed her hands and forehead against her window.

"Now *that's* more like it!" she said.

The taxi paused briefly on the corner of Fifth Avenue and Thirty-Fourth Street, waiting for a procession of police vehicles to pass by. Conner could have sworn he recognized a few people in the window of a restaurant called Cheesy Street, but he figured it was just his mind playing tricks on him. As he moved to take a second look, he dropped his wallet on the floorboard. By the time he sat back up, the taxi was already moving again.

Once the police were gone, the driver turned south on Fifth Avenue and pulled over between Thirty-Third and Thirty-Fourth Street.

"I know you wanted to get as close to the library as possible, but you may want to get out here," he suggested. "Traffic is backed up in this area because of the gas leak. It'll be faster if you just walk the rest of the way."

"That works," Conner said. "How much do I owe you?"

"That'll be sixty bucks total," the driver said.

"We have to *pay* for this ride?" Red asked in

disbelief. "For goodness' sake, a runaway carriage would have been more comfortable. We were two bumps away from having our innards scrambled!"

"Don't complain to me, lady," the driver said. "I took the smooth streets."

Conner retrieved some cash from his wallet and paid the driver. He and his friends got out of the taxi and joined the bustling pedestrians on the Fifth Avenue sidewalk. Conner looked up and down the street, but the crowds made it difficult for him to figure out where they were.

"Which way is the public library?" he asked, thinking aloud.

"I'd look it up on my phone, but I don't want my parents to track me—*it's a long story*," Bree said. "Looks like we'll have to resort to ancient methods and *ask* for directions."

Conner and Bree tried to flag someone down, but all the tourists and locals breezed right past them. There were so many people, Red couldn't see where she was walking and almost stepped on a homeless man sitting on the ground.

"Hey, Your Majesty!" he said. "Watch where you're going."

The man was scruffy and wore a janitor's uniform

under a dirty brown coat. Red smiled down at him and patted his head like he was a dog.

"Oh, bless you," she said. "Thank you for recognizing me, but there's no need for formal titles while I'm in this world."

"Red, he's being sarcastic," Bree said. "Most people in the Otherworld don't walk around in ball gowns and tiaras."

Since the homeless man was the only person on the street who wasn't in a hurry to get somewhere else, Conner figured he was their best shot at getting directions to the library.

"Excuse me, sir?" he said. "Could you tell us how to get to the New York Public Library from here?"

"Sure I *could*," the homeless man said. "Got a dollar?"

Conner shrugged and gave him a dollar. The homeless man held it toward the sun to make sure it was a legitimate bill.

"Walk north on this street for six blocks and make a left—you can't miss it," he said. "Although I doubt they're letting anyone get close after what happened last night."

"Are you talking about the gas leak?" Bree asked.

"A gas leak? Is *that* what they said happened?"

The homeless man snorted and shook his head disapprovingly. "*Typical*. They're always trying to control people by keeping them in the dark. Well, they can't control me! I was at the library last night and I saw what really happened with my own eyes."

Conner and his friends formed a half circle around the homeless man, which seemed to make him a little nervous.

"Mind telling us what you saw?" Conner asked. "We'd love to know what's really going on."

"I'd love to tell you, but a story will cost you ten bucks," the man said.

"Ten bucks?" Conner said. "But you only charged me a dollar for directions."

"Listen, kid, I didn't wind up on the streets from being a bad businessman. If I got something you want, it's gonna cost you."

Conner rolled his eyes and gave the homeless man ten dollars. Once the man had inspected the money, he tucked it away and began his story.

"It was around midnight and I was sleeping down by the library," he said. "They've got this bench near a fountain—it's my favorite place to take a snooze in the city. Anyhoo, I was dreaming about playing in the World Series when I was rudely awoken by the sound of police sirens. I was worried the library security guard had called the fuzz on me, so I hid behind some bushes. The next thing I know, some broad comes floating out of the library like a ghost! She raised her hands into the sky and *BAM! Lightning struck both the lion statues!* Naturally, once I saw that, I bolted like a rat in a cathouse. To be honest, it's not even the first time I've seen magic in this city—but hey, who's gonna believe a bum like me?"

Conner's heart was beating so hard, he could feel it in multiple parts of his body. He leaned down and looked the homeless man directly in the eye.

"The girl who floated out of the library—what did she look like?" he asked.

"She was really pale," the man said. "She had bright blue eyes and long reddish-blondish hair, and wore a white dress. Come to think of it, she looked a lot like *you*, kid."

"Alex," Conner gasped. "We were right—she's here! She's at the library!"

Without any warning, he dashed up Fifth Avenue as fast as he could, and his friends followed. They weaved through the crowds on the sidewalk until they came to a dead stop at a barricade on Thirty-Eighth Street.

The blockade was an overwhelming sight. A dozen police cars were parked in a row across the street to prevent pedestrians and traffic from going any farther. Beyond the cars, dozens and dozens of police officers were scattered throughout the vacated area. Conner tried sneaking past the barricade, but an officer blocked him.

"Whoa, whoa, whoa," the officer said. "Where's the fire?"

"Please, you have to let me through," Conner said. "It's an emergency."

"Sorry, no one is allowed past this point," the officer said. "They're clearing up a nasty gas leak up by the library. It isn't safe."

"Yes, I know that's what they're telling people, but my sister is the one at the library! I need to get to her before someone harms her!"

"Young man, the library has been evacuated," the officer said. "I promise, wherever your sister was, she's been moved to a safe location."

"No, you don't understand!" Conner yelled. "She's the one causing all this! You need to let me through so I can help her!"

As if Conner were on autopilot, he pushed the officer out of his way, squeezed between the rows of police vehicles, and made a run for the library before he even realized what he was doing. Unfortunately, he was only half a block past the barricade when he was tackled to the pavement by another police officer. Conner fought the officer off with all his might, determined to reach the library. It took two more officers to keep him pinned to the ground. They handcuffed him and threw him into the backseat of the nearest vehicle.

"You've got to let me go!" Conner pleaded. *"The whole world may be in danger if you don't let me find my sister!"*

"You're out of your mind, kid!" an officer said, and slammed the car door. "Stay in there and chill out!"

It all happened so fast, none of Conner's friends knew what to do. They were vastly outnumbered by the police officers standing nearby. If they tried to intervene now, they'd *all* get arrested. Conner looked through the window at his friends standing helplessly on the sidewalk and mouthed *"Sorry."* Now that he'd been detained in the backseat of a police car, the odds of finding Alex had plummeted. One impulsive move to save his sister might have cost them everything.

Suddenly, the ground began to vibrate. Everyone

in the area worried it was an earthquake until the vibration was accompanied by the sound of roaring engines. Conner, his friends, and all the police officers looked down Thirty-Eighth Street and discovered a long row of beige Hummers speeding toward them. The police allowed the Hummers through the barricade, and they parked side by side in an impressive straight line. Swarms of United States Marines emerged from the vehicles in camouflage uniforms with their weapons ready.

An older man with gray hair and broad shoulders stepped out of the first Hummer and all the Marines lined up behind him. Unlike the soldiers, the older man wore a green dress uniform decorated with medals. He also wore dark sunglasses and was smoking a cigar. He scanned the area like he had just stepped into a war zone and then directed his stern gaze at the police officers.

"Which one of you is Commissioner Healy?" he asked.

An older African-American man in a navy blue suit stepped out from the group of police officers.

"General Wilson, I presume," the commissioner said. "Thank you for coming, sir."

The commissioner and the general shook hands just a few feet from the police vehicle that Conner sat inside. Thanks to a slightly rolled-down window, he could hear every word the men were saying. He ducked down in the backseat so they wouldn't see him eavesdropping.

"Commissioner, will you please tell me what the *heck* is going on in your city?" the general said. "What could possibly warrant the president's decision to put boots on the ground?"

"I wish we had more answers for you, General, but we're still trying to figure it out," Commissioner Healy said. "Long story short, the library is under attack. Two of my officers responded to a distress call early this morning and discovered a young girl with strange abilities. She caused lightning to appear and somehow made the lion statues on the library steps come to life. The lions are currently guarding the library and attack anyone who tries to enter it. Once we were able to obtain photographic proof, we contacted the White House."

Interestingly, the general didn't question the commissioner's report, as Conner had expected.

"And where is the girl *now*?" the general asked.

"As far as we know, she's still inside the library," the commissioner said. "What she's doing is anyone's guess."

General Wilson took a long drag on his cigar and slowly exhaled as he absorbed this information. After a moment, he turned on his heel and addressed the Marines behind him.

"All right, soldiers—it's time to get to work," the general ordered. "I want the barricade around the library extended eight blocks in each direction. Contact the Pentagon and have them establish a no-fly zone above the city of Manhattan—I don't want anything leaking to the press. I want snipers stationed on every roof surrounding the library. Once we take our position at the base of the steps, we'll open fire on the statues and try to take them out; then we'll find the girl inside."

The commissioner was appalled by what he heard. "General, you can't shoot the lion statues! They're national landmarks!"

General Wilson removed his sunglasses and looked the commissioner in the eye.

"Thank you for your input, Commissioner, but your little backyard circus is now a matter of national security," he said. "I'll decide what measures I should or should not take to ensure that your city stays in one piece. If you have a problem with that, I'll have you placed on the other side of that barricade faster than you can say '*I Love New York.*'"

The commissioner didn't argue any further. The general nodded to his Marines and they spread out like cockroaches to fulfill his orders. The general returned to his Hummer and was driven up Fifth Avenue to get a closer look at the library. As the commissioner and his police officers watched the Hummers drive off, Jack snuck past the blockade and quietly opened the back door of the police car Conner was sitting in.

"Come on!" Jack whispered. *"Quick—while they're all looking away!"*

Once Conner had regrouped with his friends, they raced down Fifth Avenue and ducked into the first alley they could find. With one slice of his axe, Jack freed Conner from the handcuffs binding him. Conner walked around the alley in a huff and angrily kicked the side of a dumpster.

"This is getting more difficult by the second!" he moaned.

"At least we know *where* your sister is," Goldilocks reminded him. "That alone puts us in a better place than we were."

"We still have to get to her, though," Conner said. "These army guys won't care if Alex is being controlled by a witch or not—they'll *kill her* the moment they think she's a threat. We've got to get to her before they do, and I don't have the slightest idea of how to do that. And I'm sorry, Jack, but no amount of imagination or positive thinking is going to help us get past the NYPD, the United States Marines, *and* two possessed lion statues!"

Bree, Jack, Goldilocks, and Red didn't even try to persuade him otherwise. They paced around in silence as they tried to brainstorm a possible plan. Their train of thought was interrupted by the sound of someone clearing their throat—someone who wasn't in their group. They looked up and saw that the homeless man from earlier was standing a few feet away.

"Forgive the intrusion," he said. "I saw your little scuffle with the fuzz back there. I know they didn't want to listen to you, but I'd like to help if you'll let me."

"Sorry, dude, I'm out of cash," Conner said.

"This time I'm offering my services free of charge," the homeless man said. "I know I may not look like much, but I know how to get to your sister."

"No offense, but I sincerely doubt that," Conner said. "We need to get inside the public library, and every entrance is being guarded by the US Marines and two man-eating statues!"

A sly smile spread across the homeless man's face. "You're wrong," he said. "They aren't guarding *every* entrance."

Chapter Eight

THE CALVIN COOLIDGE EXPRESS

P er General Wilson's orders, the US Marines began evacuating every building within a ten-block radius of the New York Public Library. Watching the soldiers move from building to building and forcing people out of their homes and businesses made Conner feel like he was watching a scene from an apocalyptic movie. Judging from the looks on the New Yorkers' faces, everyone knew the situation wasn't a gas leak—something *far worse* was happening in Midtown Manhattan.

The homeless man led Conner and his friends covertly from alley to alley, careful not to attract the attention of the Marines. With every step Conner wondered if they were doing the right thing by following him, or if they were putting their trust in a complete lunatic.

"Where are you taking us?" Conner asked.

"*Shhhh!*" the homeless man said, and placed a finger over his mouth. "If they catch us sneaking around, we'll never get to your sister."

"Sorry—*where are you taking us?*" Conner whispered.

"We're going to a subway entrance on the corner of Fortieth and Broadway."

"We're taking the *subway*?" Conner asked. "But a train won't get us inside the library!"

"We don't need a train where we're going," the homeless man said.

The homeless man dashed across the street to hide behind a pile of trash, and the others followed him. They moved from building to building very slowly and only crossed streets when they were certain no Marines were watching. By the time they reached the intersection of Fortieth and Broadway, Midtown Manhattan was practically a ghost town and it was getting dark out. After a quick huddle behind a large delivery truck, the homeless man raced across the intersection to the southwest corner and hurried down the steep steps into the subway station. A moment later, he popped his head up and whistled to the others.

"The station's empty!" he called to them. "Hurry—while the coast is clear!"

Conner and his friends joined him underground. Their footsteps echoed off the station's title walls. The homeless man jumped over the turnstile to avoid paying, and the others copied him. Red was the least agile, and her gown got caught in the revolving turnstile. Goldilocks had to slice off a layer of her dress to set her free.

"Now everyone follow me to the end of the platform," the homeless man said.

"Wait!" Conner said. "We aren't going any farther until you tell us *exactly* where we're headed."

"Kid, I promise it'll make sense once we're there, but until then, you'll just have to trust me."

The homeless man reached the end of the long platform and jumped down onto the train tracks.

"He can't be serious," Bree said. "We're not actually going to follow him *down there*, are we?"

"What choice do we have?" Conner asked.

"Don't stop now—we're almost there!" the homeless man said.

Conner, Bree, and Jack jumped off the platform and then offered their hands to help Goldilocks and Hero, but Red took their hands first. The homeless man removed a flashlight from inside his coat and sprinted down the train tunnel.

"You might want to hurry—trains usually run through here every ten minutes," he warned.

Fearing a speeding train would hit them at any moment, Conner and his friends ran after the homeless man as fast as they could. The farther they went, the darker the tunnel became. Soon the shaky light from the homeless man's flashlight was all that was keeping them from tripping over the train tracks. Suddenly, the homeless man made a quick left turn and disappeared from sight. When the others caught up with him, they entered a different tunnel they would have never spotted on their own. Unlike the previous one, the new tunnel had no visible cables or train tracks on the ground.

"Welcome to the Calvin Coolidge Express!" the

homeless man announced. "Or at least what's finished of it."

"The *what*?" Conner asked.

The homeless man chuckled. "Don't worry, very few people know it exists," he said. "In 1928, construction began on a new transit system to take New Yorkers from Staten Island all the way to Central Park. The following year the Great Depression hit and construction came to a halt. Later, the need for steel was so high during World War Two that plans were scrapped altogether. By the time the war ended, the Calvin Coolidge Express was completely forgotten."

"Whatever it is, it smells awful," Red said. She took the can of Febreze out of her purse and sprayed the air around them.

"Unfortunately, the tunnels were built right beside the sewers, but you get used to the smell after a while."

"Why would you bring us to an abandoned subway tunnel?" Conner asked.

"*Because* one of the many stops planned for the Calvin Coolidge Express was Bryant Park," the man explained. "The city didn't want to obstruct the park, so they decided to place the stop in the base-ment of the New York Public Library."

Conner's face lit up so much, he practically glowed in the dark tunnel. He heard the man loud and clear, but it sounded too good to be true.

"So you're saying we can get to the library from this tunnel?" he asked.

"Like I said before, they aren't guarding *every* entrance," the homeless man reiterated. "See why I didn't tell you where we were going? You wouldn't have believed a bum like me unless you saw it with your own eyes."

Conner was embarrassed to admit it to himself, but the homeless man was right. If he had been just a tiny bit more critical of their guide, they would have been rounded up and sent away like all the other New Yorkers in Midtown Manhattan.

"I just realized we haven't been properly intro-duced," he said. "I'm Conner Bailey, and these are my friends Bree, Red, Jack, Goldie, and their son, Hero. What's your name?"

"The name's Rusty—Rusty Bagasarian," the homeless man said with a quick bow.

"Thank you so much for leading us here, Rusty,"

Conner said. "How did you even know this tunnel existed?"

"You learn a lot about a city when you live on its streets," Rusty said.

"Have you always been poor?" Red asked.

"Red, don't be rude!" Goldilocks reprimanded her.

"It's all right—I get that all the time," Rusty said. "Homelessness is a recent chapter for me. I used to live in Brooklyn and worked as a janitor at the Belvedere Castle in Central Park. A couple of months ago I was fired and lost everything."

"Why were you fired?" Jack asked.

"Well, to put it bluntly, I saw something *magical* and it changed my life forever."

"Was it *Hamilton*?" Red asked. "I keep seeing signs about him posted all over the city. If he's anything like Shakeyfruit's *Hamhead* I hope we get a chance to meet him."

The others rolled their eyes and ignored her.

"Earlier, when you told us about the library, you mentioned it wasn't the first time you'd seen magic in the city," Bree said. "I didn't think you were being serious, but now I'm really interested to hear about it."

Rusty let out a deep sigh before telling them. Clearly, it was a difficult subject for him to talk about.

"It happened a few months ago when I used to work night shifts at Belvedere Castle," he said. "I was in the middle of cleaning the joint when this strange vibration suddenly came out of nowhere. I figured it was just an earthquake and went back to work, but when I got home, none of the morning news stations were reporting an earthquake. I was convinced I had just imagined it, but then a few weeks later, the vibration happened again. The second time was much stronger and lasted longer than the first. I called the police to report an active fault line, but they assured me it was just a subway running underneath the castle. However, when I got home and looked at a map, I saw there *aren't* any subway lines that run below that part of Central Park. The rumbling didn't happen again until a few weeks later. The third time rattled the castle so hard, it shattered windows and left cracks all over the floor. I was nearly knocked off the balcony I was cleaning. I remember it didn't feel anything like an earthquake or a train, but like something enormous was *hatching* from an invisible egg. I looked up *and that's when I saw it*."

"*Saw what?*" Conner asked.

"The best way I can describe it is *a window into another world*," Rusty said. "For a brief second I saw a huge forest of evergreen trees and a bright starry sky. It looked like something out of a storybook— couldn't have been more different from the hustle of New York City. Then the window disappeared as fast as it had appeared."

Conner and Bree exchanged a grave look. Without any solid proof, they knew exactly what Rusty had witnessed—*the bridge between worlds was starting to form.*

"I went to the police station and filed a report about what I saw, but none of the officers believed me. A copy of the report was sent to the castle's property manager and they fired me. They thought I had caused all the damages myself and was making up a ridiculous story to cover it up. Word about my police report spread all over town, and no one wanted to hire me after that."

"That's terrible!" Bree said. "Did the window ever appear again?"

"I didn't see it again, but *others* have seen it appear all over the city," Rusty said.

"But *who*? And *where*?" Conner asked.

"You can ask them yourself," Rusty said. "Follow me."

They continued down the Calvin Coolidge Express

line. Flickering lights came into view ahead, and soon they discovered a vast underground campsite that was home to dozens and dozens of homeless people. The tunnel was full of tents, sleeping bags, and furniture made from cardboard and newspapers. The homeless people were spread out through the camp in groups; some kept warm standing over blazing trash cans, some played musical instruments, and some watched a man teaching a family of rats to fetch.

Rusty escorted Conner and his friends to a group who sat in the corner of the camp. The group included an older man in a blue suit, a woman in a fur coat, another woman in a Yankees baseball hat, and a third woman wearing a T-shirt that said READ BANNED BOOKS and tinfoil wrapped around her head. They were gathered around a radio listening to a patchy broadcast.

"There you are, Bagasarian!" the man said. "We heard there was an evacuation in Midtown. We were worried you got swept away."

"Conner and company, allow me to introduce you to my underground family," Rusty said. "This is Jerry Oswald, Annette Crabtree, Judy Harlow, and Roxie Goldberg."

"I hope you aren't from the papers!" Judy said, and hid her face behind the collar of her fur coat. "If I get included in another one of those savage *Where Are They Now* editorials, I'll just die!"

"For the hundredth time, Judy, *you aren't famous!*" Annette said.

"How dare you!" Judy said. "I was on Broadway!"

"It was Off-Broadway, and it was in the eighties," Roxie reminded her. "No one's looking for you now."

"They're not reporters, they're just trying to get inside the public library," Rusty explained. "But since we're passing through, they want to hear your stories about seeing *you know what.*"

Rusty's friends were as mortified as if he had just disclosed a nasty secret. They looked around the tunnel to make sure no one else had heard him.

"Why do you always have to bring *that* up?" Jerry asked.

"They'll only mock us like the rest of the world," Judy said.

"Haven't we been through enough already?" Annette asked.

Rusty's friends got to their feet and tried to walk away, but Conner and Bree blocked them from going too far.

"We're not here to insult you," Conner said. "We just want to know what you saw and where you saw it. *Please*, it might help us answer a lot of questions."

"And it's not like you have anything to lose," Red added.

Despite the rude comment from his friend, the homeless people sensed the sincerity in Conner's voice. They looked at one another and shrugged.

"I used to be a maid at the Plaza Hotel," Annette said. "Late one night, I went into the Presidential Suite for the turndown service. As I was making up the bed, the room began shaking. All the furniture was knocked to the floor and the guests' belongings rolled everywhere. The next thing I knew, a forest appeared out of thin air. It hovered in the sitting room for a few minutes and then vanished. The guests returned shortly after; they saw all their belongings scattered around the floor and accused me of stealing their things. They reported me to the hotel manager and I was fired. Nobody wanted to hire a maid with a history of theft, so now I live down here."

"I was on the verge of a comeback when I saw the forest," Judy said. "I had just been cast as Nurse Number Seven on the soap opera *The Cute and the Complacent*. Anyway, I was sitting in my dressing room at Rockefeller Center—that's where they film the show—when it was hit with a terrible tremor. The forest appeared over my vanity and I screamed for help. By the time a producer came to check on me, it was gone. They thought I was crazy and had my character written out of the script. I've become the laughingstock of the Screen Actors Guild and haven't been hired since."

"I was a teller at National Bank on Forty-Fourth Street," Jerry said. "I was working late one night and went into the vault to store a deposit. Suddenly, the vault started to rattle. It was so powerful it knocked all the deposit boxes open and money spilled onto the floor. The commotion set off the alarm and police arrived within the hour. Had they showed up just a moment sooner, they would have seen the forest for themselves. My boss fired me for carelessness and I couldn't find another job. I told my wife what had happened, but she didn't believe me and threw me out of the house."

Everyone turned to Roxie Goldberg, anxious to hear her story next.

"Why are you looking at me? I never saw a forest appear. I live down here because I hate paying taxes."

Conner sensed there was a pattern to the homeless

people's encounters. He paced back and forth as he thought about the information they had provided.

"How long ago did each of you see the forest appear?" he asked.

"Four months ago," Rusty said, then scrunched up his brow. "As a matter of fact, it was four months ago to this very day."

"What a coincidence," Annette said. "I saw it exactly two months ago."

"Precisely *one* month ago for me," Judy said.

"Two weeks," Jerry said.

"And how long did the apparition last?" Conner asked.

"It only lasted a few seconds at the castle," Rusty said.

"It was quick, but I'd say a minute or two," Annette said.

"Fifteen minutes at least," Judy said.

"About forty-five minutes, I suspect," Jerry said.

"Interesting," Conner said. "So the sightings are happening faster and faster, and each time the apparition appears, it stays twice as long. If it continues in this pattern, that would put the next sighting *tonight* and it could stick around for an hour or two. I just wish we could tell *where* it's gonna be."

An idea popped into Bree's head and she gasped—startling Jack and Goldilocks beside her.

"Actually, I think the locations may be just as predictable," she said.

Bree looked around the tunnel and snatched a map off a sleeping homeless person. She spread it against the wall of the tunnel and had Jack and Goldilocks hold it in place.

"Mr. Oswald, what street was National Bank on again?" she asked.

"Forty-Fourth and Fifth Avenue," Jerry said.

"And Ms. Harlow, where is Rockefeller Center located?"

"Between Forty-Eighth and Fifty-First," Judy said.

"And the Plaza Hotel?"

"It's at Fifty-Ninth and Fifth," Annette said.

"And Rusty, I know there are no streets in Central Park, but if Belvedere Castle *were* on a street, what would it be?" Bree asked.

"That's easy," Rusty said. "It's just north of the Seventy-Ninth Street Transverse."

Bree pulled a marker out of her pocket and made a note of all the locations. Once she was done, she took a step back and studied the map.

"Just what I thought," she said. "The bridge first appeared on Seventy-Ninth Street at Belvedere Castle. Next, it appeared at the Plaza Hotel—exactly *twenty blocks* south of the castle. After that, the forest appeared at Rockefeller Center—exactly *ten blocks* south of the hotel. And finally, it appeared at National Bank on Forty-Fourth Street—exactly *five blocks* south of the center. The bridge is traveling in a semi-straight line through New York City, and each time it appears, it covers half the ground it did before."

"So everything *is* a pattern!" Conner said. "That means we can trace when *and* where the bridge will appear next! According to the formulas, that would place the next appearance tonight at two and a half blocks south of National Bank on Forty-Fourth Street."

Goldilocks gulped. "So what's located between Forty-First and Forty-Second Street?"

Conner and Bree traced the map, and their fingers arrived at the same spot at the same time. They exchanged a long, fearful glance before turning to the others.

"The New York Public Library," they said in unison.

"This practically confirms everything we've

suspected," Bree said. "Whoever took Alex to the library definitely knows about the bridge between worlds. But this time, I don't think it's going anywhere. Just like the Sisters Grimm predicted, this might be the bridge's final stop. Tonight may be the night when *worlds collide*!"

Conner's eyes filled with panic. "Rusty, you've got to take us to the library," he said. *"Now."*

CHAPTER NINE

THE SCARIEST VILLAIN
OF ALL

Conner and his friends charged down the Calvin Coolidge Express tunnel as Rusty led them deeper through the abandoned subway. The homeless man ran so fast he could barely keep his flashlight steady, but even in the dark, Rusty knew the tunnel like the back of his hand. Eventually they arrived at the construction site of a small subway platform that had never been finished. Ladders, tools, and paint buckets had remained untouched since the project was halted in the 1920s.

"See that hatch above the platform?" Rusty asked, and aimed his flashlight at a circular door in the ceiling. "Climb through it and it'll take you into the lower level of the library."

"Thanks for bringing us here, Rusty," Conner said. "If we're able to save my sister, it'll be all because of you. I wish I had something to repay you with."

"It's been a long time since I felt useful," the homeless man said with a smile. "That's all the thanks I need. Good luck finding your sister, kid."

Conner and his friends shook Rusty's hand and climbed onto the unfinished platform. Jack retrieved a ladder and positioned it directly below the hatch. He climbed up the ladder and attempted to open it, but the door wouldn't budge.

"It's stuck," he called down.

"It's been nearly a century since it was opened," Rusty said. "It may need a good push."

Taking his advice, Jack pressed his back against the hatch and pushed against it with all his might. The door opened with a loud crunch, and pieces of wood fell from the ceiling. Opening the hatch punched a large hole through the floorboards and carpet above it. Jack climbed through the hole and then helped the others through the floor of the library's lower level.

The gang emerged inside a long room with colorful walls. It was filled with tiny bookshelves and miniature tables and chairs. Paintings and stuffed animals of classic literary characters smiled down at them from every corner.

"Oh my," Red said. "I didn't realize this was a library for dwarfs."

"This is the children's center," Bree said. "There's a lot more than this."

"How big is the library?" Goldilocks asked.

"It's 646,680 square feet, to be exact," Bree said. "There are four levels with over forty rooms open to the public."

Her friends were surprised she had the information so readily available.

"How do you know all that?" Red asked.

"The plane had Wi-Fi," Bree said with a shrug.

Any knowledge about the structure was useful to them, but Conner's stomach filled with knots once he heard how big the library was. Whoever had taken his sister had plenty of corners to lurk in.

"Should we split up and look for her?" Jack asked.

"No, let's stay together," Conner said. "I don't want to give Alex's kidnapper the chance to knock us off one by one—sorry, I've seen too many horror movies. We'll search each level, one room at a time, until we find her."

Conner's friends nodded and followed him out of the children's center. If they had any doubts about Alex's whereabouts, they quickly subsided as they stepped into the hallway. All the walls and floors of the library were covered in thick vines and ivy. The plants were covered in vibrant flowers that bloomed as Conner and his friends passed them. Exotic butterflies fluttered through the air from blossom to blossom. In just a matter of hours, Alex had enchanted the national landmark so that it resembled an ancient temple in the middle of a jungle.

"Strange," Jack observed. "It reminds me of when the Enchantress attacked the Eastern Kingdom and covered it in plants just like this."

"Let's pray that's where the similarities end," Goldilocks said.

They walked in a tight group as they explored the lower level of the library. Jack gripped his axe, Goldilocks drew her sword, and Red clung to her can of Febreze as they went. With all their eyes put together, there wasn't an inch of the lower level they didn't scan.

Once the lower level had been searched, they slowly moved up the stone staircase to the first floor. They searched behind every pillar and beneath each archway of the entrance hall. They looked through the aisles of merchandise in the gift shop and under all the desks in the state-of-the-art education center but found nothing out of the ordinary besides vines and ivy.

They journeyed to the next floor of the spacious structure and searched all the galleries, corridors, and research rooms. Once that level had been inspected, they climbed the stairs to the top level. They found portraits and murals, candelabras and statues, but not a trace of Alex anywhere. Soon there was only one room left to search. Conner and his friends gathered at the doors, and each took a deep breath before going inside—*this was it*.

The Rose Main Reading Room was the largest and most recognizable room in the New York Public Library. Although Conner and Bree had never seen it in person, they instantly remembered seeing it in movies and television. The room was filled with dozens of hanging chandeliers and two rows of wide tables. The high ceiling was made of beautiful wood carvings that framed painted murals of cloudy skies. The walls were lined with arched windows and two levels of bookshelves. However, all the shelves were empty because the books were floating magically through the air like a thousand balloons.

At the far end of the long room, between the rows of tables, they found Alex asleep on the floor. As soon as he laid eyes on her, Conner ran to his sister's side and scooped her up in his arms. Her face was paler than he had ever seen it and her skin felt cold as ice.

"Alex, it's me—it's Conner!" he said. "We've found you and we've come to take you home!"

Conner brushed the hair out of her face, but Alex didn't open her eyes.

"Alex, can you hear me?" he asked.

He gave her a gentle nudge, but his sister didn't open her eyes or move a muscle. Conner listened to her chest to make sure she was breathing and then checked her pulse.

"She's alive," he said. "But barely."

"Why isn't she responding?" Bree asked.

"She must be under some sort of spell," Conner said, and tapped the side of her face. "Alex, you have to fight this off so we can help you! Who's doing this to you? Who's making you enchant things and attack people?"

"She won't wake up unless I *tell* her to wake up."

Conner, Bree, Jack, Goldilocks, and Red turned to the other side of the room and discovered they weren't alone. A woman in a long black cloak, with red lips and horns like a ram, appeared out of thin air.

"Morina!" Goldilocks said. "It's *you—you're* the one who's behind all this!"

Just the sight of her filled Red with rage, and she charged toward the witch with her fists raised.

"You no-good, grass-eating, udder-sucking, hoof-stomping, wedding-crashing, friend-stealing piece of fertilizer!" she yelled. *"How dare you take my fiancé AND my friend! I'm going to rip those hideous horns right off your—"*

Morina waved her hand like she was swatting a fly, and Red went soaring across the room and landed on the second level of bookshelves. Red used the railing to get to her feet, but the metal bars magically wrapped around her body and held her in place. Morina waved her hands at the others, and they flew to the railing beside Red and were also restrained by its metal bars. Conner tried to hold on to his sister as he was forced through the air, but she slipped out of his arms and rolled back to the floor.

"I must say I'm impressed," Morina said. "I figured you might follow us, but I never expected you to make it inside the building."

"We know what you're doing here!" Bree said. "We know all about the bridge between worlds and the witches' plan to cross through it and conquer the Otherworld!"

"But you won't get away with it!" Conner said. "You and the witches won't stand a chance against this world!"

"Well, of course not," Morina said. "That's why we cursed your sister. Now that we're in control of her powers, dominating the Otherworld will be much easier. By the way, *Alex*, it's time to wake up now. Our guests will be arriving soon."

Alex levitated off the floor and onto her feet. She opened her eyes and they began to glow like lightning. Her hair rose above her head and flickered like the flames of a slow-motion fire. Once she was awake, all the books floating through the air suddenly dropped and rained down on the reading room.

"What have you done to her?" Conner yelled.

"Isn't it obvious?" Morina asked. "We cursed her just like we cursed the Enchantress."

"What are you talking about?" he asked. "Ezmia wasn't *cursed*! She became the Enchantress because she was greedy, selfish, and evil!"

"Every woman has an evil enchantress inside her—all it takes is a little curse to bring it out," Morina said. "Your sister is no exception."

"I don't believe you," Conner said. "What kind of magic could do such a thing?"

"Actually, it's an interesting story," Morina said. "You see, years and years ago, the Snow Queen and the Sea Witch discovered the Otherworld around the same time as the fairies. While the late Fairy Godmother and the Fairy Council traveled back and forth spreading stories and granting wishes in the Otherworld, the witches got together and formed a plan to conquer it. The Snow Queen and the Sea Witch weren't powerful enough to do it on their own, so they cursed little Ezmia with dust made from the glass of an evil magic mirror. It got in Ezmia's eyes and lungs and cursed her to feel anger, sorrow, and jealousy tenfold—turning her into the Enchantress we remember today.

The Snow Queen and the Sea Witch were planning to use Ezmia as a weapon against the Otherworld—but sadly, Ezmia perished before they had the chance. Once the Enchantress was dead, the Snow Queen and the Sea Witch set their sights on Alex. After a couple of attempts to curse her, they realized how much stronger she was than Ezmia. It took over ten times the amount of dust for the curse to even stick."

"That's why Alex destroyed the Witches' Brew and attacked the Fairy Council!" Conner said, understanding for the first time. "She wasn't having difficulty controlling her powers because she was overwhelmed—she was being cursed!"

"Such a good little detective," the witch said. "Luckily, the Snow Queen and the Sea Witch learned from their mistakes with Ezmia. This time, they hexed the dust so they'd have total control over whoever ingested it. Now your sister, one of the most powerful fairies ever to grace the known worlds, is a creature of rage, torment, and despair."

Conner and his friends were livid. They fought against the metal bars restraining them, but it was no use.

"You still won't win!" he shouted. "It's going to take much more than my sister and a bunch of witches to take over the Otherworld! We have armies and weapons you can't even dream of! They'll wipe you out the moment you step outside this library!"

Morina rolled her eyes as if she had heard this spiel multiple times.

"Oh yes, I know all about *those*," she said. "Unfortunately for you, I've planned accordingly. You see, the other witches have no idea what kind of world they're about to walk into. The Otherworld was *vastly* different when the Snow Queen and the Sea Witch first discovered it—they don't realize how *advanced* it's become. The witches and your sister are merely pawns in my plan to weaken the armies of this world. Once they've been wounded, my *own* army will arrive and finish them off."

"What army?" Conner asked.

The witch threw her head back and roared with laughter. "Don't tell me you haven't figured that part out yet," she said.

Goldilocks gasped. "Conner, she's talking about *the Literary Army*! She's going to bring them through the bridge, too! That's why they were lingering around the Northern Palace—it wasn't a scare tactic, they were waiting for *her*!"

Of all the possibilities Conner had predicted over

the last week, this outcome had completely escaped him. Apparently, they wouldn't need to travel into the fairy-tale world after all—the Literary Army was coming to *them*.

"It's still not enough to defeat the Otherworld!" Conner said. "Both sides will just keep fighting until there's nothing left!"

"And perhaps *that's* been my plan all along," Morina said. "The fairies have been turned into stone, soon all the witches will be slaughtered, the armies of the Otherworld will be defeated, and the Literary Army will be destroyed in the process. That leaves both worlds entirely defenseless and ready for new leadership—leadership from someone *like me*."

Conner glared at her with the most hateful gaze he had ever sent anyone in his life. He couldn't believe one person was capable of so much manipulation.

"Millions of innocent people are going to die because of you, and there won't be a drop of blood on your hands," he said. "I'd say you're a monster, but that's not fair to monsters."

Morina was tickled by that notion, and a sinister smile spread across her face. "I may not be the most powerful enemy you've made, but I'm certainly the smartest—and *that* makes me the scariest of them all," she said.

A small clock over the entryway struck midnight, and the Rose Main Reading Room began to vibrate.

"Well, it's been such a *thrill* catching up, but I'm afraid you'll all have to be quiet now," Morina said. "I don't want you spilling any secrets to our guests."

The witch snapped her fingers, and the metal bars confining them snaked around their mouths. Conner and his friends looked at one another in panic, but there was nothing they could do. Whether they liked it or not, the bridge between worlds was about to appear.

What started off as a light rumbling sensation quickly escalated into a thunderous tremor. The room shook so violently that the windows shattered and the walls began to crack. The chandeliers swung like wrecking balls before crashing to the floor. The tables slid and slammed into one another like bumper cars, and many of the bookshelves collapsed.

Suddenly, an enormous ghostly orb descended from the ceiling. It glided through the air and landed at the far end of the room. The orb stretched into a wide oval and gained color and depth, as if invisible paintbrushes were painting it. With every passing second, the image of a vast forest became clearer and clearer. Soon the image was so vibrant it didn't look like a painting of a forest, but a *doorway* to one.

The witches of the fairy-tale world peered through the opening and took their first steps into the Otherworld. Arboris, Tarantulene, Serpentina, Charcoaline, and Rat Mary led the charge and were followed by hundreds of other grotesque women. Some flew into the library on broomsticks, some galloped with hooved feet, and some crawled inside on all fours.

A wave of salty seawater spilled into the library and swirled around the room like a living serpent. The Sea Witch rode the wave into the Otherworld perched on her coral sleigh, which was pulled by a school of sharks. A sudden chill filled the air, and the Snow Queen emerged through the bridge aboard a sleigh pulled by two ferocious polar bears.

"Your Excellencies," Morina said with a shallow bow. "I'm so glad you've both successfully made it through the bridge. Just as promised, I have found the Bailey girl and cursed her with the dust from the magic mirror. With her power at our disposal, the Otherworld will be ours in no time."

The Snow Queen and the Sea Witch were shocked that Morina had pulled it off.

"Well done, Morina," the Sea Witch said. "I have to admit, we're pleasantly surprised by your competence."

The witches were so excited to finally be in the Otherworld that they didn't even notice the people tangled in the railing above them. Conner and his friends tried to warn the witches that they were walking into a trap, but they couldn't form words with the metal bars around their mouths.

"Well, what are we waiting for?" the Snow Queen screeched. *"We have a world to conquer!"*

CHAPTER TEN

THE WITCHES ARRIVE

By midnight, over a thousand US Marines had joined General Wilson on Fifth Avenue. The soldiers surrounded the New York Public Library on all four sides, but it was impossible to get close. Whenever a Marine came within ten feet of the building, he or she was quickly knocked back by one of the lion statues. Even if a soldier was on the opposite side of the structure, a lion would crawl over the building and swat the soldier away before he or she could enter.

The general watched the statues from behind a wall of sandbags in the middle of Fifth Avenue. He took a long drag from his twelfth cigar of the night and decided it was time to take action.

"All right, enough cat games!" he said to his soldiers. "I want both those lions blown to bits! Open fire on the count of three... *One... Two... Three!*"

The Marines unleashed tremendous firepower on the national landmarks. Bullets came from soldiers on all sides of the library and from snipers stationed on the rooftops nearby. The statues were shot until they crumbled into pieces and the front steps of the library were covered in their stony debris.

"Hold your fire!" the general ordered, and the shooting ceased. "Inspect the damage!"

A soldier ran up the front steps of the library and examined the debris.

"All clear, sir," he called out.

"Good," the general said. "Now send in the platoon to find the girl. If she resists arrest or retaliates with an assault, you are to terminate her immediately. That is an order, do you copy?"

"Sir, yes, sir!" the soldiers responded.

As the platoon charged up the library's front steps, they came to a sudden halt. As if the destruction of the statues were being rewound before their eyes, the debris magically reassembled piece by piece until both lion statues were fully formed again—*and the felines weren't happy.* The lions roared with such gusto that many of the soldiers' helmets flew off. With one powerful blow, the platoon was knocked down the library's steps and the soldiers rolled into the street.

"Holy reincarnation!" the general said, and the cigar fell from his mouth.

In over six decades serving in the United States Armed Forces, General Wilson had never encountered anything like *this*. The stone felines were putting up the greatest defense he had ever witnessed.

Suddenly, all three double doors at the library's entrance were blasted open from inside. Alex and the witches emerged and stood on the front steps with the lions. The witches looked around Fifth Avenue in wonder. The Otherworld was so much bigger and brighter than they'd thought. They'd expected a world similar to their own, but instead were standing in a metropolis of lights and concrete beyond their wildest dreams.

The soldiers looked at one another with the same dumbfounded expression: *Where did they all come from?* General Wilson picked up a megaphone to speak to the mysterious women.

"This is United States Marine Corps General Gunther Wilson," he said. "Whoever you are and wherever you came from, you are interfering in a matter of national security. Put your hands up and come quietly or you'll be taken by force."

The witches shared a cackle—unaware of who the soldiers were or what they were capable of.

"You heard the man, sisters," the Snow Queen screeched. *"It's time to put our hands up."*

The witch raised her hands into the air, and hundreds of enormous icicles shot up from the ground. They were so sharp that they flattened the tires of all the Hummers on the street and nearly impaled many of the soldiers.

"Attack!" the Snow Queen screeched. *"The Otherworld is ours!"*

The witches squealed in celebration and their invasion began.

The Sea Witch rode her rogue wave around the library and threw pieces of coral at the nearby soldiers. The coral latched on to their uniforms and grew rapidly around their bodies, binding their arms and legs.

Rat Mary placed open palms on the ground, closed her eyes, and whispered a spell to summon all the rats in the area. To her surprise, *thousands* of rodents crawled out of the sewers and drains, the trash cans and subways, and joined her on the front steps of the library. She directed them toward the soldiers, and the rats pounced on them like a plague of locusts.

Arboris pointed to the trees beside the library's steps. All the leaves flew from the branches into the air and rained down on the soldiers. The leaves poked and stung the soldiers like swarms of killer bees.

Smoke steamed out of Charcoaline's ears, and the cracks of her ashy skin filled with magma. A fiery geyser erupted from her mouth like a volcano, and she aimed the blast at the general. He and his soldiers dived out of the way, and their wall of sandbags exploded.

The Marines had never been trained for such attacks. They were so shocked by the witches' magic, they were practically paralyzed and didn't know how to retaliate.

"Sir? What do we do?" a soldier asked the general.

"Shoot them!" the general ordered. *"Shoot them all!"*

The witches didn't recognize the weapons the Marines were aiming in their direction. By the time they realized the objects were firearms, the soldiers had already started firing. A split second before the witches would have been shot and slaughtered on the steps of the library, Alex raised a hand, and the bullets bounced off a magical force field.

When the general realized the soldiers were wasting their bullets, he motioned for them to hold their fire. The Marines lowered their weapons and stared at Alex's magic in amazement. The Sea Witch picked a steaming bullet off the ground with her claw and examined it with her large black eyes.

"The Otherworld is not the same place it was when we discovered it," she said with a nasty scowl.

The Sea Witch held the bullet to the Snow Queen's nose. The blind witch smelled it and her brow tightened.

"They've *evolved*," she screeched. "Where is Morina? Why didn't she warn us about their development?"

The witches looked around the front steps and the entrance hall of the library, but Morina was nowhere to be found.

"She's tricked us!" Rat Mary yelled.

"Morina's sent us to our death!" Charcoaline moaned.

"How could ssshe betray usss like thisss?" Serpentina hissed.

"Silence, you fools!" the Snow Queen ordered. "We will not perish because of Morina or any human of the Otherworld! We aren't prepared for this battle—but mark my words, by sundown we will be ready for the war! All we need is a place to retreat until we gain our strength!"

The Sea Witch looked up Fifth Avenue and pointed to the southeast corner of Central Park in the distance.

"Look, up there!" she said. "It's a *forest*! I say we take cover in the woods until we are ready!"

"Yes, perfect!" the Snow Queen screeched, and turned to Alex. *"Lead the way!"*

At the witch's command, Alex clapped her hands and all the remaining soldiers went flying out of their way. She snapped her fingers and all the Hummers, the police vehicles, the lampposts, the street signs, the trash cans, and everything else in their path disintegrated into piles of ash. In one swift procession, the witches, the lion statues, and Alex marched up Fifth Avenue toward Central Park.

Once they arrived, Alex waved her hand through the air and a massive force field surrounded the entire park like a shimmering, rippling dome. The Marines tried to follow the witches into the park, but Alex's shield electrocuted anyone who got near it: *No one was going in or out.*

Alex, the lion statues, and all the witches continued their march into the heart of Central Park and disappeared from the Marines' sight. The soldiers had thought they'd seen just about everything with the moving statues, but clearly, the spectacles had only begun.

"Your orders, sir?" a soldier asked the general.

General Wilson didn't respond. He was just as stunned by the night's events as the rest of the Marines. He was going to need help with the situation, and there was only one person he could get it from.

"Sir? Your orders?"

"I'm thinking, Sergeant, I'm thinking!" the general snapped, and paced as he thought. "The whole island of Manhattan needs to be evacuated at once! Call the Pentagon and tell them we need backup! We need as many boots on the ground as possible!"

"Yes, sir!" the soldier responded.

"Oh, and Sergeant?" the general said. "One more thing—and this is the most important order of the night: *Find Cornelia Grimm—immediately!*"

CHAPTER ELEVEN

A MIRRORED ESCAPE

After a thorough inspection of all the mirrors in the Center Kingdom castle, Froggy and his mysterious young companion discovered that the castle was as empty as the mirror dimension itself. Judging by all the damaged furniture and broken artwork, the Literary Army had swept the castle and taken all the servants to the Northern Kingdom during their invasion. Most concerning of all, however, was how little Froggy recognized his former home. They peered into the chambers where he used to sleep, the dining room where he used to eat, and the library where he'd spent hours each day reading—but nothing sparked the tiniest inkling of familiarity.

"I know I used to live here, but no matter how many times I remind myself, it still seems like the home of a stranger," Froggy said.

"Where else could your friends be hiding?" the little girl asked.

Froggy tried to think of an alternative hiding spot, but he had a difficult time remembering the names of other locations altogether.

"Let's search the village outside the castle," he said. "Perhaps they're hiding somewhere less conspicuous, like one of the shops or farms."

"What are their names? I forgot to ask."

Froggy opened his mouth to respond, but the right words never emerged.

"I suppose I forgot," he said with a deep sigh. "But I'll recognize them the moment we see them. They've got strawberry-blonde hair, blue eyes, and freckles. The boy has chubby cheeks and the girl always wears her hair neatly behind a headband—or at least that's how they looked when they were twelve. I know they've matured since then, but I can't picture it."

"It's all right," the little girl reassured him. "How many twins can there be who match that description? We'll find them soon enough."

A new cluster of mirrors manifested in the distance, and they hurried to inspect them. Froggy and the little girl checked all the homes, shops, bakeries, taverns, and barns in the Center Kingdom village, but they were just as empty as the castle. They were certain the Literary Army had rounded up all the villagers, too—but an unexpected noise told them otherwise.

Froggy and the little girl followed the sound of sniffling to a mirror hung inside a small cottage. They peered inside and found a short, frumpy woman with curly red hair and a large nose. She looked at her reflection in the mirror like it was someone she despised. The woman tried smoothing the wrinkles on her forehead, flattening the bags under her eyes, and stretching her double chin as if the skin on her face were made of clay. Naturally, the adjustments never lasted, and the woman cried harder after each failed attempt.

Froggy stayed out of sight so he wouldn't frighten the woman, but the little girl was drawn to her like a magnet—*desperate* to help.

"Why are you crying?" she asked.

The woman screamed at the strange little girl appearing in the mirror. She quickly turned to look over her shoulder, expecting to find the little girl standing behind her. When she realized that the girl was only a reflection, the woman screamed again.

"How did you get inside there?" she asked. "Are you a ghost?"

"No, just cursed," the little girl replied. "I've been trapped inside the mirror for a very long time. And from the looks of it, so have *you*."

"But...but...but what is that supposed to mean?" the woman asked.

"I saw the way you were looking into the mirror just now," the little girl said. "You looked at your own face with such hatred and heartbreak. You nearly hurt yourself trying to change your appearance with your hands. If you dislike your looks to the point of hating and harming yourself, I'd say you're just as cursed and trapped in the mirror as I am."

The woman was still shocked to be speaking with a reflection, but even more overwhelmed to be analyzed by one. Tears formed in her eyes again, but this time from embarrassment.

"You've caught me in a very vulnerable moment, my dear," the woman said. "What is your name?"

"I don't know," the little girl said. "All I know is what I see, and someone should never be so distraught over something they can't control."

"I agree, but it isn't right to make judgments over one moment of weakness, either," the woman said. "My appearance has always given me grief, but that isn't the only reason I'm unhappy. My whole family was recently captured by that terrible army and taken to the Northern Kingdom. I was crying because I miss them dearly and am worried sick."

"Then why were you trying to change your looks?" the little girl asked.

"Because I desperately want to save them, but my looks are holding me back," the woman confessed. "I'm the only one in our village who escaped the army, but there are others like me in the towns nearby. I believe if we joined together we could create a plan to rescue our loved ones. However, I'm afraid no one will take me seriously because of my appearance—and I have a lifetime of experiences to validate that fear."

Froggy was certain the woman's situation would

be far too complicated for the little girl's expertise, but even in this dilemma, the girl knew the exact advice to give.

"No one ever changed the world by being beautiful," she said. "If you want to make a difference, you can't let something as trivial as *appearance* get in your way. A daisy doesn't need the roses' permission to bloom—and neither do you."

"I may not need permission, but I do need support," the woman argued. "I can't fight an army on my own—I'll need others to join me. But I'm afraid they'll only see my looks and won't listen to my words. I'm afraid they'll only laugh at my hopes of rescuing my loved ones."

The little girl placed her hands on her hips and stared at the woman with the confidence of someone twice her age.

"Only idiots listen with their eyes," she said. "If people don't hear your words, then *shout* them. If people silence you, then write your message with fire. Demanding respect is never easy, but if something you love is at stake, then I'd say it's worth the price. Besides, if you can't get villagers to take you seriously, you'll never defeat an army! Sometimes we're meant to face the demons at home so we know how to fight the demons abroad."

The little girl had waited years to give someone that advice, and it appeared to do the trick. As if a sudden electric charge had run through the woman's body, she stood taller and straighter, and her eyes beamed with determination.

"You're right, child," she said. "With all the energy I've wasted moping in front of the mirror, I could have accomplished great things by now. Well, I'm going to stop moping at once and get to work."

The woman was so reenergized that her hands trembled as she gathered her coat and her hat. She was so eager to begin that she completely forgot she wasn't alone. Only when the woman had one foot out the door did she remember that the little girl was still standing in the mirror.

"Thank you for the encouragement," the woman said. "Whatever curse you're under, I hope someone can free you from the mirror. You've certainly freed me."

The woman left her cottage and hurried to the next village at a determined pace. Froggy was floored by the little girl's counseling abilities. He applauded her and they journeyed away from the cottage mirror.

"That was quite the motivational speech," he said. "With just a few words, you may have changed that woman's life forever. Boy, I sure wish our paths had crossed when I was younger. I could have used that same inspirational—"

Suddenly, the cottage mirror behind them started to glow. It became brighter and brighter until it shined with the power of the sun. Froggy and the little girl both shielded their eyes from the strange phenomenon.

"What's happening?" he asked.

"I don't know," she said. "I've never seen a mirror do that before!"

Rays of light shot out from the mirror like ribbons and wrapped around the little girl's wrists, ankles, and waist. The light pulled her closer and closer to the mirror until her body was pressed against the glass. Just when Froggy didn't think she could go any farther, the little girl passed through the plate of glass as if it were a sheet of water. She collapsed on the cottage floor, and all the light faded. Froggy tried to follow her, but the glass between worlds became solid again.

"You're on the other side!" Froggy exclaimed. "You've been *freed*!"

"But how?" she asked in disbelief. "What broke the spell?"

Froggy thought about it, but it was a mystery to him, too. There was only one possible conclusion he could come up with.

"Maybe it's just like the woman said," he suggested. "Perhaps the key to freeing yourself from the mirror is freeing someone else first."

The little girl got to her feet, but when she turned back to the mirror, she wasn't a little girl anymore. A beautiful middle-aged woman with long raven hair was now standing before Froggy.

"I'm so *old*," she said. "Why have I aged so much?"

"This must be the age you were when you went inside the mirror," Froggy said. "The longer you were trapped, the more you faded into a little girl."

The woman stared at her reflection, and after a moment, it astonished her. She looked into her own eyes as if she were seeing a long-lost friend. Suddenly, a wave of memories illuminated her mind like a swarm of fireflies flying into a dark cave.

"I *remember*," she said. "I remember where I was

born, I remember where I grew up, I remember all the places I lived, I remember the faces of my loved ones . . . and I remember my *name*."

"What is it?" Froggy asked.

"Evly," she gasped.

Her face quickly filled with shame upon the discovery. It was so overwhelming that she had to take a seat on a small stool.

"Why the long face? This should be a happy moment for you."

"Because it wasn't the *only* name I had," Evly said.

She walked around the cottage and recited her memories as they came to her, as if she were narrating a film she saw behind her eyelids.

"When I was very young, I was kidnapped by an evil enchantress and forced to work as her slave. I was deeply in love with a young man named Mira, who tried to rescue me. The Enchantress caught Mira and imprisoned him inside a magic mirror as punishment. I was devastated and quickly planned my own escape from her. I poisoned the Enchantress and ran far away, dragging Mira's mirror into the forest beside me. And then I made a decision that turned me into a *monster*. . . ."

Froggy laughed. "I have a hard time believing that."

"No, I mean it," Evly said. "I was so heartbroken over Mira, I had a witch cut out my heart and turn it into stone. It made all the pain go away, but it also turned me into an irrational, unsympathetic, and cruel woman. I devoted the rest of my heartless life to freeing Mira from the mirror. I married a king in hopes of using his resources, and I tried killing my stepdaughter. The world found out and hated me for it, and I became known throughout the kingdoms as *the Evil Queen*...."

The name should have sent shivers down Froggy's spine, but he remained completely unaffected. He listened to Evly's memories as if they were a story he had never been told, completely unaware that the two of them shared some of these memories.

"Years later, I tried freeing Mira using the Wishing Spell. By the time I collected all the items the spell needed, Mira had faded into nothing but a reflection. He died in my arms just a few moments after being freed. There was a big battle at the time. Soldiers had found me in an abandoned castle, cannons were being blasted outside, the castle began to crumble. The magic mirror crashed over me and I've been trapped inside ever since."

Evly covered her eyes and cried as if the story she had been watching had come to a tragic ending.

"And what about your heart?" Froggy asked. "Is it still made of stone?"

Evly placed a hand over her chest and gasped.

"No, I can feel it beating!" she said. "How is this possible? What sort of magic could restore someone's heart?"

"I understand completely," Froggy said with a smile. "It's called a *second chance*. After a lifetime of sorrow, the mirror dimension has granted you an opportunity to start over."

"I don't deserve a second chance," Evly said. "After all the pain I've caused over the years, I deserve to spend eternity inside a prison cell."

"Then perhaps it's a chance for *redemption*," he suggested. "You were too late to free Mira, but that doesn't mean it's too late for everyone else. There are plenty of people who feel trapped in the mirror and could use all the advice you've been storing."

"But why me?" Evly asked. "Surely there are much more suitable candidates than an evil queen."

"Well, maybe not," Froggy said. "Maybe you were

meant to go through all that pain and heartbreak so you could save others from their own. Maybe the Evil Queen is just a chapter in your life and not the whole story. Maybe the world has dreamed bigger plans for you than you've dreamed for yourself."

Tears filled Evly's eyes as she thought it over. It was difficult to accept kindness from a world she thought so cruel.

"I should take my own advice and stop feeling sorry over the things I can't control," she said. "Thank you for guiding me through it. As much as I'd like to continue looking for your friends, I suppose I'm quite useless to you from this side of the glass. Good luck to you, whoever you are."

Evly kissed the mirror near Froggy's cheek and left the cottage, taking her first steps toward a new beginning. Once she was gone, Froggy left the mirror and wandered into the darkness of the mirror dimension.

"What a nice lady," he said to himself. "I wonder which friends she was talking about. . . ."

CHAPTER TWELVE

THE UNEXPECTED RESCUERS

Conner and his friends could hear the commotion between the witches and the Marines as if it were happening right in front of them. It was terrifying knowing his sister was outside in the line of gunfire, and pure torture knowing there was nothing he could do to help her. Conner fought against the metal bars wrapped around his body until his skin bruised, but the railing never budged.

Just as a thunderous round of gunfire commenced,

Morina reappeared in the Rose Main Reading Room. She sauntered through the room to the bridge between worlds without even looking at the captives twisted in the railing above her. Conner and the others called her every foul name they could think of as she passed by, but the metal bars across their mouths muffled their words.

"Save your strength—you're going to be up there for a *very* long time," Morina said with a laugh. "Now that my pawns are in place, it's time to secure a checkmate. Enjoy these moments while you can—it'll be the last time the Otherworld belongs to you."

Morina blew them each a kiss and the metal bars wrapped around their bodies even more tightly. The witch stepped into the fairy-tale world and disappeared in the forest on the other side.

Conner and his friends squirmed in their painful constraints. They were pinned so tightly they could barely breathe and were starting to lose feeling in their limbs. Hero was woken by his mother's frantic twisting and began to cry—but the infant's crying was drowned out by Red's high-pitched weeping.

There hadn't been many moments in Conner's life when he'd felt completely out of luck, but this was one of them. With his sister under a terrible curse, his friends imprisoned around him, and no way to contact anyone outside the library, Conner thought the Otherworld might be doomed.

Suddenly, the conflict outside went dead silent and Conner feared the worst. Either the Marines had exterminated the witches and his sister, or the battle had moved. Footsteps entered the Rose Main Reading Room, and Conner worried that the witches were retreating into the library. Since his head was stuck facing forward, he looked out of the corners of his eyes until the muscles in his sockets were strained. He saw the shapes of four familiar young women— and they were the *last* people on earth he was expecting to find.

"As I live and breathe," said a familiar voice. "If it isn't *Conner Bailey* . . . and he's *exactly* where I've always wanted him—vulnerable and in need of a favor!"

Mindy, Cindy, Lindy, and Wendy walked farther into the Rose Main Reading Room and stood where Conner and the others could see them clearly. The Book Huggers stared up at him and his friends with matching smirks, crossed arms, and devious expressions. The teenage girls looked like vultures surrounding a pack of injured animals.

"Hmm hmmhmhm?" Bree mumbled in disbelief.

"Oh, look, girls!" Cindy said. "Bree Campbell and Conner are in a suspicious circumstance together! What a surprise—*NOT!*"

"Hmmmm hmm hm hmm hmmm!" Conner grunted.

"What's that, Conner? After all these years you finally have *something to say*?" Mindy asked. "Wish I could hear you through the all *lies* and *trickery* you've planted in my head!"

"HMMM HMM HMMM!" Conner grunted angrily.

"Lindy, go back to the abandoned subway tunnel," Mindy ordered. "I believe there was a handsaw on the platform. That should help Conner *loosen his lips*."

Lindy followed the command and promptly left the reading room. Conner wasn't sure if the Book Huggers' plan was to free him or torture him with the saw, and judging by their questionable behavior in the past, either was possible. A few minutes later Lindy returned carrying a foot-long handsaw like it was a poisonous snake.

"Great work. Now remove the bar covering his mouth," Mindy instructed.

Lindy paused nervously. "Maybe Wendy should do this? She was the only one of us who didn't fail woodshop."

Wendy nodded confidently and took the tool from her friend. The quietest Book Hugger placed the handsaw between her teeth and climbed a bookshelf toward Conner like a pirate ascending the side of a ship. With two quick strikes on each side, the metal bar across Conner's face fell to the floor.

"What the HECK are you guys doing here?" he asked.

"We're on vacation with our families," Cindy said. "That *was*, until we saw you in a taxi outside Cheesy Street! Then pleasure quickly turned into business."

"We've been following you ever since," Lindy said. "We told our parents the pizza bagels gave us diarrhea. They still think we're in the bathroom."

"The homeless janitor didn't want to tell us where you went, but his friends weren't so loyal," Mindy said. "They sang like canaries for a couple of granola bars and a box of Tic Tacs."

Conner had never thought he'd be so grateful for his eccentric stalkers. Usually he found just the mention of the Book Huggers quite repulsive, but now he looked upon the girls as if they were each wearing a superhero's cape. They were his only hope of rescuing Alex and saving the Otherworld.

"I never thought I'd say this, but I'm *genuinely* happy to see you guys," Conner said with a thankful smile. "Now you've got to saw off the rest of these bars and let me down! It's kind of an emergency!"

Wendy started sawing the bars around Conner's legs, but Mindy held up a hand to stop her.

"As much as it pains me to see you like this, I'm afraid we can't help you just yet," Mindy said. "You see, we've had questions about you and your sister for a long time now—questions only *you* can answer. So if you want us to scratch your back, you've got to scratch ours first."

"Are you crazy?" Conner snapped. "I just said it's an emergency! People are going to get hurt unless you help me down!"

"PEOPLE HAVE ALREADY BEEN HURT!" Mindy yelled, and slammed her hands on the nearest table. "Do you know what it's like to have your parents, peers, and school administrators treat you like a lunatic? It's HURTFUL! Do you know what it's like to be the laughingstock of conspiracy blogs and chat rooms? It's also HURTFUL! Do you know what it's like to get blocked on social media *personally* by the mayor, the governor, state representatives, and the

Pentagon? It's *really* HURTFUL! Despite our overwhelming catalog of evidence, our valid suspicions and valiant quest for the truth have left us humiliated, stigmatized, and institutionalized at every turn—but *still* the Book Huggers persist! Now, if you ever want your feet to touch the ground, you're going to give us the information we desire and deserve! You've kept the truth from us for four years, *Conner Bailey*, but your web of deception ends today!"

Despite their uncomfortable restraints, everyone in the Rose Main Reading Room froze and stared at the Book Huggers in silence. Even Hero was taken aback by the teenagers' emotional display.

"Okay, *fine*," Conner said. "I'll tell you everything you want to know as long as you help me down afterward."

The Book Huggers were so anxious to finally get answers, they practically vibrated. They shined a reading lamp directly in Conner's face and their interrogation began.

"I'm going to ask you a series of questions and I want you to respond with either a yes or a no," Mindy instructed as she paced below him.

"Wouldn't it be faster if I just told you everything—"

"*I'll ask the questions!*" Mindy roared. "In the sixth grade, you and your sister missed school for two weeks. According to a note we found in the nurse's office, which a source confirmed was written in your mother's handwriting, you and Alex were both absent due to *chicken pox*. But you weren't really sick with chicken pox, were you?"

"No," Conner said with a sigh.

"Precisely what I predicted," Cindy said.

"In the seventh grade, your sister allegedly moved to Vermont to attend a school for advanced learners," Mindy said. "Shortly before her departure, we witnessed Alex talking to a book in the school library and whispering covert messages like *'Take me back'* and *'I don't want to be here anymore.'* The transferral paperwork we obtained indicated she was going to live with her grandmother, but after a thorough scan through public documents, we discovered your grandmother didn't own any property in Vermont. So, Alex never moved to Vermont, did she?"

"No," Conner replied with a massive eye roll.

"I knew that was a lie!" Lindy said with a fist pump.

"In the eighth grade, you and Bree abandoned our school trip on the way home from Germany," Mindy said. "Bree has claimed several different motives for committing the stunt, ranging from underground concerts to food festivals. But you didn't run off for music or cuisine, did you?"

"No," Conner said.

Wendy used the handsaw like a guitar, indicating she had known all along.

"The following year you never returned to school," Mindy said. "Mrs. Peters informed us that you had transferred to Vermont to live with your grandmother and sister, but we all know you didn't move to Vermont, either, right?"

"No," Conner said, and began to lose his patience. "Will you please get to the point? You're wasting time!"

"One more question," Mindy said. "Recently, the girls and I were innocently walking by your house on Sycamore Drive when we saw a group of strange people in the window. We were afraid your house was being robbed, so we took a closer look—*and that's when we saw pirates and a massive ship appear out of a beam of light connected to your binder!* We were told they were just actors and set pieces, but they weren't actors and set pieces, *were they?*"

"*No!*" Conner snapped. "You guys were *spying* on my house? That's illegal!"

"This leads us to believe that everything from your strange school absences, to your phony transfers, to your European excursion, and even the evacuation happening right now in New York City, are all related!" Mindy declared. "Admit it! You and your sister have been involved in an interdimensional conspiracy for years, and the Book Huggers have been right to question you every step of the way!"

"YES!" Conner shouted. "YOU'VE BEEN RIGHT ABOUT EVERYTHING! FOR THE LAST FOUR YEARS MY SISTER AND I HAVE BEEN TRAVELING BACK AND FORTH BETWEEN THE FAIRY-TALE WORLD, THE WORLDS OF CLASSIC LITERATURE, AND THE WORLDS OF MY CREATIVE WRITING! THAT IS THE TRUTH—ARE YOU PSYCO-PATHS HAPPY NOW?"

Judging by the sheer bliss surfacing in their faces, the Book Huggers were more than happy. They jumped for joy, glad tears filled their eyes, and Wendy climbed down to join the girls in a massive group hug. After years of mistreatment, disrespect, and false diagnoses, the Book Huggers' entire existence had finally been validated.

When their embrace was over, Lindy removed a

folded piece of paper from her pocket and read a chart printed on it.

"All right, time to see who won the Bailey Twins Disappearance Pool," she said.

"What is the Bailey Twins Disappearance Pool?" Conner asked.

"We made bets in the sixth grade about where you and Alex were sneaking off to," Mindy explained.

"I guessed alien abduction, tunnel to China, and wizards," Lindy read from the chart. "Mindy had Illuminati, Bigfoot's cave, and vampires. Cindy predicted an international kidnapping ring, lost continent of Lemuria, and the mines of mole people. Wendy had government espionage facility, Swedish cover band, and—well, what do you know—*worlds of fiction!* Wendy wins!"

Mindy, Lindy, and Cindy each handed Wendy twenty bucks.

"I was really hoping for the lost continent of Lemuria, but I'm not mad at worlds of fiction," Cindy said.

"How do you get to the worlds of fiction, anyway?" Lindy asked.

"There's lots of different methods," Conner said. "Like that enormous hole in the back of the room leading to a forest."

Until that moment, the Book Huggers hadn't paid much attention to anything or anyone in the Rose Main Reading Room besides Conner. The four girls turned to the bridge and gasped when they realized just how out of the ordinary it was.

"*I thought that was just a big plasma screen!*" Lindy said.

"Nope, it's a bridge into another dimension," Conner explained. "And soon, thousands of terrible beings are going to charge out of it and attack our world. So, if you're done asking questions, *cut me down so I can do something to prevent it*!"

Wendy hurried up the bookshelf and sawed off the remaining bars around Conner's body. He took the tool from her and freed Jack, who used his axe to free Bree, Red, and Goldilocks. Once everyone was back on the floor, Conner and Bree went to the bridge between worlds and started brainstorming ways to close it.

"There's got to be a way we can seal this thing before the Literary Army arrives," Conner thought aloud.

"I don't think there's anything we can seal it with that the Literary Army can't get through," Bree said.

Conner angrily kicked the bridge, but his foot just went into the fairy-tale world and he almost slipped.

"I don't know how we're going to stop Morina!" he said. "She's, like, one hundred steps ahead of everyone else!"

"That's not entirely true," Goldilocks said. "Morina revealed a lot about her plot to take over the Otherworld, but she never mentioned anything about our recruits at the hospital. I don't think she knows we have an army of our own!"

"That stupid cow!" Red said. "Morina was probably so fixated on kidnapping Alex she didn't even notice the people from Conner's stories!"

"In that case, our odds haven't really changed," Jack said. "We knew we'd have to face the witches and the Literary Army, we just didn't realize we'd be facing them in the Otherworld. I say we send for the others at the hospital and try to track down your sister in the meantime."

Conner nodded. "Mindy, Cindy, Lindy, and Wendy," he said. "I need you to go back to the abandoned subway and get as far away from here as possible. Once you're someplace safe, find a phone and call my mom. Tell her we need backup and we need it fast. She'll know what to do."

To Conner's complete surprise, the Book Huggers saluted him and left the reading room at once—cooperating with him for the first time in history. Conner, Bree, Red, Jack, and Goldilocks followed them out of the room and down the staircase. As the Book Huggers descended toward the library's lower level, Conner and his friends headed to the entrance hall on the first floor.

As soon as they stepped into the hall, their stomachs dropped at the sight of all the destruction. The doors had been blown open, the front steps were covered in bullets, and the streets were filled with sharp icicles, but luckily, there were no bodies to be found—living or dead. The witches were gone, but not a single Marine was near the library, either. Conner and his friends stepped into the middle of Fifth Avenue and looked up and down the street for a sign of where the battle had moved.

"Look!" Red said. "All the soldiers are up the road by those trees!"

"It looks like they're trying to get inside Central Park!" Bree said. "But what's that weird bubble in their way?"

Conner recognized his sister's magic instantly. "It's a force field," he said. "The witches must be inside the park, and Alex has put a shield around it."

"Good thing the park is closed at night," Bree

said. "Otherwise the witches would have hundreds of hostages."

Central Park's strict curfew was a minor relief, but once Conner remembered *why* he knew the park's hours so well, he was consumed by a horrifying feeling in the pit of his stomach.

"The park's *not* empty!" he said. "The Boy and Girl Scouts of America are having a huge camp-out in the park *tonight*! The little boy I sat next to on the plane told me all about it!"

"You mean there are *children* trapped inside the park with *witches*?" Red asked.

"Yes! And we have to help them!" Conner said.

"How are we going to get into the park if Alex has put a force field around it?" Jack said.

"If we can't get through it, maybe we can go under it," Conner said. "Rusty said the Calvin Coolidge Express was going to stop in Central Park—let's go back to the tunnel and pray we find another hatch beneath it. But we have to hurry—God only knows what the witches could be doing to those kids right now!"

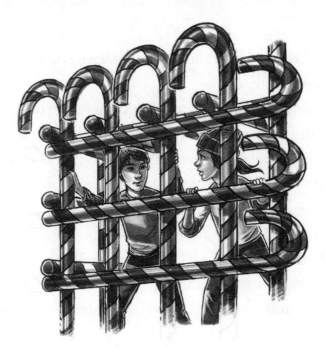

CHAPTER THIRTEEN

SOMETHING'S COOKING

Conner and his friends returned to the Calvin Coolidge Express tunnel beneath the New York Public Library. Jack found an old lantern on the unfinished platform, along with some matches, and lit it so they could see where they were going. Bree used a compass app on her phone to be certain which direction was north. The gang ran up the abandoned subway tunnel as fast as they could toward Central Park, hoping and praying they would find a way into it.

Strangely, only when Goldilocks started running did Hero finally settle down and go to sleep. The more tense and bumpy the situation, the more relaxed the infant became. His aunt Red, however, was fussing enough for both of them. The farther they ran through the tunnel, the more tears ran down her face.

"Red, why are you crying?" Bree asked.

"Physical exertion," Red confessed. "It never agrees with me."

After over a mile and a half of spotting nothing in the tunnel but bricks and the occasional rat, Conner and his friends finally arrived at another unfinished platform. The words CENTRAL PARK were written in chalk on the wall beside it.

"We're here!" Conner said. "Does anyone see a hatch to crawl through?"

Jack raised the lantern toward the ceiling and they saw a circular door that opened inward. Conner found a ladder to the side of the platform and positioned it directly below the door. He climbed the ladder and pulled on the door's handle, but it wouldn't open.

"The door's bolted shut!" he said. "We're gonna need a jackhammer or something powerful to get through this."

Bree, Jack, Goldilocks, and Red looked around the platform but didn't find anything except some rope and masking tape. Their chances of getting through the door seemed very slim. Red, defeated, took a seat on the edge of the platform and pouted.

"So, we just ran a mile down a filthy, smelly tunnel for *nothing*?" she said, and sprayed her Febreze in the air around her. "This rescue mission isn't going very well, is it?"

The others walked around the platform as they tried to think of alternative ways into the park. Bree, however, stood very still, and her eyes never moved from Red. An idea blossomed in her mind and a smirk grew across her face.

"Red, can I borrow your Febreze?" she asked.

Before Red had the chance to answer, Bree snatched the can of air freshener out of the queen's hands. She picked up a roll of masking tape, plucked a long strand of twine from the rope, and climbed the ladder. Bree then taped the can of Febreze to the circular door, near the bolts keeping it shut. She broke off the tip of the canister and stuck the twine down the tube.

"Does anyone have a lighter?" she asked.

Jack handed her the matches he'd found on the previous platform. Bree lit a match and set the loose end of the twine on fire. Conner climbed halfway up the ladder to take a closer look at whatever contraption she was making.

"Bree, what are you doing?" he asked.

"Making a bomb," Bree said casually. "We might want to take cover—*quickly!*"

Jack, Goldilocks, and Red jumped off the platform and ducked into the tunnel. Bree and Conner hurried down the ladder and joined the others. The flame flickered up the twine and into the can of Febreze and *BAM!* The canister exploded and the circular door fell from the ceiling.

"I've saved the day!" Red cheered, and applauded herself.

Jack and Goldilocks rolled their eyes and gave Bree a congratulatory pat on the back. Conner just stared at her with his mouth hanging open.

"What?" Bree asked.

"You just built a *bomb*!" Conner said in shock.

"And?"

"I just realized what a horrible influence you are," he said.

Bree shrugged. "At least it smells better down here."

The gang returned to the platform and stared up at the fresh hole in the ceiling. The explosion appeared to have blown through a layer of dirt and grass above the door. Conner climbed the ladder and crawled through the hole, and his friends followed close behind him.

Had Conner not known Central Park was above them he would have thought they were entering a forest in the fairy-tale world. He emerged from the tunnel at the bottom of a grassy hill sprinkled with large boulders. New York City's skyscrapers were barely visible behind all the trees surrounding the area. Conner looked up and saw Alex's magic shield stretching across the night sky like a jiggling, sparkling dome.

For whatever reason, Conner's friends were taking their time climbing up from the tunnel. It took Bree, Jack, and Goldilocks a couple of minutes each to surface into the park, and almost five minutes passed before Red joined them aboveground. Conner thought this was a little peculiar, given the urgency of the situation.

"About time, *Red*," he said.

"What are you talking about?" Red asked. "I was right behind you."

"It doesn't matter," he said. "Let's search the park and find where the witches went. They could be *anywhere* or disguised as *anything*, so everyone keep a sharp eye out. Speak up if you see something even remotely suspicious."

His friends nodded, and they formed a tight circle, just as they had when searching the library. They found a cement path beside the grassy hill and cautiously followed it deeper into the park. Central Park was enormous, and each time they passed a new directory they were shocked by how little ground they had covered since the previous one. Every now and then they would step through a clearing and see the city's skyline peeking above the trees, but other than the twinkling buildings, they found nothing out of the ordinary. There wasn't a witch or a Scout in sight.

Conner found a discarded map on the ground and used it to navigate the labyrinth of pathways snaking through the park. They agreed that the witches had most likely retreated to the heart of the park after battling the Marines, so Conner guided his friends down a trail leading to the park's center. The closer they got to the park's core, the more densely the air filled with smoke and a rich aroma.

"Does anyone else smell that?" Jack asked.

"Yes," Goldilocks said. "It smells like gingerbread—*fresh* gingerbread."

"The witches are probably building gingerbread houses to lure the Boy and Girl Scouts of America," Bree said.

"If so, that is *such* a witch cliché," Red said.

"Not all witches are cannibals, though," Conner said. "Whatever they're cooking, I don't think it's *houses*."

The group eventually came to a large fountain on the edge of a small lake. The fountain had a wide, circular pool of shallow water and an angel statue perched at the top. It faced an impressive terrace that was flanked by two enormous staircases. Underneath the terrace was a spacious walkway that was lined with arches and pillars. The area looked like a piece of Rome.

"What's this place?" Jack asked.

"The Bethesda Fountain and Terrace," Conner read from the map.

"It's pretty iconic," Bree added. "They use it in a lot of movies and television shows."

"New York is such a strange place," Red said. "One minute I'm completely repulsed, then the next I feel right at home. Did the *Old* York inspire such mood swings?"

Before Conner could answer her, he was distracted by something moving underneath the Bethesda Terrace. A thin woman wearing a headband, a bright pink tank top, and matching sneakers was peeking out from behind one of the pillars in the walkway. The woman nervously eyed the park around them and frantically gestured for Conner and his friends to join her.

"Pssst," she whispered. *"Come over here—quick!"*

From the way she was dressed, Conner assumed the woman was a native of the Otherworld. Still, he and his friends approached the walkway with the utmost caution. The woman in pink led them into the walkway, and they discovered she wasn't alone. A man in a headband, a green tank top, and matching tennis shoes was hiding behind another pillar. Another man wearing a blue helmet and black biker shorts was ducking behind a trash can. A third man, in a janitor's uniform, was crouched in the corner and staring into space with his hands over his head.

"It isn't safe to be wandering around the park in

the open like that," the woman in pink told them. "If they find you, they'll capture you and take you back to their base."

"You must be talking about the witches," Conner said. "Do you know which part of the park their base is in?"

"They're gathered somewhere between the lake and the reservoir. On the Great Lawn, I suspect," the man in green said. "But they search the park every couple of hours to look for escapees."

"What are you guys doing in the park so late?" Bree asked.

"My husband and I were out for a late jog," the woman in pink explained. "We used the Seventy-Ninth Street Transverse as a shortcut to get home, and that's when *the shield went up*. We tried to get through it, but it zapped us."

She and her husband showed Conner and his friends the burn marks covering their arms.

"We searched the park for help and saw the witches wandering through it," the man in green said. "So we hid in Belvedere Castle, and that's where we met *him*."

He nodded to the janitor in the corner.

"I was working a night shift at the castle," the

janitor said. "We tried calling the police but couldn't get a signal or a dial tone on any of the phones. When the coast was clear, the three of us made a quick dash to Tavern on the Green."

"And that's where they met me," the biker said. "My friends and I were cycling around the perimeter of the park and also took a shortcut to get home. After the shield went up, we hid from the witches in Tavern on the Green with other people who got trapped in the park. We thought we were safe there, but eventually they found us. We're the only four who escaped!"

"The rest were captured and taken to the witches' base," the woman in pink said. "We've been hiding under the terrace ever since."

The janitor began to laugh, but not because he was amused. He started rocking back and forth as if he was on the verge of losing his sanity.

"You know, the guy I replaced was fired for making wild claims about magical things in the park," he said. "We all thought old Rusty was just insane, and now here I am, cowering like a toddler from a bunch of *witches*. Funny how the tables have turned."

The people under the terrace looked exhausted, and they trembled as they spoke. Obviously they had been through quite an ordeal, but something about their story wasn't adding up.

"You guys make it seem like you've been here for days," Conner said. "The witches have only been in the park for an hour at most. How have you covered so much ground?"

The joggers, the biker, and the janitor all exchanged bewildered looks.

"Sweetie, we *have* been here for days," the woman in pink said.

"What?" Conner said. "How is that possible?"

"Ever since the shield went up, time in Central Park started moving much slower than in the rest of the city," the man in green said. "All the clocks on Fifth Avenue have barely moved, and it's been two days since any of us saw the sun!"

"An hour inside the park is like a second outside it," his wife said. "Whenever we see people on the other side of the shield, they're barely moving—like they're stuck in slow motion!"

Conner felt like his heart had stopped beating. Now he understood why it had taken his friends so long to crawl out of the tunnel—Alex wasn't only shielding the park, she was altering its time, too!

Whatever the witches were up to, they had bought themselves plenty of time to get it done.

"Wait, why are you so surprised to hear this?" the biker asked. "Haven't you been in the park for just as long?"

"No, we just got here," Conner said.

"You mean there's a way *out* of the park?" the janitor said, and jumped to his feet. *"You've got to take us there! I'm going to lose my mind if I have to stay here another—"*

"Quiet!" Goldilocks whispered. "Someone's approaching!"

Conner, his friends, and the escapees quickly hid behind the pillars in the walkway. They heard footsteps, and soon four figures appeared in the distance. Rat Mary and Serpentina were escorting a Boy Scout and a Girl Scout to the Bethesda Fountain. The witches pushed, kicked, and called the Scouts foul names as they went. The children looked terrified and even more exhausted than the escapees under the terrace. They each carried two large wooden buckets and placed them in the fountain's pool.

"Now fill them up, you filthy hobgoblins!" Rat Mary ordered. "And hurry! The Mistresses are waiting for their refreshments!"

The Scouts followed her commands and filled their buckets with water from the fountain. Serpentina scanned the water with a peculiar expression.

"Thisss doesn't look any better than the water in lakesss or pondsss," she hissed. "The Mistressesss requested *clean* water."

"What the Mistresses don't know won't hurt them," Rat Mary said. "Besides, the Snow Queen and the Sea Witch promised us that life in the Otherworld would be different. So far, it doesn't seem to be any different from back home. We're *still* doing all the work while they sit on their thrones and do nothing."

"You know, Morina may have intentionally led usss all to our deathsss, but I'm starting to ressspect her," Serpentina said. "Ssshe's probably back in the kingdomsss enjoying being the only—"

Even though no one made a sound under the terrace, both witches suddenly snapped their heads toward it. Conner, his friends, and the escapees all held their breath and tucked themselves as far as possible behind the pillars.

"I thought I heard something," Serpentina said.

"Probably more humans—*yuck*," Rat Mary said. "I look forward to exterminating them all. They're the true vermin of this world."

"Ssshould we round them up and take them back to the bassse?" Serpentina asked.

"No, we've done our task," Rat Mary said. "We'll send another witch to come back for them."

The Scouts finished filling their buckets, which became so heavy that the children could barely carry them. The witches shoved the Scouts back in the direction they'd come from and disappeared into the park. The escapees under the terrace waited a couple of minutes before moving, just to make sure the witches were gone.

"That was a close one," the woman in pink said. "Let's get out of here before other witches come back to capture us."

The group of escapees hurried through the walkway and away from the terrace. They climbed a flight of stairs leading to a path on higher ground and heard a loud *POP* from above them. They looked up in terror to see Rat Mary glaring at them from the top of the stairs. The witch roared with laughter and exposed her tiny, sharp teeth.

"You didn't actually think we'd leave you here, did you?" she said.

The escapees turned around and ran back toward

the terrace, but after another loud *POP*, Serpentina appeared and blocked their way.

"You aren't going anywhere!" she roared. "Sssay, I recognize sssome of you from our home world! You're the friends and brother of the Bailey girl! Oh my, the Mistressesss will be ssso pleasssed we captured you!"

"We aren't coming quietly!" Jack shouted.

He raised his axe and Goldilocks raised her sword, but Rat Mary and Serpentina snapped their fingers and the weapons flew into the witches' hands. The BabyBjörn, with Hero inside, also unfastened itself from around Goldilocks, flew to Rat Mary, and wrapped around her torso. The witch looked down at the strange holster and was pleasantly surprised to find an infant attached to it.

"It's my lucky day," Rat Mary said. "There are so many potions I've always wanted to make that require an infant as the main ingredient."

"NOOOO!" Goldilocks yelled.

She charged up the stairs to rescue her son, but Serpentina's long tongue wrapped around Goldilocks's leg and dragged her back down the steps.

"If you even think about hurting him, I'll teach

you a new definition of pain!" Goldilocks warned the witches.

Rat Mary and Serpentina shared a menacing laugh.

"I sincerely doubt you'll get the chance," Rat Mary said. "Not where you're going, at least."

With no way to escape and no one to save them, Conner, his friends, and the Central Park escapees were taken prisoner. The captives followed the Boy and Girl Scout through the park while the witches watched them from the rear. The witches forced them to walk in a straight line, and whenever someone stepped out of line, they were either whipped by Serpentina's tongue or scratched by Rat Mary's long nails.

They journeyed deeper and deeper into the park, traveling more than half a mile. Soon the smell of gingerbread became so strong and the air became so smoky that it was difficult to breathe. Conner and the other captives stepped onto the Great Lawn in the heart of Central Park and instantly knew they had arrived at the witches' base.

What was usually fifty-five acres of open grassy

fields and baseball diamonds was now the location of one nightmarish scene after another.

Hundreds of Boy Scouts and Girl Scouts were scattered across the Great Lawn and were being forced to bake some sort of gingerbread creation. There were rows of huge cauldrons where Scouts mixed ingredients and stirred dough. The dough was scooped out of the cauldrons by other Scouts and spread out on metal sheets as big as king-size mattresses. Once the dough was flat, Scouts cut it with enormous cookie cutters, making human-size gingerbread men. Then the Scouts transferred the metal sheets to one of a dozen enormous brick ovens along the west side of the lawn.

Charcoaline kept the ovens blazing with her fiery breath. Arboris, Tarantulene, and all the other witches walked among the Scouts like prison guards. They smacked and scolded every child who wasn't working to their level of satisfaction—which was *all* of them. Just like the Boy and Girl Scout collecting water at the Bethesda Fountain, all the children on the Great Lawn were terrified and exhausted and moved about like zombies. Conner saw Oliver, his companion from the plane, stationed at one of the cauldrons. Oliver was too afraid to look up and kept his eyes on the dough he was mixing.

"Why are they baking such enormous ginger-bread men?" Red asked.

"Isn't it obvious?" Goldilocks said. "They're making gingerbread soldiers—the witches are cooking up an army!"

"If we get out of this alive, I never want to hear the word *army* again," Conner said.

At the north end of the Great Lawn, the witches had constructed a tall hill made of jagged bedrock. It loomed over the lawn like a rocky watchtower. The bottom of the hill was guarded by the lion statues from the library, the polar bears from the Snow Queen's sleigh, and a thin moat where the Sea Witch's sharks swam. At the top of the bedrock, the Snow Queen sat on a throne made of ice, and the Sea Witch was perched on a throne made of coral.

Alex stood between the Snow Queen and the Sea Witch at the peak of the hill. Her eyes were still glowing like lightning, her hair was still floating above her head like a slow-motion fire, and she faced the roof of her massive force field. She seemed less like a person and more like a *generator* stuck in a mindless state, producing magic that protected and benefited her commanders. His sister's lifelessness brought tears to Conner's eyes, and he wondered if she could even be saved, or if, like Morina had said, she was cursed past the point of no return.

Rat Mary and Serpentina directed their prisoners toward the northeast corner of the Great Lawn to a row of cages made from candy canes. The cages were filled with Scout leaders, Central Park staff, tourists, and other New Yorkers the witches had rounded up. The witches pushed the joggers, the biker, the janitor, Jack, Goldilocks, Red, and Bree inside a small cage—but right before they could grab hold of Conner, he dashed toward the hill to get to his sister.

Just the way he'd felt at the barricade on Fifth Avenue, Conner was consumed by a powerful desire to save his sister and lost all common sense. Rat Mary and Serpentina chased after him, but Conner was much faster than the witches. He ran in an erratic pattern between the cauldrons and barely missed being lassoed by Serpentina's tongue. Conner leaped over the moat at the base of the hill and hiked up the bedrock as fast as he could.

"Alex!" he shouted. "It's me—it's your brother! The witches have invaded the Otherworld! You've got to fight off the curse or else—"

Before Conner could get anywhere close to his sister, one of the library lions knocked him off the hill. He soared over the moat and landed painfully hard on the ground. The wind was knocked out of him, and he gasped for air.

"CONNER!" Alex screamed.

For just a brief moment, her concern for her brother overpowered the curse. Her eyes stopped glowing, her hair stopped floating, and the shield around Central Park disappeared. The Snow Queen and the Sea Witch looked at each other in panic— they hadn't thought *anything* could break the curse.

"Keep the shield up, you stupid girl!" the Snow Queen screeched.

Alex immediately returned to her bewitched state, and the shield reappeared over Central Park. Rat Mary and Serpentina dragged Conner to the cage and threw him inside it with his friends.

"Conner, are you hurt?" Goldilocks asked him.

"I'll be okay," he groaned.

"That was so stupid of you!" Bree berated him. "What were you thinking? You could have gotten yourself killed!"

"I knew exactly what I was doing," Conner said. "Now we know Morina was wrong—Alex *hasn't* been cursed past the point of no return! She's still in there—*we can still save her!*"

CHAPTER FOURTEEN

THE CURSED AND THE COURTEOUS

A powerful rainstorm traveled down the western coast of the fairy-tale world and drenched the Dwarf Forests. Luckily, most of the residents and animals were already in hiding from the Literary Army, so the woods were virtually empty when the storm hit. But there was still one creature that got caught in the rain and scuttled through the forest in search of shelter.

The creature was shivering, soaked to the bone, and a complete stranger to the woods. After traveling in circles all night, it spotted a cottage by the side of a stream. The cottage appeared to be empty, as there was no light shining through the windows or smoke rising from the chimney. The creature hoped the cottage's looks weren't deceiving—not for the creature's own sake, but for the sake of any poor soul who might be inside. The creature had a reputation for leaving an impression on whomever it crossed paths with.

The creature broke down the front door and stepped out of the storm. The cottage was unlike any place it had ever seen. The walls, the floor, the ceiling, and the furniture were all painted white. The front room was lined with shelves of tiny glass bottles filled with colorful liquids.

The creature was parched from its trek through the vicious storm. It took a bottle from a shelf, twisted off the small golden cap, and smelled the red liquid inside. The fluid smelled like a fruity juice, so the creature threw its head back and downed the bottle in one gulp. Not only did the liquid instantly quench the creature's thirst, but it also reenergized the creature and made it feel warm inside. The creature inspected the bottle and saw that the word

REJUVENATION was engraved on the glass. It checked the other bottles on the shelves and discovered similar engravings. The blue liquids were labeled YOUTH, the pink liquids were labeled BEAUTY, the purple bottles were labeled VIBRANCY, and the turquoise bottles were labeled STAMINA.

The strange engravings aroused the creature's curiosity. It searched the cottage for more clues about what kind of establishment it had stumbled into.

In the back of the room the creature found a wall covered by a curtain. It pulled a tassel and the curtain separated, revealing a large mirror with a golden frame. As soon as the creature realized it was a mirror, it quickly shielded its eyes to avoid its reflection. Looking into the creature's eyes instantly turned any observer into *stone*—and the creature itself was no exception.

If someone managed to get a glimpse of it before being turned into stone, they would see she was a woman with glowing red eyes, fangs, and a long, scaly body. Instead of hair, the woman had a head full of hissing snakes that constantly fought one another for dominance. The monster's name was Medusa, and she was from a world far beyond the realm of fairy tales.

Strangely, as Medusa shielded herself from her reflection, she noticed that something was very different about her appearance. The powerful glow that was usually emitted by her eye sockets had disappeared. She peeked through her fingers at the mirror, and her gaze drifted up her body and landed on her face—but miraculously, Medusa wasn't turned to stone. Instead of the bright red pupils that infamously turned people into statues, Medusa saw a pair of brown eyes she hadn't seen in a very long time. She glanced down at the empty bottle in her hand and realized that the liquid inside wasn't juice, but a *potion*.

As Medusa gazed into her new eyes, her reflection started to transform, too. She watched in amazement as the hideous creature in the mirror slowly turned into a beautiful woman. Her head of snakes became a head of thick, sandy hair, her scaly skin became smooth and tanned, and her long coiled body became a voluptuous figure under a crimson toga. The Mirror of Truth had only changed Medusa's reflection, but for the first time in decades, Medusa saw the woman she was *before* she was turned into a monster.

Medusa wondered what other kinds of sorcery the cottage might contain. A door caught her eye on the other side of the room, and she went to it. Although it had several locks and bolts, the door was wide open and led to a steep staircase descending into a basement. Medusa slithered down the steps and discovered the twenty sleeping children under Morina's dark spell.

"Hello!" said a polite voice behind her.

Medusa looked over her shoulder and found another mirror leaning against the basement wall. A cheerful frog man wearing a three-piece suit waved at her from inside it. For a brief second, Medusa instinctively covered her eyes to spare the frog man from being turned into stone, forgetting that the potion had transformed her eyes. It had been so long since Medusa had communicated with another living thing, she'd almost forgotten how.

"Who are you?" she asked.

"Your guess is as good as mine," the frog man said.

"What in Zeus's name is that supposed to mean?"

"Unfortunately, I've lost my memory," he explained. "I've been searching for someone who might recognize me and help me remember, but so far you're the only person I've found."

"Sorry to disappoint you, but we've never met,"

Medusa said. "Believe me—I would know if we'd crossed paths."

"Well, that's a shame," the frog man said. "I guess I'll have to keep searching. I've looked practically everywhere, but everything is empty. It makes me wonder if there's a sale happening somewhere."

"How did you get inside the mirror?" Medusa asked.

"Oh, I was cursed," he explained. "I can't remember who or what put me in here, nor when or how it happened, but I do know I was *very* upset about it."

"Was this cottage your home?" she asked.

"Hmmm," the frog man said as he looked around the basement. "It seems very familiar, but I don't think it was *my* home, per se. I know very little about myself, but I can't imagine I was the type who kept unconscious children in the basement."

Medusa took a second look at the mysterious children. For the first time, she noticed that their skin had a light glow, and even though they were all the size of children, many had the wrinkles and crow's-feet of people much older.

"What happened to them?" she asked.

"Looks like they're under some sort of spell," he said.

"I suppose that makes *all* of us kindred spirits."

"You mean, you're cursed, too?" the frog man asked.

Medusa shot him a look—*wasn't it obvious?*

"Well, it would be rude to just *assume*," the frog man said. "Who cursed you, then? Was it the same person who cursed me or the children?"

"That's very unlikely," Medusa answered. "I was damned by a jealous goddess in my home world. She turned my hair into snakes, covered my body in scales, and cursed my eyes to turn anyone they saw into stone. I was so ashamed of myself and terrified of harming people that I secluded myself on an island called Sarpedon. I lived on the island for years until I was captured and brought to this world."

"Who captured you?"

"A terrible army of pirates, winged monkeys, and card soldiers," she said. "They kept me blindfolded in a cage and used me to turn their enemies into stone. Eventually I escaped and have been searching the woods for a place to isolate myself ever since. The longer I roam, the more lives I ruin."

"If your eyes turn others into stone, how am I not a statue?" the frog man asked.

"I drank a potion upstairs that returned my eyes to

normal," Medusa explained. "I'm not sure how long the potion will last, but there are hundreds more where it came from. They're engraved with words like *youth*, *beauty*, and *stamina*—all the things I'm lacking."

"That's wonderful!" the frog man said. "Suppose you drank *all* the potions—do you think it would turn you back into your human form?"

Medusa hadn't thought about it, but the idea mesmerized her.

"It's certainly worth a try," she said.

A mutual smile stretched across their faces, but the frog man's smile faded when a troubling thought crossed his mind.

"Say, where do you think all that youth, beauty, and stamina came from?" he asked.

Medusa was so pleased with the results, she hadn't stopped to wonder how the potions were made. Her eyes wandered back to the sleeping children, and it dawned on her just how drained of youth, beauty, and stamina they appeared to be. It suddenly became clear where the potions were coming from, and Medusa felt sick to her stomach.

"Hera Almighty," she gasped. "It's coming from the *children*! Their life force is being drained into potion bottles!"

The mythical monster was overwhelmed with guilt. She knelt on the floor and began to weep. With no handkerchief to dry her eyes, Medusa used the empty bottle of *rejuvenation* to collect her tears. She cried so hard, it wasn't long before the bottle was overflowing.

"There, there," the frog man comforted her. "It was just an accident. You wouldn't have drunk the potion if you'd known what it was."

"But I *would*!" Medusa confessed. "For the first time in decades, I've found a way to break the curse! I've found a cure for this miserable existence! There's *nothing* I wouldn't do to get rid of the monster I've become! I just wish it didn't have to come at such a terrible price!"

Medusa's admitted selfishness made her cry even harder than she had before. For reasons unknown to him, the frog man sympathized with her dark confession. He went silent for a few moments and gathered the right words to advise her with.

"If you ask me, there are two options at hand. Both will change you, but only *one* will get rid of the monster forever."

"What's the first option?" she asked.

"You can drink all the potions upstairs and return

to the woman you were before the curse. You'll never turn another soul into stone and never see a monster in the mirror again. But if you steal from these children, you won't *look* like a monster anymore—you'll just *be* one. And that's much worse, in my opinion."

"And the second option?"

"You can restore all the bottled youth, beauty, and stamina to their rightful owners," the frog man explained. "It won't change how you look, but it *will* change how you look at yourself. From then on, every time you pass a mirror and see your reflection, you won't see a hideous monster; you'll see a woman who chose to help others instead of helping herself. And anyone who looks into a mirror and sees *who* they are, over *what* they are—well, it's impossible to curse someone like that."

Medusa thought about the frog man's words and knew he was right. She wiped her tears, lifted herself from the floor, and slithered up the stairs. A few moments later she returned with as many potion bottles as she could carry. She made several trips up and down the stairs until every bottle was in the basement. One by one, she twisted off each golden cap and poured the potions into the mouths of the sleeping children.

Little by little, the stolen youth, beauty, and stamina returned to their rightful owners. The children's skin stopped glowing; they opened their heavy eyes and looked around the basement in a daze. They were too groggy to get up or keep their eyes open for long, but each child felt Morina's curse disappear from their body. One of the little boys stayed conscious long enough to look up at Medusa. She cowered in the corner of the basement, afraid her appearance would frighten the child. The boy wasn't scared at all; on the contrary, he smiled at her.

"You must be an angel," he whispered. "Thank you for saving us."

Just like all the other children, the boy closed his eyes and began to sleep off the lingering effects of the curse. Medusa had been called many things since being cursed, but this was the first time someone called her an *angel*.

"The children must be delirious if they think I'm an angel," she said.

"I'd say it's quite fitting, actually," the frog man said. "It takes a very special person to commit such a selfless act."

Although she was too modest to agree, Medusa nodded.

"You were right," she said. "From now on, every time I pass a mirror, I won't see my hideous reflection, I'll only be reminded of helping these children."

Suddenly, the mirror began to glow as brightly as the sun. Beams of light wrapped around the frog man's body and pushed him through the plate of glass as if it were made of water. The frog man collapsed on the basement floor and the mirror returned to normal.

"I'm . . . I'm . . . *I'm free!*" he cheered. "The curse is broken!"

As soon as he got to his feet, the frog man's memories returned like a river bursting through a broken dam.

"I can *remember*!" he announced. "I remember where I was born, I remember where I grew up, I remember all the places I lived, I remember the faces of my loved ones—*and I remember my name!*"

"What is it?" Medusa asked.

"Charles Carlton Charming, but my friends call me Froggy."

The restored frog man paused as a very critical memory surfaced.

"Oh my word—*Alex and Conner!* I was trying to warn them about the Literary Army when my memory faded! I was searching for a place where they might be hiding! I need to find them and the royal families before it's too late!"

"Did you say *royal families*?" Medusa asked. "Because I could have sworn I saw a bunch of royal families in an abandoned mine not far from here. They were hiding with loads of other people, but they all turned into stone before I could get a good look at them."

Froggy's heart practically fell into his stomach at the thought of his friends and family being turned into statues.

"Is there a way to transform someone back after they've been turned to stone?" he asked with large, desperate eyes.

"Actually, there might be," Medusa said. "After the goddess transformed me into a monster, she said *only tears of the damned can soothe the eyes of the cursed*. I thought it was just vindictive banter, but perhaps it was *instructions*. Take the bottle of my tears, pour them into the eyes of the statues, and it may reverse the damage."

She handed him the *rejuvenation* bottle filled with her teardrops.

"Thank you!" Froggy said. "How do I get to the abandoned mine from here?"

"I'll take you there, but first, I need a favor from you," she said.

"Yes, of course! Anything!"

"Eventually the rejuvenation potion will wear off and my old eyes will return," Medusa said. "I need someplace to go where I won't harm others—a place I can live where no one will ever find me."

"I know just the place," Froggy said. "I used to live in a hole up the river from here. It's not much, but it's very cozy. There are hundreds of books there and a nice chair beside a fireplace where you can sit and keep warm. As a matter of fact, most of the books in my collection were on the subject of *curses*—there may be a remedy for yours within their pages! If you take me to the abandoned mine, I'll tell you exactly how to find it."

Medusa was delighted by the description. "It sounds like a paradise," she said. "Now follow me—I'll show you to the mine."

NEWS II STORM WATCH IN ◆ II BREAK!<<

Chapter Fifteen

BACKUP

Conner had only been gone for eighteen hours, but his friends and characters at the Saint Andrew's Children's Hospital had grown twice as restless since he left. It was almost ten o'clock at night and all the pirates, superheroes, Cyborgs, mummies, literary characters, and fairy-tale characters were wide awake. Every passing hour spent in the commissary felt like it was longer than the one before. They were itching for something productive to do and running out of ways to entertain themselves.

After their *I Love Lucy* marathon was finished, the pirates of Starboardia discovered a steamy soap opera on Telemundo. Auburn Sally, Admiral Jacobson, and the entire *Dolly Llama* crew couldn't look away from the Latin American actors' passionate performances. They felt their faces blush at every turn of the scandalous story.

"Does anyone know what they're saying?" Winking Wendy asked.

"I don't understand a word, but I *feel* everything," Somersault Sydney said.

Across the commissary, the characters from "The Adventures of Blimp Boy" passed the time by teaching the characters from the Sherwood Forest how to gamble. It didn't matter how many times Beau Rogers and his great-aunt Emgee repeated the rules, the Merry Men had a hard time soaking up the concept of poker.

"AHA! THE ODDS ARE IN MY FAVOR AGAIN!" Robin Hood boasted. "I HAVE THREE KINGS AND TWO ACES! GOOD LUCK BEATING THAT!"

The archaeologists folded their cards before they even had a chance to look at them.

"Robin, for the tenth time, you're not supposed to reveal your cards until the end," Beau said. "The whole point is to make us *think* you have a good hand—you don't just come out and say it."

The Prince of Thieves let out a haughty laugh. "BUT I *HAVE* FOOLED YOU," he said, and revealed his cards. "BEHOLD, *A PAIR OF TWOS*! NOT ONLY HAVE I DECEIVED YOU, BUT I'VE DONE IT IN RECORD TIME! I DARE SAY THE STUDENT HAS BECOME THE TEACHER. NOW SLIDE OVER MY EARNINGS!"

The superheroes from "The Ziblings" were in the middle of a heated round of charades with the space explorers from "Galaxy Queen." Blaze, Whipney, and Morph were one team, while the Cyborg Queen, Commander Newters, and Professor Wallet were on the other.

"It's an elephant!" Blaze called out.

"That's right!" Morph said, and quickly moved on.

"It's a satellite dish!" Whipney guessed.

"Yes!" Morph said, and went to the next paper.

"It's a toy box!" Blaze said.

"That's it!" Morph said. "Boy, we're really good at this!"

"Of course you're doing well!" the Cyborg Queen complained. "You're *literally transforming* into whatever the paper says! I don't see how this is a fair game!"

Meanwhile, Trollbella got roped into playing a game of hide-and-seek with the Lost Boys from Neverland. The troll queen counted to a hundred while the boys hid, but when she was done counting, instead of searching for them, Trollbella had a seat and flipped through a magazine.

"Aren't you going to find them?" the Tin Woodman asked her.

"I was, but then I had an epiphany," Trollbella said. "If I want boys to stop playing games with me, I've got to stop playing games with boys."

"Even *hide-and-seek*?" the Tin Woodman asked.

"*Especially* hide-and-seek," Trollbella said in total seriousness. "Who we are on the playground is who we are in life, and I'm done being a seeker. If someone wants to be my Troblin King, he's just gonna have to find *me*."

Charlotte stood by the window and watched the characters getting fresh air outside. Peter Pan and

Bolt competed in several rounds of a questionable activity they called *Who Can Fly Closest to the Moon Without Passing Out*. Lester, the Rosary Chicken, and Blubo were picking at bugs in the lawns surrounding the hospital. Bones, the mummified dog from the Pyramid of Anesthesia, buried the parts of his body that fell off. Unbeknownst to him, Clawdius was digging them back up and burying them in other spots.

The Blissworm inched up a tree, hung upside down from a branch, and blew Charlotte a kiss goodbye, and then its soft body slowly hardened into a cocoon—which was very surprising, since Conner had never mentioned anything about it having a metamorphosis. The space worm even placed a DO NOT DISTURB sign on the corner of its chrysalis.

Although there was plenty to distract her, nothing could take Charlotte's mind off her children. Every additional hour she didn't hear from Conner was more torturous than the previous one. The delayed communication made her fear that something was wrong—*very* wrong.

The commissary doors swung open and Bob entered with a mummy who had slipped out without Charlotte noticing.

"Look who I found in the emergency room," Bob said.

The mummy had two large burn marks on the wraps covering his heart.

"What happened to his chest?" Charlotte asked.

"Apparently two paramedics found him roaming the parking lot," Bob said. "They checked his pulse and took him to Emergency right away. The nurses were trying to revive him when I got there. I had to make him sign a DNR to get them to stop."

"He must have walked right past me," Charlotte said. "I've been trying to keep everyone stimulated while we wait to hear from Conner, but there's only so much they can do. You know things are dull when the dead start wandering off."

"Don't be so hard on yourself—you've got a lot on your mind," Bob said. "Speaking of which, any word from Conner?"

"Nothing," she said with a heavy sigh. "I've tried calling a dozen times, but no one is answering. I know I worry about them constantly, but I can't fight a feeling that something terrible has happened. For the first time in as long as I can remember, I feel like they both *need* me."

Bob and Charlotte were distracted when the

pirates from Starboardia started moaning at the television.

"What's going on?" Charlotte asked.

"Some lady came on the screen and interrupted our show!" Fish-Lips Lucy grumbled. "And Maria was *just* about to catch José being unfaithful!"

Bob and Charlotte glanced at the screen to see what they were talking about. President of the United States Katherine Walker was sitting at her desk in the Oval Office, about to give a national address.

"That *lady* is the president," Bob said. "She only comes on TV when something important is happening."

"But it's past midnight on the East Coast," Charlotte said. "What could be so important?"

"Beats me," Bob said. "Turn it up, guys."

The pirates turned up the volume and everyone in the commissary gathered around the television. The characters outside could tell something was going on and came in to see what the big deal was. The Bliss-worm even peeked out from its cocoon.

"My fellow Americans," President Walker said to the camera. "By now I'm sure you've heard about the situation unfolding in New York City. There are many outlandish reports circulating in the news and social media, so allow me to present the facts and calm the frenzy. Early yesterday morning, a massive gas leak was discovered at the main branch of the New York Public Library. Local authorities were called to the scene and quickly ordered an evacuation of the surrounding area. After carefully assessing the damage throughout the day, that evacuation has now been extended to the entire island of Manhattan. I understand this poses an inconvenience of immeasurable proportions, but nothing, I repeat, *nothing*, is more important than the safety of the American people. We assure you the situation is being taken care of by highly trained professionals and there is no need to panic...."

Charlotte instantly began to panic.

"She wouldn't be reassuring the country if there were nothing to worry about," Charlotte said. "Now I know I wasn't just being paranoid—*something's definitely happened! The twins are in danger!*"

Just then, Charlotte's cell phone started buzzing in her pocket. She retrieved the phone and saw an incoming call from an unfamiliar number. Charlotte immediately answered the phone, praying she'd hear the voices of her children on the other end.

"Conner, is that you?"

"Mrs. Gordon? Oh, thank God, I've finally got you! I've been trying to get a signal for hours but there's a lot of people using their cell phones around here!"

At first Charlotte didn't recognize the young voice, but she could tell that the caller was standing in a crowded area.

"Who is this?" she asked.

"It's Mindy—Mindy McClowsky," Mindy said.

"And Cindy Strutherbergers!" Cindy added.

"And Lindy Lenkins!" Lindy announced.

Wendy performed a quick clap-snap combo to announce her presence.

"Wendy Takahashi is with us, too," Mindy said. "You're on speaker with the Book Huggers from Willow Crest High School."

Charlotte was automatically annoyed. "Girls, I really don't have time to talk about whether or not Alex and Conner are interning at Area 51—"

"You don't have to!" Mindy said. "We just saw Conner and he told us all about your family secret! Our mission is complete—we're totally in the loop now! And boy, do you guys have enough drama to fill a week of talk shows, or what!"

"Wait a second, did you say you *just saw Conner*?"

"Yes!" Mindy said. "We were just at the library

with him and his friends—and by the way, don't believe a word anyone says about a *gas leak*. That is *totally* not what's going on!"

The news overwhelmed Charlotte and she sat down. The pirates turned off the television so they could eavesdrop on her conversation.

"Where is Conner now? Is he or Alex with you?"

"No, he and his friends went to find Alex, but we're not sure where they went," Mindy explained. "Come to think of it, I'm not sure where we are, either. After we crawled out of the abandoned subway tunnel, we got shoved into a bus by police officers and they drove us off the island."

"I think we're in Brooklyn," Lindy said.

"No, this is definitely Queens," Cindy said.

Wendy pointed to a sign that clearly stated they were in Hoboken, but no one paid attention to her.

"It's impossible to tell," Mindy said. "Anyway, this weird bridge-thingy appeared in the library that leads directly to the fairy-tale world. I guess a bunch of witches came out of it earlier and something way worse is coming soon. It's like a bad episode of *Doctor Who* over here! Conner asked us to call you and say they need backup—he said you'd know what to do!"

Like a firefighter at the sound of an alarm, Charlotte hopped to her feet and began gathering her purse, Conner's binder of short stories, the fairy-tale treasury, and the flask of Portal Potion.

"We'll leave right away!" she said. "Thank you for calling, Mindy!"

"You're welcome!" Mindy said. "Oh! And Mrs. Gordon? One last thing. My fellow Book Huggers and I will absolutely accept your apology for lying to us over the years whenever you feel it's an appropriate—"

Charlotte hung up the phone before Mindy could finish her sentence. She turned back to the others and saw they were gathered right behind her—desperate to know the details of her call.

"Well?" the Tin Woodman asked.

"Conner needs us," Charlotte announced. "I'm not sure how, but the witches have crossed into the Otherworld and the Literary Army isn't far behind. We've got to get to New York and stop them before they destroy the city!"

The commissary erupted in celebration—not at the news of the approaching army, but because they were finally leaving the hospital.

"How are we going to get there?" Bob asked. "I've

got some frequent flyer miles left, but not enough for *all* of us."

"We don't have to worry about transportation, silly!" Bolt said. "The Ziblings have a jet!"

"Aunt Emgee and I have a blimp!" Beau Rogers said.

"The Cyborgs have an intergalactic spacecraft," Commander Newters said.

"And *we* have the *Dolly Llama*—the fastest pirate ship in the Caribbean Sea!" Auburn Sally proclaimed.

The characters scratched their heads at the odd idea of taking a pirate ship across the country.

"Sally, New York City is three thousand miles away," Charlotte explained. "You can't get there by boat."

"Oh yes you can!" Peter Pan declared. "We'll make the ship fly with fairy dust. I have just enough left to make it soar! And once we sail the skies to New York City, *we'll rescue Tinker Bell from the miserable Captain Hook*!"

"We'll defeat the Wicked Witch of the West and free the Winkies and the flying monkeys from her magic spell!" Blubo said.

"We'll dethrone the Queen of Hearts, and perhaps earn a heart of our own!" the Tin Woodman said.

"WE'LL BURN THE UGLY WITCHES AT THE STAKE—BUT KEEP THE ATTRACTIVE ONES!" Robin Hood said.

"We'll save Butterboy from the clutches of the Breemonster!" Trollbella said. "Sorry, I meant from *the bad guys*!"

Charlotte appreciated the characters' spirit, but she knew they were wasting time.

"All right, enough declarations," she said. "*Let's go save the world!* But before we go, someone needs to grab the Blissworm."

Morina was standing in the Dwarf Forests a few yards away from the bridge between worlds. Earlier, she had sent a crow to the Northern Kingdom with a message informing the Literary Emperors that the first phase of their plan was complete. She instructed them to meet her in the woods with their armies at sunrise, and their invasion of the Otherworld would begin.

Strangely, the witch had not received a response confirming that they had gotten the message. Morina grew more impatient the longer she waited to hear back. Finally, a few hours after sending word, she got a reply—but it wasn't the response she was expecting.

The ground began to rumble and the trees started to sway as something enormous moved through the forest. Soon the sound of marching feet echoed through the woods, moving closer and closer to the witch.

Soon the Wicked Witch of the West, the Queen of Hearts, and Captain Hook appeared in the distance with their entire army following behind. Thousands of Winkies and card soldiers stood in two very neat rows behind their emperors; the *Jolly Roger* and its rambunctious crew drifted in the air above them like a giant balloon; and the sky surrounding the floating pirate ship was filled with swarms of flying monkeys.

The emperors led their army through the woods until they stood face-to-face with the witch.

"Hello, emperors," Morina said. "What a surprise to see you arrive so soon. I wasn't expecting you until sunrise. I hope you received the message with my instructions."

The Wicked Witch, the Queen of Hearts, and Captain Hook exchanged a sly smile.

"Your message was received, but we thought it would be best to respond in person," the Wicked Witch said.

"Oh?" Morina asked. "Is something wrong?"

"Not at all," Captain Hook said. "We were very pleased to hear that the witches have successfully crossed into the Otherworld. However, there's been a change of plans. Instead of waiting for the witches to weaken the Otherworld's defenses, we've decided to enter the Otherworld *now* and take it by surprise."

Morina was infuriated that they had altered the agenda without consulting her first. She was so enraged, her eyes turned red and her veins visibly blackened. Still, the witch tried to stay as calm as possible, knowing the emperors wouldn't respond to anger.

"My lords, I understand you're eager to invade, but I beg you to follow the plan I've created," she said. "If we cross into the Otherworld before the witches are exterminated, you'll be battling the witches *and* the Otherworld's armies."

"I think we can handle a gaggle of witches," the Wicked Witch cackled.

"Certainly," Morina said. "But as I first explained, it'll be much easier to secure domination if we wait for the witches to perish in—"

"NO MORE WAITING!" the Queen of Hearts roared. "We want to conquer the Otherworld and we want to *conquer it NOW!* Step aside or you'll be the first casualty of the night!"

Morina knew it was useless to reason with them. The emperors were like toddlers waiting to play with a new toy. As much as she wanted to stop them, she wasn't powerful enough to take on the Literary Army by herself.

She reluctantly stepped out of the way and allowed the Wicked Witch, the Queen of Hearts, Captain Hook, and their army to march toward the bridge.

The emperors were making a catastrophic mistake by entering the Otherworld early. However, Morina knew her plan wasn't doomed to fail just yet. There was still someone in the equation who *was* powerful enough to take on an army—*several armies*, if they were directed properly.

So the witch remained quiet as a new strategy unfolded: If she could just get to *Alex* before the witches were slain, there was still a chance Morina could succeed. . . .

CHAPTER SIXTEEN

THE TEARS OF MEDUSA

Froggy hopped around the abandoned dwarf mine and poured Medusa's tears into the eyes of all the statues. He was surprised to see there were just as many stone animals in the mine as there were men, women, and children. The statues were pale, solid as rocks, and frozen with such terrified expressions that Froggy didn't recognize any of the faces. He prayed the teardrops would reverse the magic and the Bailey twins would appear among them.

Once he finished pouring Medusa's teardrops into each pair of stone eyes, Froggy took a step back and waited with bated breath. Like chicks hatching from their eggs, the statues slowly started to wiggle and crack. Arms and legs began moving, heads began turning, and the stone chipped away like it was nothing but a thin shell. The men, women, children, and animals brushed themselves off and cleared dust from the back of their throats.

Froggy was relieved to see so many familiar faces appear around him. He saw his brothers, Chance, Chase, and Chandler; their wives, Cinderella, Sleeping Beauty, and Snow White; and his nieces, Hope and Ash. Froggy also recognized Empress Elvina, Queen Rapunzel and Sir William, Hagetta, the Traveling Tradesman, Red's granny, the Little Old Woman from the Shoe Inn, Rook and Farmer Robins, Sir Lampton, Sir Grant, and soldiers from the Charming and Northern Kingdoms. He even saw Cornelius, Porridge, Buckle, and Oats once they uncovered themselves.

The people and animals looked around the abandoned mine in a daze. The last thing they remembered was the bright eyes of a horrifying monster, and now they were brushing layers of stone off their bodies.

"What happened to us?" Snow White asked.

"You were turned into stone by a creature named Medusa," Froggy explained. "I poured her tears into your eyes and it reversed the spell!"

Everyone's confusion doubled when they realized Froggy was standing beside them.

"Charlie, is that *you*?" Chance asked in disbelief.

"Hello, brother!" Froggy said. "Words can't describe how wonderful it is to see all of you!"

Froggy gave his brothers and their wives enormous hugs and kissed his nieces on the cheek.

"You're out of the mirror!" Cinderella said. "But how did you escape it? Red told us it was impossible to free you!"

"That's what I thought, but I've happily been proved wrong," Froggy said. "Getting here was an awfully big journey, and I promise to tell the story one day, but right now it's urgent I find Alex and Conner."

Froggy looked around for the Bailey twins, but they weren't inside the crowded mine.

"Wait a second, where are the twins?" he asked.

"They aren't here," Chandler said. "They went into the Otherworld."

"And what about Red? And Jack and Goldilocks?" Froggy asked.

"They're with the twins," Chandler said. "Don't worry, they're safe as far as we know."

"I don't understand," Froggy said. "Why would they all be in the Otherworld?"

The Charming brothers looked at one another with very concerned expressions. They wanted to fill Froggy in but didn't know where to begin.

"Oh, Charlie, so many terrible things have happened since you've been gone," Chase said. "The Masked Man stole a potion from the late Fairy Godmother's chambers and used it to travel into the books from your library. He recruited a terrible army that attacked our world and imprisoned the citizens from every kingdom. He almost executed all the royal families, but thankfully Jack and Goldilocks saved us and brought us to the abandoned mine. After we escaped, the Masked Man's army turned on him, and now three horrible emperors are in power!"

"Unfortunately, I'm quite familiar with the emperors," Froggy said. "I saw the Wicked Witch, the Queen of Hearts, and Captain Hook through a mirror in the Northern Palace. I overheard them making plans to invade and conquer the Otherworld next— that's why I need to find the twins immediately! I need to warn them the emperors' army is coming!"

"The twins went into the Otherworld to recruit their own army," Sleeping Beauty explained. "Jack, Goldilocks, Red, and Trollbella went to help them assemble it. They've already enlisted people from the worlds of literature, like the Tin Woodman from Oz, the Lost Boys from Neverland, and the Merry Men from the Sherwood Forest."

Froggy thought his ears were deceiving him. "Did you say *Oz*? *Neverland*? *The Sherwood Forest?*" he repeated. "Well, they've certainly had quite an adventure without me. What sort of army are they assembling?"

"The twins are recruiting characters from Conner's writing," Rapunzel said.

Froggy's mouth dropped open. "That's *remarkable*," he said. "But why go to such extremes? Aren't there enough people in *this* world to fight the Literary Army? Surely, the Fairy Council could do something to help—"

"The Fairy Council was turned into stone long before us," Sir Lampton said. "The Literary Army attacked the Fairy Kingdom first before ambushing the others. They came so quickly in the middle of the night, there was nothing we could do to prepare ourselves."

Froggy had known things were bad, but he had no idea they were *this* bad. He sat on a boulder as the magnitude of the situation sank in.

"Just for the record, I'd like to remind everyone that I predicted *all* of this," the Traveling Tradesman said. "Remember when I was using the Lost Boys' marbles to foresee the future? I specifically said *worlds would collide*, and now look what's happening—*worlds have collided, all right!*"

Hagetta rolled her eyes at the silly man. "Oh, shut up, you old geezer," she said. "If you're such a gifted psychic, then where was the warning about the Literary Army? Or the monster who turned us all into statues for a week?"

Regardless of the challenging times, Froggy still needed to warn the twins about the Literary Army's next conquest. He leaped to his feet, more determined to find them than before.

"I need a way into the Otherworld," he said. "How do the twins manage to get back and forth?"

Hagetta looked around the mine and retrieved

the emerald-green *Land of Stories* treasury from the ground.

"They've been using this," she said, and handed Froggy the book. "It's been splashed with the Portal Potion. When the book is opened, a powerful beam of light projects from its pages. Step through the beam and you'll enter the Otherworld."

"Thank you," Froggy said. "I just hope I'm not too late."

"Do you want us to come with you?" Sir Grant asked.

"No, this world needs you more than I do," Froggy said. "Once the Literary Army has crossed into the Otherworld, the rest of you should use their absence to liberate your people from the Northern Kingdom. There's also a cottage just a few miles east of here by the river. You'll find the missing children from the Corner Kingdom and Charming Kingdom in the basement. Take them with you and reunite them with their families."

The royal families and the soldiers nodded—eager to finally be of service to their people again.

Rook stepped forward. "I want to come with you," he said. "If Alex is even remotely in danger, I'm willing to do whatever I can to help her."

"That's out of the question," Farmer Robins said. "An enormous army is headed for her world, Rook! It's too dangerous! I won't let you put yourself in harm's way!"

"You don't understand—I *have* to!" Rook declared. "I'm partly to blame for this whole mess. If I hadn't led the Grande Armée to the royal families, the Masked Man would never have had the opportunity to steal the Portal Potion! I betrayed Alex and I've had to live with the guilt of a hundred men because of it. The only way I can redeem myself is by making things right. This may be my last opportunity to make it up to her—so I'm going and there's nothing you can do to stop me."

After seeing the determination in Rook's eyes and hearing the passion in his voice, Farmer Robins knew there was no arguing with his son. Instead of debating him any further, the farmer clasped his son in a tight embrace.

"Be safe," he said tearfully. "You're all I've got left, Rook."

"I will," Rook said, and hugged his father back.

"Your father is right about one thing," Sir Grant said. "The Otherworld is going to be significantly more dangerous once the Literary Army enters it.

Even if the twins have secured an army to fight them, the two of you shouldn't make the trip alone."

Froggy couldn't have agreed more. "We'll take the Fairy Council with us," he decided. "I have just enough tears left to free them. But we need to hurry—as far as we know, the army could already be headed to the Otherworld."

"Then we'll take Cornelius to the Fairy Kingdom," Rook suggested. "He'll get us there three times as fast as any horse could."

Rook whistled and the chubby unicorn stepped out from the group of animals. Cornelius loved being singled out and neighed arrogantly. Porridge, Buckle, and Oats grunted—there was nothing more annoying than a big-headed unicorn.

"Splendid," Froggy said. "We'll leave at once."

Froggy and Rook climbed aboard Cornelius and steered him out of the mine. The unicorn galloped as fast as a race car. They charged through the Dwarf Forests and sped across the Charming Kingdom, and within two hours of their departure, they were already approaching the Fairy Palace in the Fairy Kingdom—or at least what was left of it.

The destruction was a devastating sight. The golden pillars and arches of the majestic palace had been blown to pieces by the *Jolly Roger*'s mighty cannons. The vibrant gardens surrounding the palace had been burned to a crisp and were covered in debris. In the center of the ruins, Froggy, Rook, and Cornelius found the statues of Rosette, Tangerina, Xanthous, Emerelda, Skylene, Violetta, and Coral. The colorful Fairy Council was just as pale, stiff, and frozen with fear as the people had been in the abandoned mine.

"What kind of monster is capable of *this*?" Rook asked.

"It wasn't her fault," Froggy said. "It was the monsters *behind* the monster—they're the ones to blame."

Froggy jumped down from Cornelius's back and approached the statues with his bottle of Medusa's tears. Just as he was about to pour the first teardrop into Emerelda's stone eye, the sound of approaching footsteps came from behind him. Froggy turned and saw a group of strange men walking toward them.

"Quick," he whispered. *"We need to hide."*

Froggy, Rook, and Cornelius dived behind a fallen pillar—although it was much more difficult for the chubby unicorn to crouch behind it. They watched the strange men as they entered the palace ruins. There were eleven men in total, each wearing the armor of a knight. They inspected the damage with their swords raised. The men also carried large shields, but Froggy didn't recognize the crest painted across them.

"Who are they?" Rook whispered.

"I have no idea," Froggy said. "They aren't from any kingdom I'm familiar—"

"DON'T MOVE!"

Froggy, Rook, and Cornelius cautiously looked over their shoulders and saw that a twelfth knight had snuck up behind them. He was a very handsome and muscular young man. He held his sword just a few inches from their faces.

"I've found a couple of scoundrels hiding in the debris!" he called to the other knights.

"I beg your pardon," Froggy said. "Who do you think you're calling a scoundrel?"

"Who do you think you're talking to?" the knight asked.

"Who do you think *you're* talking to?" Froggy repeated.

"I happen to be a *king*, thank you ever so much," the knight declared.

"Well, *so am I*!" Froggy announced.

"Then *you* must be responsible for damaging the

palace!" the knight said, and raised his sword, preparing to strike.

"ARTIE, CUT IT OUT! HE'S WITH US!"

A split second before being sliced open, Froggy was saved by a familiar raspy voice. He looked into the singed gardens and saw an elderly couple approaching the ruins. Froggy recognized the woman the moment he laid eyes on her.

"Mother Goose!" he yelled.

"Hey, Charlie!" she said. "Long time no see!"

Mother Goose gave Froggy a hard but friendly pat on the back.

"Hey, Merlin," she called to the old man behind her. "This is the guy I was telling you about—the prince who was cursed as a frog, then got kidnapped at his own wedding, and then got thrown into a magic mirror!"

"Oh, my poor tragic fellow," Merlin said, and vigorously shook Froggy's hand. "It's such a pleasure to finally meet you! And my condolences, you know, *about your life.*"

"Hey, Charlie, how'd you get out of the mirror?" Mother Goose said.

"I escaped," he said. "It's a long story—where have *you* been all this time?"

"Oh, I moved to another dimension," Mother Goose said. "Alex and I got trapped in the world of Camelot while we were chasing the Masked Man. I took one look at *this* handsome devil and knew it was time to settle down."

Mother Goose winked flirtatiously at Merlin, and the wizard kissed her hand.

"Wait a moment, you mean that's *the real Merlin*?" Froggy asked in disbelief.

"The one and only," Mother Goose said. "And this is our squire, Artie—oops, I mean *King Arthur*! Sorry, Artie, old habits die hard."

"*You're* King Arthur?" Froggy asked.

Arthur became defensive. "Yes," he said. "Is there a problem?"

"Not at all," Froggy said. "You just seem so… *young*. I always imagined King Arthur as an older man with a beard and an unpleasant scowl."

"Artie wasn't supposed to be king until he was much older," Mother Goose explained. "He started having nightmares about Alex and wanted to come check on her. I told him if he finished his training I'd take him to the fairy-tale world to see her. Well, I didn't think he was serious about it, but the kid pulled the sword from the stone and founded the Knights of the Round Table in just a couple of days!"

"Knights are much easier to persuade when they're teenagers," Arthur said.

"We had never heard of a *round table*, but we didn't have anything else better to do," one of the knights said with a shrug.

"Right—what was your name again?" Arthur asked him.

"It's *Lancelot*, Your Grace," he said. "Anyway, a crusade sure sounded like fun—so here we are."

Rook looked Arthur up and down, instantly intimidated by the young king.

"So you and Alex are *friends*?" he asked.

"I'd say we're more than just *acquainted*," Arthur said with a telling grin.

"Well, *I* was her first kiss," Rook bragged.

"Well, *I'll* be her last," Arthur quipped.

Rook roared and charged toward Arthur, intending to tackle him. In one swift motion, Arthur threw Rook over his shoulder and pinned him to the ground under his boot.

"Boys, knock it off!" Merlin said. "We don't have time for an adolescent love triangle—there are *much* bigger issues in this story."

"Speaking of which, *what the heck happened to the Fairy Palace*?" Mother Goose said. "This place looks like New Year's Eve at Pompeii! And the Fairy Council is as stiff on the outside as they were on the inside! Charlie, what's going on in this world?"

Froggy let out a deep sigh. "It's been attacked by an atrocious army of literary characters," he explained. "The Wicked Witch from Oz, the Queen of Hearts from Wonderland, and Captain Hook from Neverland have joined forces and taken over the kingdoms! And recently, they've set their sights on the Otherworld. I'm on my way there to warn the twins the army is coming!"

"Then it wasn't a dream," Arthur said. "Alex really *is* in trouble! We've got to save her!"

"All right, all right, all right," Mother Goose said. "Artie, you can say *I told you so* later—but right now we've got to get our keisters into the Otherworld and help the twins! Lead the way, Charlie—we're coming with you!"

"I'm glad to hear it," Froggy said. "But first, I need to *loosen up* the Fairy Council."

"Good luck," Mother Goose said with a snort. "I've been trying to loosen up those broads for centuries."

Froggy hopped to the statues in the center of the destruction and placed two drops of Medusa's tears in each of their eyes. Just like the people in the mine, the Fairy Council began to wiggle, shake, and crack. With seven bright, colorful blasts, the stone covering their bodies exploded and the council was finally free. The fairies looked around at their ruined home in shock. Emerelda, however, remained as stoic as ever. As if she had been deep in thought during her entire time as a statue, the leader of the Fairy Council emerged from the spell knowing exactly what needed to be done next.

"*Alex,*" Emerelda said sharply. "*We need to find Alex.*"

CHAPTER SEVENTEEN

WORLDS COLLIDE

Within a few hours after the witches occupied Central Park, the number of US Marines under General Wilson's command had doubled, and more were on their way from military bases around the country. The soldiers formed a line that stretched along Central Park's six-mile perimeter, and snipers were repositioned on the balconies of penthouse apartments facing the park. There was no possible way anything could escape the park without going through the Marines—not that anything could get through Alex's magic shield. They had only seen the shield disappear once all night, but it had been reinstated so quickly, the Marines thought it was wisest to keep their distance.

Unfortunately, General Wilson had positioned his soldiers in the wrong location. The witches still had several hours before their gingerbread army was finished baking. The real threat was approaching from *behind* the Marines—but by the time they saw it coming, it was already too late.

"Sir, I have good news!" a soldier reported to General Wilson.

"What is it?" the general asked.

"We've located Cornelia Grimm," the soldier replied. "She should be here within the hour."

"Thank you, Sergeant," General Wilson said. "I want to be notified the minute she arrives."

Suddenly, Fifth Avenue started to rumble with the power of an earthquake. The Marines searched the street to see what was causing the commotion but didn't see anything out of the ordinary. However, the soldiers felt the tremor grow stronger and stronger the closer they walked to the New York Public Library.

As they approached the library's front steps, a

thunderous explosion prompted all the Marines to dive to the ground. They looked up and saw a massive pirate ship burst out of the library's roof and soar into the air. The ship was followed by swarms of winged creatures—*monkeys*, as far as they could tell. Once the sky was filled with the mysterious beasts, fleets of strangely shaped soldiers charged out of the library's damaged entrance with their swords and staffs raised above their heads.

"General, we're under attack—again!" shouted a Marine. "What are your orders, sir?"

General Wilson watched in total shock as the literary characters emerged from the library. Apparently the witches were just the prelude of a painfully long performance, and for the first time all night, the general doubted they'd make it to the curtain call.

"Sir, your orders?" the Marine asked again.

"*Pray*, Sergeant," the general ordered. "At this point, it's all we *can* do."

As the sun rose over New York City, a floating procession of fictional proportions flew over northern New Jersey. An enormous spacecraft, a large blimp, a colorful jet, and a flying pirate ship transported

Conner's family, friends, and characters toward the Empire State.

"We should start looking for a place to land," Charlotte said from inside the blimp. "Look over there—it's *Liberty Island*! That's perfect!"

Emgee gave her a thumbs-up and gradually steered the blimp toward the lawns behind the Statue of Liberty. Once the *Charlie Chaplin* landed safely, the *BASK-8*, the *Dolly Llama*, and the Ziblings' jet joined it on the island.

Charlotte, Bob, Trollbella, the Tin Woodman, and Lester rode aboard the blimp with Beau Rogers and Emgee. Unfortunately, they also had to share it with Bones and all the mummies from the Pyramid of Anesthesia. After traveling across the country with the undead in a tight space, the smell was almost unbearable. Trollbella yanked opened the door and jumped out of the blimp before it came to a complete stop.

"Thank the Troblin Heavens—fresh air!" she gasped. "I don't think I'll ever get the stench of death out of my clothes! I smell like the Breemonster's breath!"

The *BASK-8* lowered its ramp and the Cyborg Queen rolled out of the spacecraft with Commander Newters and the Cyborg soldiers following behind her. Captain Auburn Sally kicked down her ship's gangplank and she, Admiral Jacobson, their crew, the Merry Men, and the Rosary Chicken exited the *Dolly Llama*. The Blissworm's cocoon had been hung at the top of the mast beside the ship's flag.

The Ziblings lowered the steps of their jet, and the superheroes climbed down with Professor Wallet, Blubo, Peter Pan, and the Lost Boys.

"That! Was! AWESOME!" Tootles cheered. "Can we ride the jet again?"

"If you think *that* was fast, you should see the Ziblings' rocket our dad is building!" Bolt bragged.

Riding the Ziblings' jet made the Lost Boys euphoric, but Peter Pan looked like the saddest boy in the world.

"Peter, what's wrong?" Professor Wallet asked.

"Oh, it's nothing," Peter said with a sigh. "I just never thought people would invent *machines* that could fly. I mean, it sort of defeats the purpose of *me* if everyone can do it."

"My dear boy, who do you think the rest of the world has been trying to catch up with all these years?" Professor Wallet said with a twinkle in his eye.

Once everyone had exited their various methods of transportation, Charlotte gathered Conner's binder of short stories, the emerald-green treasury, and the Portal Potion, and led the characters to the grassy field directly below the Statue of Liberty. They looked across the Hudson River at the island of Manhattan and could see smoke bellowing from somewhere in Midtown. After closer inspection, they could see the *Jolly Roger* and flying monkeys snaking through the city's skyscrapers.

"Oh no!" Charlotte gasped. "The Literary Army is already here!"

"What should we do now?" Bob asked.

"I'm trying to think," Charlotte said. "Call me crazy, but I've never orchestrated a *war* before."

The emerald-green storybook suddenly started to glow in her hands. Charlotte dropped the book on the grass and it opened, shining a beam of light toward the sky. Froggy hopped out of the beam and looked around Liberty Island. His mouth dropped open at the sight of the New York skyline across the river and the Statue of Liberty towering above him.

"So *this* is the Otherworld," he said in amazement. "I can't imagine why the twins would ever leave a place like this."

"Froggy, how did you get here?" Charlotte asked.

"The twins told me you were trapped in a magic mirror!"

"Hello, Mrs. Gordon," he said. "I'd love to stay and catch up, but it's urgent I speak with the twins! Where might they be?"

Charlotte pointed to the New York skyline. "They're in there somewhere."

Froggy looked toward Manhattan and noticed the smoke, the flying monkeys, and the *Jolly Roger* hovering above Midtown.

"The army's already arrived!" he said. "We're too late!"

"You mean, you're not alone?" Charlotte asked.

As soon as she asked the question, Charlotte had the answer. Mother Goose, Merlin, Arthur, and the Knights of the Round Table emerged from the beam of light in a straight line. Cornelius galloped out of the beam next with Rook on his back, followed by the seven members of the Fairy Council.

"Well, take a look at all these theatrics," Mother Goose said as she scanned the island. "Are these the characters from Conner's short stories or am I back at Burning Man?"

Lester was overjoyed to see Mother Goose.

He wrapped his wings around her and the two embraced.

"Squawk!" the gander said as he nuzzled his beak under her chin.

"I've missed you, too, Lester," Mother Goose said. "Gosh, I leave you alone for a couple of weeks and the whole universe starts falling apart!"

"You guys sure are a sight for sore eyes," Charlotte said. "We could really use your help. New York City is under attack! The witches and the Literary Army have crossed into the Otherworld!"

"The *witches*?" Emerelda asked. "What on earth are they doing in the Otherworld?"

"I imagine the same thing as the Literary Army," Mother Goose said. "Come on, Emerelda, you can't be *that* surprised. It's just like the kids say: *Witches be witches*."

"They kidnapped Alex a week ago and have put her under some sort of spell," Charlotte informed them. "Conner and his friends came to the city yesterday to find her, but now we're not certain where any of them are. Before she was kidnapped, Alex helped Conner assemble an army from his short stories to fight the Literary Army, but I'm not exactly qualified to lead them."

If there was ever a moment where someone with

natural leadership skills would be of use, this was it. Arthur looked at Merlin and the wizard nodded—*it was the young king's time to shine.* Arthur scaled the side of the Statue of Liberty's platform and whistled down to get everyone's attention.

"Everyone listen up," he said. "We've got people to find and an army to defeat. We'll accomplish neither of these things if we just stand around scratching our heads. So first things first—*Lester,* I want you to do a lap around the city and see if you can spot either Alex or her brother. Come back to us the moment you see something."

Lester saluted the young king and took off at once.

"As for the rest of you, we'll need to split up into *four* teams," Arthur instructed. "*Team one* will go after the witches, *team two* will face Captain Hook and his pirates, *team three* will confront the Wicked Witch, the Winkies, and the flying monkeys, and *team four* will track down the Queen of Hearts and her card soldiers."

All the characters were confused. None of them had the slightest clue who this bossy young man was.

"EXCUSE ME, BUT WHO DO YOU THINK YOU ARE? THE KING OF ENGLAND?" Robin Hood asked.

"That's *exactly* who he is," Mother Goose announced. "Everyone, meet King Arthur! He just pulled the sword out of the stone back in Camelot!"

"OH," Robin Hood said. "IN THAT CASE, *CARRY ON!*"

Arthur let the disrespect roll off his back and dived into planning mode.

"Before we storm the city, it's crucial we know how to defeat the villains we're up against," he said. "Does anyone know how to defeat Captain Hook or the Queen of Hearts or the Wicked Witch?"

Liberty Island went completely silent as everyone thought about it. The Lost Boys, Blubo, and the Tin Woodman had always *dreamed* about destroying the villains from their home worlds, but none of them knew how to actually go about it.

"Gosh, it's been so long since I read those books," Charlotte said.

"Oh, I know!" Bob announced. "Wait—never mind, that was how they did it in the movie, not the book."

"Oh come now," Arthur said encouragingly. "There's got to be *someone* who knows about their weaknesses!"

To the rest of the crew's surprise, Catfish Kate

raised a hand. "Master Bailey knew how to defeat Smoky-Sails Sam," the pirate said. "I bet *he* would know exactly how to defeat Captain Hook, the Queen of Hearts, and the Wicked Witch!"

"You idiot," High-Tide Tabitha said. "That was because Smoky-Sails Sam was Master Bailey's character—the captain, the queen, and the witch aren't his creations."

"Then who *is* their creator?" Arthur asked. "We must speak to him immediately!"

"You can't," Bob said. "James M. Barrie, Lewis Carroll, and L. Frank Baum have all been dead for decades."

Charlotte didn't want to give up just yet, so she imagined what Alex or Conner would do to get the answers they needed. Her eyes were drawn to the binder of short stories and the flask of Portal Potion in her hands.

"Wait a second," she said. "Maybe it *is* possible to speak to them. If we wrote a story where the authors came back to life, we could use the Portal Potion to enter the story and ask them how to defeat their characters!"

"Holy Mary Shelley," Mother Goose said. "It's both brilliant and immoral—just like me!"

"I'm more than willing to break some morality clauses if it means saving the world," Charlotte said. "Who's got a pen?"

Beau Rogers handed Charlotte a pen from inside his leather jacket. She sat on the ground and quickly jotted down the short story she had in mind on a blank page in Conner's binder. Once she was finished, Charlotte poured a few drops of the Portal Potion on the story, and a beam of light shot out from it.

"Here goes nothing," she said.

Charlotte stepped through the beam and entered a bright and endless space. The words from her story floated in the air all around her. She watched in wonder as the words started to stretch and gain color and texture. Soon Charlotte found herself in a dark room with three empty chairs. The words *James M. Barrie, Lewis Carroll,* and *L. Frank Baum* slowly transformed into the men they described, and the authors materialized before her eyes.

"Hello, gentlemen," Charlotte said. "We need to talk."

Chapter Eighteen

FAIRIES VS. WITCHES

Once the battery on Bree's cell phone died, Conner and his friends had no way of tracking the time. They felt like they had been trapped in the candy cane cage for days, but whether that was due to the time alteration or their anxiety was anyone's guess. The escapees they'd met under the Bethesda Terrace and the captives in the other cages all sat silently. They watched the horrible events around them as if they were trapped in a nightmare they couldn't wake from.

Goldilocks hadn't sat down once since they were put inside the cage. Her eyes never left Hero as he bounced around in the BabyBjörn attached to Rat Mary. Eventually, the infant became hungry and started to cry. Instead of giving him back to his mother, Rat Mary tried feeding him a bottle of bright green elixir—a potion Conner and his friends didn't recognize. Hero smelled the liquid and wisely refused it.

"Attaboy," Goldilocks whispered.

After the ovens were filled to capacity with baking gingerbread soldiers, the witches gave the Boy Scouts and Girl Scouts of America a new task. All the cauldrons and trays were moved to the side of the Great Lawn and replaced with piles of candy. The witches gave the Scouts welding tools and ordered them to make weapons out of the sweets. The children made candy cane swords, lollipop axes, licorice whips, candy apple ball and chains, and gummy bear nunchakus. The Scouts piled their finished creations in the center of the lawn, and the arsenal grew a foot taller with every passing hour.

To say that the Boy Scouts and Girl Scouts were exhausted was an understatement—it was a miracle they were still conscious. The children had been working non-stop since before Conner and his friends had even arrived at the witches' base. Many of the Scouts started nodding off as they made the candy weapons, but they would quickly sit up before one of the witches could punish them. Although Conner's adrenaline kept him alert, watching the tired Scouts put him in touch with his own fatigue. He leaned his head against the bars of the candy cane cage and, against his will, fell into a deep, deep sleep.

Conner dreamed he was standing in his old neighborhood in front of his old house. It wasn't the boxy rental house the twins had moved to after their father died, but the house their family lived in while he was still alive. It was painted blue with white trim and had so many windows, the house looked like it was wearing a pleasant smile. The front yard was groomed to perfection, and there was a large oak tree the twins loved climbing when they were little.

Oblivious to the horrors in his waking life, Conner smiled at the lovely sight of his former home.

"I must be stressed about something," he said to himself. "I only dream about this house when I'm upset."

Conner walked up the winding path through his

mother's rose garden and entered the house through the front door. He expected to step into a cozy living room with tufted sofas, a small white piano, and all the other furniture they'd had to sell when they moved. But the front of their old house was barely recognizable because the entire room was covered in papers. Handwritten notes were taped to the walls, pinned to the sofas, and spread across the floor and all the surfaces. Not an inch of the living room was visible.

"Well, that's odd," Conner said. "I must have eaten something funky right before bed to be dreaming this. I wonder what it's supposed to symbolize."

The handwriting was the same on all the notes and looked very familiar, but it wasn't his own. Conner pulled one off the wall to read it:

Conner,

I've been trying to contact you for days but we're never asleep at the same time. If things escalate to what I'm afraid of, then I know you'll be dreaming about our old house eventually—you always do when you're troubled. Please forgive the mess I made in your subconscious, but it's very important I get this message to you.

This won't be easy to read, but please hear me out. As you know by now, I've been cursed—probably with the most powerful curse that's ever been created. It's turned me into an angry, vengeful, and miserable person. It's as if the witches have transformed me into Ezmia, and it makes me wonder if they were the ones behind her undoing all along.

Unlike the Enchantress, the witches have found a way to keep me entirely in their control—and that's what worries me the most. They've forced me to do so many terrible things already, but I'll never be able to forgive myself if I harm someone I love. So I'm begging you, *don't give the witches the chance.* You can't stop the curse, but you can prevent me from doing the unthinkable, by stopping *me*.

I understand that what I'm asking is a burden no brother should ever be asked to bear, but you're the only person I can trust to get it done. You've seen the magic I'm capable of when I'm upset; if the witches unleash it, the Otherworld could be destroyed. That's why you and you alone must make sure it doesn't happen. By taking my life, you'll be saving the lives of millions, and we both know it's a worthy sacrifice.

I've had a wonderful life, Conner. The adventures we've shared over the years are what dreams are made of. I can't imagine having a better family, better friends, or better memories. That's why I can willingly "return to magic" without any reservations. I look forward to watching over you and Mom with Dad and Grandma at my side.

I love you with all my heart and am forever proud to be your sister,

Alex

Conner knew he was experiencing much more than a dream. He ripped up the note as if it would make the request disappear, but every note in the sitting room was scribbled with the same message. Conner whirled through the house and tore every paper he could get his hands on, but the message rang out loud and clear: *Alex was asking Conner to kill her.*

Even in his sleep, the thought of harming his sister made Conner's heart race and beads of sweat run down his face. Soon he felt two pairs of hands on him, shaking him awake.

"Conner, wake up!" Jack said.

"Sorry!" Conner gasped, and quickly sat up. "How long was I out?"

"An hour or two," Bree said. "Then you started going full *Exorcist* on us."

"I was having a nightmare, but it wasn't *just* a nightmare," Conner said. "Alex has been trying to communicate with me in our dreams. She covered our childhood home in letters asking me to *kill her*! She thinks the only way we can save the Otherworld is by taking her life!"

"That's terrible!" Red said. "Just because someone is dangerous doesn't mean they have to be *killed* to be stopped. Think about the Evil Queen—oh wait, I suppose that mirror thing was worse than death.... Well, think about the Enchantress—oh yeah, never mind.... But General Marquis—oops, he *really* died.... Well, the Masked Man didn't—oh, that's right, he *did*.... Sorry, I thought there were plenty of examples. You know, maybe Alex has a point—"

"We're *not* killing my sister," Conner said. "I refuse to believe there isn't a way to break the curse she's under! Alex's emotions are being affected right now and she's jumping to conclusions. We'll find a way to help her."

"Yes, we will," Goldilocks said confidently. "I know exactly what's going through Alex's mind right now. It wasn't long ago that I was in her shoes. She's feeling scared, embarrassed, and guilty, and she thinks there's no coming back from the place she's at. But luckily for her, she's got us to set her straight."

"Oh, it's *Goldilocks*!" Red declared with a snap of her fingers. "*She's* the example I was looking for! Goldie was a lonely, miserable, and ill-tempered thief when we first met. But thanks to my friendship, she's turned her life around and become a social, happy, and balanced woman."

Goldilocks sighed. "What can I say? I owe it all to you, Red."

"You're quite welcome," Red said. "What I did for Goldilocks is exactly what we need to do for Alex. If she insists on being killed, then we'll just have to *love her to death*."

Conner and his friends nodded politely and gazed outside the cage, hoping Red wouldn't come up with any more nonsensical anecdotes. On the west side of the Great Lawn, they watched Charcoaline as she inspected the giant ovens. The gingerbread soldiers had been baking for hours, and Conner had been wondering how much time they needed. Charcoaline cackled with delight and rang a large bell.

"Your Excellencies! Our army is finished!" Charcoaline announced.

The Snow Queen and the Sea Witch stood up from their thrones, and eerie smiles spread across their faces.

"Release them from the ovens!" the Snow Queen commanded. "And line up the children. They must *greet* the army they've created."

The witches rounded up the Boy and Girl Scouts and forced them to stand in groups facing the ovens. Charcoaline pulled open the door of each oven, and smoke filled the air. Like something straight from a horror movie, hundreds of gingerbread soldiers slowly crept out of the smoky ovens like zombies, moaning like the ghosts of tortured souls. They were tall, their bodies were burned, and they left behind trails of crumbs as they walked.

"You must be starving," the Sea Witch hissed. "Come, have a snack and gain your strength before the big battle."

The gingerbread soldiers skulked toward the

groups of Scouts. The children tried to step back from the frightening cookies, but none of them could move. They looked down and discovered that Tarantulene had sprayed the grass with her web—*the Scouts' feet were stuck to the ground!* Conner and his friends didn't understand the point of this, but as they watched the gingerbread soldiers approach the children, it all made sense.

"They're going to feed the Scouts to the gingerbread soldiers!" Conner exclaimed.

"That's horrible!" Red said.

"Obscene!" Goldilocks said.

"We have to do something!" Bree said.

Conner and his friends jumped to their feet and shook the bars of their candy cane cage, but no matter how hard they shook them, the bars never budged. The Boy and Girl Scouts started screaming as the gingerbread soldiers crept closer. The demonic cookies opened their wide mouths and revealed their sharp candy corn teeth.

"Alex, you've got to help those kids!" Conner yelled at her. "The sister I know and love would never stand by as innocent children were devoured— no matter what kind of curse she was under! Come on, you've got to fight it! You've got to save them!"

For a brief moment, the expression on his sister's face changed. Alex tightened her brow, clenched her jaw, and made fists with her hands. Conner could tell she was fighting the curse with every fiber of her being. Her glowing eyes started to fade, her floating hair started to fall, and the shield she was keeping up around Central Park began to flicker like a dying lightbulb, until it finally disappeared.

"Don't let him distract you!" the Snow Queen screeched at her. "Keep the shield steady!"

The command reinforced the curse. The expression faded from Alex's face, her eyes glowed brighter than before, her hair floated back above her head, and the shield reappeared around Central Park. However, the brief moments she had managed to let the force field down had been long enough for a few familiar characters to sneak through it. A split second before the gingerbread army took their first bite out of the Boy and Girl Scouts, a colorful cavalcade suddenly charged out of the trees.

Mother Goose and Merlin swooped onto the Great Lawn aboard Lester's back, and the Fairy Council soared through the air beside them. On the ground below, Froggy and Rook rode in on Cornelius, while Arthur and the Knights of the Round

Table stormed onto the lawn on foot. Conner and his friends were shocked and ecstatic to see their friends arrive.

"Am I seeing things or is that Mother Goose and the Fairy Council?" Jack asked.

"It is—and they've come in the nick of time!" Goldilocks cried.

"And Charlie's with them!" Red shouted in disbelief.

"How is this possible?" Conner asked. "The Fairy Council were statues, Mother Goose was in Camelot, and Froggy was trapped in a magic mirror!"

"Who cares?" Red snapped. "After all the crap we've been through, just be glad we have some happy questions for a change!"

The Scouts had no idea who any of the newcomers were, but their flashy entrance was enough to distract the gingerbread soldiers from eating them. The unexpected company infuriated the witches beyond belief. They had come so far; they weren't going to let anything stop them now. The Snow Queen, the Sea Witch, Charcoaline, Arboris, Tarantulene, Serpentina, and Rat Mary formed a line at the south end of the Great Lawn, preventing the newcomers from coming any closer. The other witches cowered at the sight of the Fairy Council and hid behind the ovens.

The Fairy Council, Mother Goose, Merlin, and Lester landed on the lawn in front of the witches. Froggy, Rook, Cornelius, Arthur, and the Knights of the Round Table joined the fairies and stood by their sides. The fairies and the witches stared at one another for a tense moment before anyone said a word.

"Release these children and surrender your army at once!" Emerelda demanded.

"Or *what*?" the Snow Queen asked.

"Or we'll remove them from you," Xanthous said.

The witches glanced at one another and roared with cocky laughter.

"Is that so?" the Sea Witch asked. "And how exactly is that going to happen? After all, fairies can only use their magic to help others."

"Witch, *please*," Mother Goose said. "We're the ones who write the rules, and we can break them just as easily as you."

"This is your last warning," Skylene said. "You *will* surrender and go back to the kingdoms where you belong."

"Don't be foolish and make this worse than it needs to be," Tangerina said.

"The witches are *not* going back to the old world!" the Snow Queen screeched. "We're sick of your limitations, sick of your regulations, and sick of your laws! Your kind has forced us into the shadows for centuries— so we left the kingdoms before you could suppress us into oblivion! We've found our own world to rule as we please, and there isn't room for fairies here!"

"You mistake our mercy for mistreatment," Emerelda said. "If our goal was to exterminate you, we would have done it a long time ago. Your survival is thanks to our *generosity* and nothing more. We've never *suppressed you*, we've simply protected the innocent people you harm without remorse—and a new world isn't going to stop us."

"Then let's settle this once and for all," the Sea Witch hissed. "If the universe isn't big enough for both the fairies and the witches, it's high time we take our proper place on the magical food chain! Sisters, if we want a world for ourselves *we must destroy the fairies*!"

The witches charged toward the fairies, and an overdue battle of good versus evil began. Each member of the Fairy Council paired with a witch and spread out across the Great Lawn to duel.

Arthur and the Knights of the Round Table dashed toward the gingerbread soldiers with their swords raised. The soldiers collected weapons from the candy arsenal and fought the young king and his knights. The gingerbread soldiers were easy to disarm and slay, but they greatly outnumbered Arthur and his knights; battling the giant cookies wasn't going to be a piece of cake.

Alex's location was no longer a mystery to any of the newcomers. She was clearly visible on the hill at the north end of the Great Lawn. So while the fairies and witches were dueling, Froggy hopped around the lawn looking for Conner and the others. The only thing on Rook's agenda was getting Alex to safety, so he cautiously steered Cornelius through the fighting knights and soldiers toward the hill. Mother Goose and Merlin raced to the groups of Boy and Girl Scouts. With a snap of their fingers, the spiderweb around the Scouts' feet vanished and the children were free.

"As I said to the Children's Crusade of 1212: *Get out of here, kiddos! This isn't your fight!*" Mother Goose said.

In true Boy and Girl Scout fashion, before running to safety, the Scouts ran to the candy cane cages and freed the witches' prisoners. Oliver used a lollipop axe to slice the lock off the cage that held Conner and his friends.

"Hey, I know you!" Oliver said. "You guys were on my flight!"

"Oliver, you've got to get all these other people out of here," Conner said. "Take everyone to the southwest corner of the park. You'll find an opening to an abandoned subway tunnel at the base of a hill. Crawl into the tunnel and follow it as far away as you can get!"

"But what about you and your friends?" Oliver asked.

"We'll be okay," Conner said. "Believe it or not, we're actually used to this kind of stuff. Now hurry— before the witches see you!"

Oliver nodded and saluted Conner. Once he got their attention, Oliver led all the Scouts, their troop leaders, the escapees from the Bethesda Fountain, and all the other captives off the Great Lawn and toward the southwest corner of Central Park.

"What should we do now? Get Alex?" Bree asked.

Conner glanced up at his sister, but she hadn't moved a muscle since the battle had started.

"She'll be fine for the time being," he said. "But those dudes fighting the gingerbread soldiers look like they could use our help!"

Conner and his friends dashed to the arsenal of candy weapons. Conner and Goldilocks picked up candy cane swords, Jack took a lollipop axe, Bree chose a licorice whip, and although she had no idea what they were, Red selected gummy bear nunchakus. Once they were armed, Conner and his friends joined Arthur and the Knights of the Round Table and helped them battle the gingerbread soldiers.

"You must be Alex's brother!" Arthur said as he decapitated a soldier.

"That's me," Conner said. "Who are you?"

"I'm King Arthur and these are my Knights of the Round Table," Arthur said.

"From *Camelot*?" Conner asked. "What are you guys doing in Central Park?"

"Long story short, I'm sort of your sister's boy-friend," the young king disclosed.

"Boyfriend?" Conner asked as he sliced a soldier in half. "Alex never mentioned she had a boyfriend!"

"Well, we haven't defined the relationship yet," Arthur said.

This surprised Conner more than anything else in the park so far.

"If we survive this, you and I are going to have a chat about your intentions," he warned.

As their friends fought the gingerbread soldiers, Jack and Goldilocks saw Rat Mary and Hero on the other side of the lawn. The couple moved through the soldiers in the direction of their son, slicing through them as if they were overgrown weeds. Bree seemed to be enjoying the fight; she giggled as she swung the licorice whip around her like a lion tamer.

"Is that your girlfriend?" Arthur asked Conner.

"Sort of," Conner said. "We haven't defined our relationship, either."

Bree cracked the whip with such gusto that all the gingerbread soldiers were afraid to get near her. Even Conner kept his distance.

"Wow," Arthur said. "If I were you, I'd have someone ask her about *her* intentions."

Red tried getting as involved in the fight as her friends, but she had no idea how to use her gummy bear nunchakus. Every time she tried swinging them, she ended up whacking herself in the face. The awkward movement made her easy to spot in the crowd.

"Red, there you are!" Froggy said. "I've been looking everywhere for you!"

"Charlie!" she exclaimed. "I've missed you so much!"

Red jumped into Froggy's arms and kissed him all over his green face. A gingerbread soldier snuck up behind the couple and raised his lollipop axe above their heads. Red was outraged by the interruption.

"Excuse me? Can't you see we're in the middle of a reunion?" she asked.

Instead of using her gummy bear nunchakus, Red smacked the gingerbread soldier in the face with her purse. The blow knocked off the soldier's head, and its body crumpled to the ground.

"I swear, these purchases are the gifts that keep on giving," Red said.

Conner saw Froggy and worked his way through the gingerbread soldiers to greet him.

"Froggy! I'm so glad to see you!" he said.

"Likewise, my friend," Froggy said. "I've spent days searching for you! I was trying to warn you the Literary Army was coming, but they beat me to it. Fortunately, your mother and the characters from your stories have also arrived and are dealing with the army as we speak."

"Thanks for the update," Conner said. "Let's hurry up and defeat these witches so we can join them—they're gonna need our help."

While Conner and his friends finished off the

gingerbread soldiers, the duels between the fairies and the witches were intensifying by the second.

Rosette and Arboris were going head-to-head in a heated brawl. The witch pointed at the grass, and large tree roots snapped up from the ground and knocked the fairy backward. Rosette retaliated by throwing a handful of seeds at the witch. A family of Venus flytraps immediately rose out of the dirt around Arboris's feet and pinned the witch to the ground with their snapping mouths.

Bugs crawled out of Arboris's skin and chewed on the flytraps until the witch was free. Arboris then hit the ground with her fist and sent a massive wave through the grass that knocked Rosette on her back. The fairy waved her hand, and a cluster of rosebushes with enormous thorns grew in a circle around the witch.

Rosette spun her finger, and the rosebushes began to twirl around Arboris like the blades of a blender. The witch screamed as the thorns scratched and sliced her. By the time the roses stopped spinning, Arboris had been decomposed into nothing but a pile of mulch.

"Even this rose has her thorns," Rosette said, and blew on her fingertip like it was a smoking gun.

Tangerina and Tarantulene were locked eye-to-eye as they fought. The witch kicked the fairy with all four of her legs and hit her with all four of her hands. A swarm of bees flew out of Tangerina's beehive and circled Tarantulene, stinging her arms and legs wherever they could.

The witch sprayed the bees with spiderweb and then showered the fairy with it—sticking Tangerina's whole body to the ground. Tarantulene then stood over the fairy, preparing to strike her with her long fangs. But Tangerina managed to free one of her hands from the web, and she pointed at the witch. Honey erupted from the fairy's finger and covered Tarantulene from head to toe. The honey quickly hardened and trapped the witch inside a large golden blob.

"It's *honey* that attracts the flies, darling," Tangerina said. "You should try it."

Across the Great Lawn, Xanthous was caught in a battle with the Snow Queen. Unfortunately for him, *nothing* about their fight was heated. The witch pointed her cane at the fairy, and sharp icicles shot out of it like bullets. Xanthous dived out of their path, but there were too many to avoid. One icicle pierced his shoulder and another pierced his thigh, pinning poor Xanthous to a tree. The fairy screamed in agony and the witch cackled with satisfaction. The flames on Xanthous's head and shoulders spread across his body until he was completely covered in fire and the icicles impaling him melted away.

The witch lifted the cloth covering her eyes, and an icy chill blew out from her empty eye sockets. Xanthous shielded himself with a wall of fire, but he struggled to keep it up. The wind grew stronger and stronger while the temperature became colder and colder. It was so cold, the Snow Queen's face started to freeze, and soon her whole body was covered in ice.

"I always loved extinguishing little flamers like you!" the Snow Queen said.

"Do you know what they say about icy old queens?" Xanthous asked. "The colder the heart, the easier she melts."

A ball of fire appeared in Xanthous's hand, and he threw it at the Snow Queen. The fireball collided with the witch and exploded. The heat was so severe, it melted all the ice covering the Snow Queen's body, and the witch vanished.

The Snow Queen's polar bears were furious at seeing their mistress destroyed. They charged across the Great Lawn, intending to rip Xanthous limb from limb. Mother Goose and Merlin stepped into the bears' path and blocked the beasts from attacking the fairy.

"My dear, I think it's time to *grin and bear it*." Merlin chuckled.

"Oh, Merlin, your jokes are *unbearable*." Mother Goose laughed.

The couple transformed into a pair of ferocious grizzly bears and wrestled the polar bears to the ground. After a series of body slams, headlocks, and pile drivers, the polar bears gave up and tapped out of the fight.

In the opposite corner of the Great Lawn, Emerelda had a beastly challenger of her own. The Sea Witch snapped her claws, and a wall of salty water surrounded Emerelda. The witch snapped her claws again, and the wall filled with great white sharks—*Emerelda was trapped!* The Sea Witch opened her mouth, and an enormous electric eel slithered out from the back of her throat. The eel wrapped around Emerelda and shocked the fairy as it pinned her arms to her sides. The witch then pelted Emerelda with pieces of coral that grew over the fairy and confined her even more tightly.

"You won't get away with this!" Emerelda shouted. "You can surround me with every fish in the sea, but good will always prevail over evil!"

"That's the beauty of this world," the Sea Witch hissed. "In the Otherworld, the evildoers can win!"

The Sea Witch clapped her claws together, and the wall of water caved in on the fairy. The water formed a sphere around Emerelda, and she couldn't breathe. The fairy struggled against her fishy constraints but couldn't break free. Emerelda's eyes fluttered shut as she appeared to drown.

Before she celebrated her victory, the Sea Witch wanted to make certain the fairy was dead. She snapped her claws again, and the coral and eel disappeared and the fairy's lifeless body rolled out of the watery sphere. As the witch leaned over her, Emerelda suddenly snapped back to life and grabbed the Sea Witch's claw. The witch's body was infected by Emerelda's touch; inch by inch, the Sea Witch was covered in an emerald glow that transformed her body into sea glass. When the transformation was complete, Emerelda blasted the Sea Witch with a bright green light and she burst into thousands of pieces, showering Central Park with tiny shards of sea glass.

The Sea Witch's sharks angrily lunged toward Emerelda, and the giant sphere of salt water rolled toward her. Before the sharks could harm the fairy, Mother Goose and Merlin pushed Emerelda out of the way and jumped inside the sphere. The couple transformed into a pair of giant squid and beat the sharks senseless.

Nearby, Violetta was having a difficult time keeping up with Serpentina's swift attacks. The witch wrapped her tongue around the fairy's ankle and dragged her through the mud. In retaliation, Violetta simply threw a small rock at the witch, but missed. Serpentina flung Violetta into the air, and the fairy landed with a heavy thud on the ground. Once again, all Violetta did to defend herself was throw another rock at the witch, and it, too, missed by almost a foot. The fairy repeated her poor defense over and over, but it only annoyed her opponent.

"Oh, come on! You're not even trying! Have sssome ssself-ressspect and fight back!" Serpentina hissed.

Violetta smiled and pointed to the sky above Serpentina. The witch looked up and saw that all the rocks were hovering above her head—but they had all grown to the size of boulders. Violetta snapped her fingers, and the boulders collapsed on top of Serpentina.

Across the lawn, Skylene was clashing with Charcoaline. A geyser of lava erupted from Charcoaline's mouth, and she aimed it toward the fairy. Skylene reached out her hands and blocked the lava with an equally powerful geyser of water. The water made a rainbow appear over the Great Lawn, not that anyone had a spare moment to enjoy it. Charcoaline used all her strength to hit Skylene with the most powerful geyser she could muster. The witch's whole body filled with lava, and it flowed through the cracks of her ashy skin.

Skylene spotted the Central Park Reservoir out of the corner of her eye and had an idea. The fairy kept her watery geyser flowing with one hand and pointed to the reservoir with the other. An enormous wave of cold water spilled out of the reservoir and drenched everyone and everything across the Great Lawn. When Skylene looked up, Charcoaline had disappeared. The fairy looked at the ground and discovered that her opponent had been cooled into a mound of singed charcoal.

Not only did Skylene's wave defeat the witch, it also dissolved all the remaining gingerbread soldiers. Conner, his friends, and the knights from Camelot cheered in victory. With the soldiers gone, Rook and Cornelius were free to approach the hill where Alex stood. The lion statues from the New York Public

Library growled down at them—there was no way they were getting past Patience and Fortitude.

"Cornelius, you stay here and distract the lions," Rook said. "I'm going to sneak up the hill behind them."

Meanwhile, Jack and Goldilocks raced to the end of the Great Lawn where Rat Mary was dueling with Coral. The witch repeatedly scratched and bit the young fairy, but Coral was afraid that if she fought back, she'd injure the infant strapped to the witch's chest.

"Give us back our son, you miserable rodent!" Jack said.

"If you think I'm miserable, you should meet my friends," Rat Mary said.

The witch placed both hands on the ground and summoned all the rats and mice in Central Park. The rodents came in droves until there were thousands and thousands at Rat Mary's command. The witch pointed at Jack, Goldilocks, and Coral, and the rodents attacked. The rats and mice crawled over their bodies, scratched their faces, and chewed on their hair. Jack and Goldilocks tried to knock the vermin off with their weapons, but there were too many to keep up with.

"Hey, *Buckteeth McRabies*," Mother Goose called out. "Why don't you pick on someone your own size?"

Rat Mary roared with laughter. "What are you going to do, *Granny*?"

Mother Goose cringed at the insult. "You know, I've been called a lot of names in my day, but you want to hear what they used to call me in Hamelin?"

"Let me guess," Rat Mary said. "Was it *Mother Time*? *Rip Van Wrinkles*? *Old Woman River*? *Lady MacDeath*?"

"Not even close," Mother Goose said. "They called me *the Pied Piper*!"

Mother Goose removed a small pipe that was tucked into her bonnet. She pressed the instrument against her lips and played a charming melody. As soon as the first three notes rang out, all the rats and mice attacking Jack, Goldilocks, and Coral froze. They immediately formed a line and scurried across the Great Lawn toward the reservoir. The rodents dived into the water and never resurfaced.

Rat Mary's eyes widened with fear. She scanned the Great Lawn and discovered that the only witches left were the ones hiding behind the ovens—it was the *witches* who were outnumbered now.

"Sisters, we must leave this foul place!" Rat Mary declared. "If the fairies want the Otherworld so much, they can have it! We'll find another world to call home, but now *it's time to fly*!"

Rat Mary held out a hand, and a broomstick flew into it. The witches cowering behind the ovens quickly retrieved their own brooms.

"Lower the shield, girl!" Rat Mary shouted at Alex.

Alex did as she was told, and the force field surrounding Central Park disappeared. The witches straddled their brooms and rose into the air like a flock of crows. Rat Mary led the witches toward the New York City skyline with Hero dangling from her chest.

"HERO!" Goldilocks shouted.

Jack whistled for Lester, and the gander hurried toward him.

"Lester, we need your help!" Jack said. "Follow those witches!"

Jack and Goldilocks hopped aboard Lester's back, and the giant bird soared into the air and followed the witches toward the city.

Now that the shield was down, everyone was finally free to leave the park, but they were also vulnerable to the dangers outside it. A sniper stationed on the rooftop of a building just east of the park had been waiting all night and all morning for this moment to come.

"General, I've got a clear shot on the girl from the library," he said into his radio. "She seems to be the one generating the shield over the park. Do I have your permission to shoot before it reappears?"

"We're a little busy with monkeys and flying ships over here," the general replied. "Fire at your own discretion!"

"Target is locked," the sniper said. "Preparing to fire in three...two...*one!*"

The sniper pulled the trigger, and in a split second, a bullet traveled more than a thousand feet from the rooftop and pierced the beating heart of an unsuspecting misunderstood teenager. Conner and his friends heard the gunshot echo through the park and looked up at the hill in terror.

"*NOOOOOO!*" Conner screamed.

The sound of her brother's panicked voice broke Alex's curse for another brief moment. She looked down at the Great Lawn and saw Conner, Bree, Froggy, Red, Cornelius, Arthur, Mother Goose, Merlin, the Knights of the Round Table, and the Fairy Council staring up with horrified expressions—but they weren't looking at her. Alex turned to her left and saw Rook standing by her side with blood dripping from a small hole in his chest.

"Alex..." he gasped. "I hope...I hope...*I hope this will make things right.*"

Rook collapsed, rolled down the side of the hill, and never got up. He had gone to the hill hoping to save Alex. Tragically, his mission was even more of a success than he'd intended. Alex stared down at her friend's body in shock.

"Rook?" she said softly. *"Rook, please get up! Please get up!"*

The farmer's son didn't move, and Alex realized that her worst nightmare had come true: Someone she loved had been hurt. A tsunami of emotion rushed through her body, and the witches' curse returned. Her eyes glowed brighter than ever, her hair flickered above her head like the flames of a rocket, and power she had never possessed before surged through her veins.

Alex pointed at the sniper in the distance, and the building he stood on imploded underneath him. The man jumped and made it to a nearby rooftop only a moment before he would have plummeted to the ground.

"Alex, please, you need to calm down!" Conner yelled up at the hill. "You've got to control your emotions before they control you!"

His sister clapped her hands, and a bright spiral of light like the Milky Way Galaxy appeared above her. Alex and the lion statues disappeared inside the light, and the spiral whirled out of Central Park. With no witches to control her, the curse had transformed Alex into a destructive force without bounds—*and she was loose in New York City.*

"We need to find her at once!" Emerelda told the others. "If we can't find a way to break the curse, Alex could destroy the city—and maybe herself in the process!"

Conner, Bree, Froggy, Red, Mother Goose, Merlin, and the Fairy Council ran out of Central Park and headed in the direction of Alex's light. Arthur and the Knights of the Round Table knelt beside Rook's body to pay their respects. Cornelius nudged his friend with his snout and waited for him to wake up, but Rook never opened his eyes again.

CHAPTER NINETEEN

WAR OF THE WORLDS

While the fairies battled the witches in Central Park, General Wilson and his Marines were up against the fight of their lives. The Literary Army had the strongest, fastest, and most efficient opposition the United States soldiers had ever faced. The flying monkeys swooped in from the sky and yanked the Marines' weapons out of their hands before they even knew what was happening. The *Jolly Roger* blasted their cannons at all the

Marines' Hummers and tanks, and at the rooftops where the pirates spotted snipers. Once they were virtually defenseless, the Winkies and card soldiers rounded up all the Marines in Midtown Manhattan and forced them to kneel in the middle of Fifty-Ninth Street on the edge of Central Park.

The Winkies and card soldiers surrounded the captured Marines while the *Jolly Roger* and the flying monkeys watched them from the air above. The literary soldiers only parted as the Wicked Witch, the Queen of Hearts, and Captain Hook came to have a word with the prisoners.

"Which one of you is in charge?" the Queen of Hearts asked.

Against his sergeant's advice, General Wilson got to his feet and addressed the literary villains.

"I am," he announced. "I'm General Gunther Wilson of the United States Marines. Who the heck are you people?"

"Now, now, General," the Wicked Witch said. "That's no way to speak to your new commanders."

"The United States Marines only answer to *one* commander—and that's our commander in chief," General Wilson said.

"And where is he?" Captain Hook asked, and

looked around the New York street. "He must step forward immediately and surrender the Otherworld to us!"

"*She* is in Washington, DC," General Wilson said. "And I hate to be the bearer of bad news, but you'll *never* get close to her. You see, we're just a fraction of the United States military; the rest of it is surrounding the city as we speak. The minute you step off this island, you'll all be annihilated."

The Wicked Witch, the Queen of Hearts, and Captain Hook were amused by the general's remarks. The villains looked at one another and howled with menacing laughter.

"Then we'll disarm them just as easily as we've disarmed *you*," the Queen of Hearts said. "This isn't the first world we've conquered, General, and it won't be the last. Soon the heads of your precious military and commander in chief will be mounted on our wall!"

"But you and your men don't have to perish in the process," the Wicked Witch said. "You and your men could join our army and be part of our great empire."

General Wilson took off his sunglasses so the villains could see every inch of his disgusted and impassioned scowl.

"We'd rather *die* than join the likes of you!" he shouted.

"So be it," Captain Hook said. *"Mr. Smee, prepare the cannons!"*

The pirates aboard the *Jolly Roger* loaded the ship's cannons and aimed them at the Marines. The general and his soldiers closed their eyes and braced themselves for a massacre.

"On my count of three!" Captain Hook ordered. "One...two..."

Suddenly, the *Dolly Llama* descended from the sky and shielded the Marines from the *Jolly Roger*'s cannons. The floating ships were so close to each other, the pirates could see the whites of one another's eyes. Peter Pan stood beside Captain Auburn Sally and Admiral Jacobson on the upper deck.

"Oi! Codfish!" Peter Pan called down to Captain Hook. "Miss me?"

The sight of Peter Pan made Captain Hook growl like a wounded animal.

"Peeeter Paaan?" he roared. "What are you doing in the Otherworld?"

"I couldn't let you have all the fun without me, now could I?" Peter Pan taunted him. "Leave these

Marines alone, Captain. Finish your fight with me before you pick another one."

Captain Hook glared at the Boy Who Wouldn't Grow Up with so much hatred, it was a miracle his face didn't catch fire.

"Smee, drop a ladder!" Captain Hook ordered.

Mr. Smee rolled a rope ladder off the side of the ship and it touched the ground. Captain Hook grabbed hold of the ladder and pointed to the *Dolly Llama* with his hook.

"After that ship!" he commanded.

Peter Pan stuck his tongue out at Captain Hook. Admiral Jacobson spun the *Dolly Llama*'s wheel, and the ship rose higher into the sky, with the *Jolly Roger* soaring after it. The flying monkeys also flew after the *Dolly Llama* to assist the *Jolly Roger*, but the creatures came to an abrupt stop when the Ziblings' colorful jet zipped into their path. The superheroes and their adoptive father waved at the monkeys from inside the cockpit.

"Attention, Hominidae-Accipitridae hybrids," Professor Wallet said through the aircraft's speaker. "Resist your animalistic urges and spare yourselves from a cataclysmic fate!"

The flying monkeys scratched their heads and looked at one another in confusion. The Ziblings rolled their eyes at the professor's terminology, and Bolt took the microphone from him.

"In translation: *Just 'cause monkey see, don't mean monkey should do*," Bolt said. "Ditch the flying ship and come with us! We'll make it worth your while!"

Morph transformed into a pile of bananas to tease the monkeys. The winged creatures were tempted to go after the Ziblings' jet, but they glanced down at the Wicked Witch for permission first.

"Tear that flying chunk of metal apart!" the Wicked Witch ordered them.

Since the flying monkeys were under the witch's spell, they had no choice but to obey her. The winged creatures hurtled after the Ziblings' jet with their claws raised and their sharp teeth exposed. The superheroes yanked on their aircraft's gears, and the jet zoomed into the clouds.

"I DARE SAY, MERRY MEN," shouted a boisterous voice. "WHAT SORT OF SELF-RESPECTING MAN REFERS TO HIMSELF AS A *WINKIE*?"

The Wicked Witch looked down Fifty-Ninth Street and saw Robin Hood, Little John, Alan-a-Dale, Will Scarlet, and Friar Tuck standing at Columbus

Circle. The circle was a New York City landmark and had a tall statue of Christopher Columbus in the center of a roundabout connecting Fifty-Ninth Street to Broadway.

"WOULD YOU LOOK AT THAT HIDEOUS WOMAN THE WINKIES TAKE ORDERS FROM," Robin Hood said. "DO YOU KNOW WHAT WE IN LOXLEY CALL A WOMAN WITH ONE EYE, TERRIBLE CLOTHES, AND A HAGGARD FACE?"

"I don't know, Robin," Little John said. "What do you call her?"

"*SINGLE!*" the Prince of Thieves declared.

The Merry Men burst into a fit of haughty laughter. The Wicked Witch grunted at the insult, and steam piped out of her ears.

"*After those arrogant men!*" she ordered.

Also under the witch's spell, the Winkie soldiers immediately sprinted down the street and dashed after the Prince of Thieves. The Wicked Witch sat sidesaddle on her magic umbrella and flew above her soldiers. Robin Hood and the Merry Men hightailed it out of Columbus Circle and ran north on Broadway, leading their followers to another part of the city.

As the Queen of Hearts watched the Wicked

Witch and the Winkies race off, a stiff hand unexpectedly tapped her on the shoulder.

"Excuse me, ma'am?" asked a voice behind her. "Would you happen to know how to get to Grand Central Station from here?"

The Queen of Hearts turned around and discovered the Tin Woodman standing behind her. The queen had never seen a man made of metal before, and a delighted squeal escaped her lips. She stepped toward the metal man with eyes like a predator.

"My word, what a remarkably rare *head* you have," she said, and stroked the side of his face. "It would be a wonderful addition to my collection."

"Come again?" the Tin Woodman asked.

"GUARDS, SEIZE THIS MAN AT ONCE!" the Queen of Hearts shouted. *"AND OFF WITH HIS HEAD!"*

"And *this* is why you don't ask for directions in strange cities," the Tin Woodman said to himself.

The Ozian ran from the deranged queen as fast as his tin legs would carry him. He took a sharp turn on Fifth Avenue, heading south into the city, and the card soldiers hurried after him. The Queen of Hearts snapped her fingers, and two of her soldiers joined hands, scooped her up, and carried her with them as they chased after the Tin Woodman.

Unbeknownst to the Literary Army, they had just been strategically lured away by Conner's friends and characters—and the villains had taken the bait like a hungry school of fish. Now that the *Jolly Roger* was flying after the *Dolly Llama*, the flying monkeys were following the Ziblings, the Winkies were running after the Merry Men, and the card soldiers were chasing the Tin Woodman, the general and the Marines were left completely unattended on Fifty-Ninth Street.

The Marines looked around the street in total bewilderment—how had they gone from facing certain execution to freedom so quickly?

"Sir, what just happened?" a Marine asked.

"That was called *luck*, Sergeant," General Wilson responded. "Let's not press it any further."

"Your orders, sir?" asked another Marine.

"Evacuate Manhattan immediately," General Wilson said. "And someone get the president on the phone at once. We need authorization to wipe out these barbarians before they disperse."

"Sir, what does that mean?"

"I'm saying we are at DEFCON-2, Sergeant,"

the general barked. "We need to vaporize this island while those savages are still on it. In less than an hour, New York City will only exist in our memories."

The *Dolly Llama* snaked between the city's buildings with the *Jolly Roger* hot on its tail. The pirates fired their cannons at one another, but the ships floated so freely, it was difficult to hit their targets. Cannonballs slammed into the high-rises they sailed past, leaving a trail of shattered glass, broken antennas, and busted corporate logos throughout Midtown Manhattan.

"Enough cat-and-mouse games," Captain Auburn Sally announced. "It's time to confront these scallywags face-to-face!"

The *Dolly Llama* set sail for the Empire State Building, then made a dramatic turn. Admiral Jacobson tied down the ship's helm, and the *Dolly Llama* began circling the Empire State Building. The *Jolly Roger* mimicked the maneuver and also revolved around the building.

Captain Auburn Sally and her crew swung onto the observation deck while Admiral Jacobson and his fleet manned the cannons. Captain Hook and his men joined the women on the observation deck, leaving Mr. Smee to operate all the *Jolly Roger*'s cannons on his own. The men of the *Jolly Roger* and the women of the *Dolly Llama* formed lines at opposite ends of the observation deck and drew their weapons.

"Men like you give pirates a bad name," Captain Auburn Sally said.

"You aren't *pirates*," Captain Hook said with a laugh. "You're just a bunch of little girls with attitude!"

"Then I feel sorry for you, Hook," Auburn Sally said. "Because you and your men are about to get your booty handed to you by a bunch of little girls. *Ladies, charge!*"

The pirates from Starboardia and the pirates from Neverland clashed in a swashbuckling spectacle eighty-six stories above the ground. Cannonballs flew above their heads as the circling ships sparred in the air. The sounds of clanking swords and firing cannons echoed in the streets of New York City.

The crew of the *Dolly Llama* were gifted swordswomen, but they also used some of their signature moves to battle the men of the *Jolly Roger*. Winking Wendy made her opponents sick by flashing the empty socket under her eye patch. Fish-Lips Lucy gave her adversaries painful hickeys when they least expected it. Somersault Sydney tumbled across the observation deck and knocked down the men in her path like they were bowling pins. Stinky-Feet Phoebe held her smelly feet against her challengers' faces until the fumes made them lose consciousness. Too-Much-Rum Ronda broke empty bottles of rum over the pirates' heads—and after a long week at the Saint Andrew's Children's Hospital commissary, Ronda had *a lot* of empty bottles.

While the pirates battled on top of the Empire State Building, Peter Pan covertly flew over to the *Jolly Roger*. He quietly searched all the ship's decks for Tinker Bell, but the fairy was nowhere to be found.

"Looking for *this*, Peter?" Captain Hook called to him.

Peter Pan jerked his head toward the sound of Hook's voice. The captain was standing on the edge of the observation deck with a jar dangling from his hook, and Peter saw Tinker Bell trapped inside it.

"Give her back!" Peter Pan shouted.

"If you want her, come and get her!" Captain Hook yelled.

Peter Pan removed the dagger from his boot and met Captain Hook on the edge of the observation deck. The literary characters fought each other with more intensity than ever before. The more they fought, the higher they climbed, and soon they were dueling on the roof of the observation deck. Captain Hook climbed a ladder up the side of the building's spire while Peter hovered in the air beside him—all while blocking deadly blows from the other's weapon. Finally, the captain reached the very top of the building's spire and couldn't climb any higher.

"Hand over the fairy," Peter Pan demanded.

The captain couldn't tell if Peter was deliberately taunting him, but he still cringed at the word *hand*.

"Do you know what I wish I could do more than anything else in the world, Peter?" Captain Hook asked.

"Clap?" Peter Pan guessed.

"What?" the captain asked. *"No!"*

"Do a handstand?"

"NO!"

"Play the piano?"

"STOP IT! STOP MAKING APPENDAGE JOKES!"

"Why? Is it getting out of *hand*?"

"YOU ARE SO IMMATURE!"

"Captain, now is not the time to *point the finger*."

Peter Pan was beside himself with laughter. Captain Hook growled angrily and got back to his point.

"More than anything, I want to see you lose something you love," the captain said. "But since it's impossible to hold you down and cut off *your hand*, I've decided to hit you where it hurts the most. You want Tinker Bell back? *Catch!*"

Captain Hook threw Tinker Bell's jar into the air, and it plummeted toward the streets below. Peter Pan dived after the jar—and as he passed the *Jolly Roger*, Mr. Smee fired a cannon at him. Instead of a cannonball, though, a wide net erupted from the cannon and wrapped itself around Peter. The boy landed on the roof of the observation deck and was too firmly tangled in the net to save Tinker Bell.

"TINK!" Peter Pan screamed.

The Rosary Chicken hadn't moved from the deck of the *Dolly Llama* since the battle began, but as she watched the helpless fairy fall to her death, the chicken knew this was her moment to contribute. The Rosary Chicken plunged toward the jar, but just as she clutched the jar's handle with her beak, the chicken suddenly remembered *she couldn't fly!*

"SQUUUUAW!" the Rosary Chicken squawked as she fell toward her own certain death.

Fortunately, her desperate chirps were heard by another one of Conner's characters. At the top of the *Dolly Llama*'s mast, the Blissworm emerged from its cocoon to save its friend. However, the Blissworm didn't exit its chrysalis as a smiling, squishy space worm. Instead, a massive creature slipped out of the cocoon and landed on the deck of the *Dolly Llama* with a loud thud. The creature had bulging biceps, defined abdominal muscles, three feathered antennas, and a wide set of wings whose pattern, when they stretched open, resembled a sad face. The Blissworm had evolved into the next phase of its metamorphosis: a ferocious Mad Moth.

The Mad Moth got to its feet, roared like a Tyrannosaurus rex, and beat on its broad chest like a gorilla. The creature was such a fascinating sight, all the pirates on the Empire State Building stopped fighting to watch it—some even took a seat. The Mad Moth leaped off the *Dolly Llama*, using the entire ship as a diving board, and whooshed toward Tinker Bell and the Rosary Chicken. The Mad Moth caught up to the chicken and the fairy within a few feet of the street below.

"SQUAAAAAAAAAAAAAAW!"

The Rosary Chicken was more afraid of the Mad Moth than the fall. The massive insect returned to the *Dolly Llama* and gently placed the chicken and Tinker Bell's jar on the deck. Peter Pan and the characters from Starboardia cheered the Mad Moth's bold rescue. It was so impressive, even a few of the *Jolly Roger* pirates clapped along.

"*NOOOOOO!*" Captain Hook yelled. *"He was supposed to lose something he loved!"*

The livid captain slid down the Empire State Building's spire and landed beside Peter Pan on the roof of the observation deck. The boy was still trapped in the net and couldn't move. Captain Hook raised his sword over Peter's head, preparing to strike him with a final, fatal blow. Right before the captain would have slain the Boy Who Wouldn't Grow Up, Auburn Sally somersaulted across the roof and sliced off Captain Hook's remaining hand. The captain's sword (and his hand) fell to the ground.

"*AAAAAAAAAHHHHHHHH!*" Captain Hook roared in agony.

Strangely, instead of blood gushing from the captain's veins, the only thing that came out was *words*. All the adjectives that James M. Barrie used to describe the horrible Captain Hook spewed from the captain's severed wrist.

Captain Hook tucked his wounded arm into his

shoulder and lost his balance. He fell over the railing of the observation deck and plunged toward the ground. The captain hit the street with such a powerful thump that the entire block rattled. When the pirates looked down, instead of seeing the captain's body, they saw more of James M. Barrie's words splattered across the pavement. The words slowly sizzled into smoke and disappeared.

After witnessing their captain's fall to his death, the *Jolly Roger* pirates raised their hands in surrender. Peter Pan was cut free from the net and was happily reunited with Tinker Bell. Not-So-Jolly Joan burst into tears and blew her nose in Peg-Leg Peggy's shoulder.

"What's wrong, Joan?" Peg-Leg Peggy asked.

"Oh, it's nothing." Not-So-Jolly Joan sniffled. "I just love a happy ending."

The Ziblings' jet zipped through the sky above New York City, but no matter how inconsistently they piloted the aircraft, the superheroes couldn't lose the flying monkeys trailing them. Blubo joined the swarm of winged creatures as they soared after the jet, but not because he was under the Wicked Witch's spell. The little monkey was looking for his family and spotted his parents at the front of the flock.

"Mom! Dad! It's me—it's Blubo!" he shouted.

"Blubo!" his mother cried. "What are you doing here?"

"You were supposed to stay at the witch's castle in Oz!" his father said.

Despite the concerned expressions on their faces, Blubo's parents never slowed down to greet their son or even turned to see him. Like all the other monkeys, they kept their eyes fixed on the Ziblings' jet.

"I met some friends who are going to stop the Wicked Witch!" Blubo told them. "Those superheroes are with us—they're good guys! You've got to stop chasing them before someone gets hurt!"

"I wish we could, son," his father said. "As long as the Wicked Witch is wearing the golden cap, the monkeys are under her control."

"I know, but can't you fight the spell?" Blubo asked.

"We've tried, sweetheart, but it's no use," his mother said. "The Wicked Witch's magic is too powerful. You should get out of here and enjoy your life while you still can. Once you get older, you'll be under the witch's control, too."

Despite his parents' advice, Blubo wasn't ready to give up just yet. The little monkey left the flock and glided toward the city on a daring mission to save himself, his parents, and his species.

Eventually, the flying monkeys caught up with the Ziblings' jet. The creatures landed on the aircraft's wings and began ripping it apart panel by panel. A loud alarm sounded inside the cockpit to warn the passengers.

"That's not good," Professor Wallet said. "Those chimps are going to make us crash if we don't intervene!"

"Don't worry, Dad, we'll take care of it!" Bolt said. "You stay inside and steer; we'll go outside and save the jet before this flight goes *bananas*. Get it? Because they're *monkeys*."

Blaze, Whipney, and Morph sighed at their little brother's joke.

"You've really got to work on those one-liners, Bolt," Whipney said.

"Yeah, it's kind of crucial if you want to be remembered," Blaze said.

"But more importantly *merchandized*," Morph said.

The Ziblings crawled out of a hatch at the top of

the cockpit to handle the flying monkeys outside. The aircraft was speeding at hundreds of miles per hour, and Blaze, Whipney, Morph, and Bolt had to hold on tightly to the edge of the wings so they didn't fly off.

Blaze hit the flying monkeys with fiery blasts from the tips of his fingers. Whipney whipped the winged creatures off the jet with her long braids of hair. Morph transformed into a giant octopus and knocked the monkeys off the aircraft with his enormous limbs. Bolt zapped the monkeys with bursts of electricity, but since they were all clinging to a metal object, every time he missed, he accidentally electrocuted his brothers and sister.

"BOLT!" they yelled in unison.

"Sorry—my bad!" he apologized.

Soon there were so many flying monkeys covering the jet, the aircraft looked like a large black bird flying through the air. One of the monkeys ripped off a panel and found a bundle of wires underneath it. The monkey sliced the wires with its teeth, and the jet's engines stopped working. The Ziblings' jet suddenly dropped from the sky and plunged toward the streets below.

"Hold on tight, children!" Professor Wallet's voice

called from the speakers. *"It's going to be a bumpy landing!"*

Their mission complete, the flying monkeys abandoned the wings of the jet. Morph transformed into a giant parachute to ease the approaching impact, but the jet was too heavy. The Ziblings' jet smashed through the roof of a Broadway theater and nose-dived into the orchestra pit. The rough landing knocked the wind out of the superheroes, and they slid down the aircraft and rolled onto the theater's stage. Professor Wallet crawled out from a mountain of airbags and rested beside his children.

Bolt looked around the theater as he caught his breath. "It could have been worse," he said. "We could have landed *Off-Broadway*."

The smallest superhero snickered at his own joke, and to his surprise, his brothers and sister laughed, too.

"Much better," Blaze said.

"Now, that's a good line," Morph agreed.

"See, it just takes practice," Whipney said.

Suddenly, high-pitched screeching echoed inside the theater. The Ziblings looked through the fresh hole in the roof and saw that the flying monkeys were headed toward the theater—*they weren't finished with the superheroes yet*. The other Ziblings were still catching their breath, so Bolt leaped to his feet and flew toward the ceiling.

"I'll be right back," Bolt said. "I've got some *monkey business* to take care of!"

His brothers and sister groaned.

"Annnnnd you lost me," Blaze said.

"Less is more," Morph said.

"Should have stopped at *Off-Broadway*," Whipney said.

Bolt rocketed out of the theater and soared right past the flying monkeys. Just the way a bird protects her nest from a predator, the distraction worked, and the monkeys followed Bolt instead.

The superhero flew east and spotted the Chrysler Building in the distance. The sparkling skyscraper gave Bolt an idea. He landed at the very tip of the building's sharp spire, and the winged creatures landed below him. The monkeys charged up the sides of the building toward the little superhero, intending to tear him apart like the Ziblings' jet.

Bolt waited until all the flying monkeys were on the Chrysler Building's metal-coated roof; then he looked up at the clouds and summoned a powerful bolt of lightning from the sky. The lightning hit the spire and sent a wave of electricity through the building. The extreme voltage made every lightbulb burst, every window shatter, and it electrocuted all the flying monkeys. The winged creatures were zapped so hard they looked like balls of fur with wings. The monkeys fluttered to the ground and passed out as soon as they hit the street.

"Well, that'll put a *monkey wrench* in their day!" Bolt chuckled.

The little superhero was so proud of himself for defeating the flying monkeys, he didn't even need his siblings to approve his one-liner. He threw his head back and laughed until his belly hurt.

The Winkies and the Wicked Witch followed Robin Hood and the Merry Men up Broadway to Lincoln Center. The center was home to five large theaters that sat around a spacious courtyard with a large fountain in the center. Robin Hood and the Merry Men sprinted up the steps of the courtyard, and although there were plenty of places to run, they stopped at the edge of the fountain. The Winkies quickly filled the courtyard and surrounded the Merry Men with their weapons raised.

"You morons give up so easily," the Wicked Witch remarked.

"DO YOU HEAR THAT SHRILL SOUND, MERRY MEN?" Robin Hood asked. "THE WITCH'S VOICE IS EVEN UGLIER THAN HER FACE, AND I DIDN'T THINK THAT WAS POSSIBLE."

"Silence!" the Wicked Witch commanded.

"I MEAN, LOOK AT HER," Robin continued. "THE WITCH IS SO UGLY, WHEN SHE WAS BORN, THE DOCTOR PROBABLY SLAPPED HER TWICE BECAUSE HE DIDN'T KNOW WHICH END WAS WHICH."

"All right, that's enough—"

"THE WITCH IS SO UGLY, SHE WENT TO A FUNERAL AND THE CORPSE GOT UP AND RAN AWAY!"

"If you don't shut up, I'll—"

"THE WITCH IS SO UGLY, SHE WAS VOTED THE NATIONAL ANIMAL OF SCOTLAND!"

The Wicked Witch tapped her umbrella on the ground, and a dirty sock appeared in Robin Hood's mouth.

"I'm going to enjoy watching you die!" the witch declared. "Winkies, kill this pompous man *and* his imbecile followers! And do it *slowly*...."

The Winkies lunged toward Robin Hood and his Merry Men, but before they could strike the Prince of Thieves, they were distracted by a large object overhead. The *Charlie Chaplin* rose over Lincoln Center like an inflatable sun. Beau Rogers stood in the doorway of the blimp's gondola wearing the Lost Talisman of Pharaoh Eczema around his neck.

"You aren't the only one who's into mind control, milady," Beau Rogers announced. "Allow me to introduce you to *my* batch of brainwashed warriors!"

All the mummies from the Pyramid of Anesthesia crept out from behind the structures of Lincoln Center and surrounded the Wicked Witch and her Winkies.

"My soldiers have already met their maker—*now it's your turn!*" Beau said.

"Nice quip, kid!" Emgee called from the blimp's steering wheel.

"Thanks, Aunt Emgee," he said. *"Mummies, attack!"*

The undead soldiers approached the Winkies at a leisurely pace—which was as fast as the mummies could move. Unfortunately for Beau and the Merry Men, their surprise assault didn't go as well as they'd hoped. The Winkies were exceptional fighters and tore through the mummies like they were made of cotton. Within a few minutes, the Winkies had defeated the mummies and trapped Robin Hood and the Merry Men again.

The Wicked Witch let out a deafening cackle. "Any last words?" she asked.

"WELL, MERRY MEN, IT LOOKS LIKE THIS IS THE END," Robin Hood declared. "I NEVER THOUGHT WE'D PERISH AT THE HANDS OF SOLDIERS WITH SUCH RIDICULOUS NAMES AND MORE FLAMBOYANT CLOTHING THAN OUR OWN. NONETHELESS, IT'S BEEN AN HONOR TO TRAVEL THE UNIVERSE AT YOUR SIDE!"

"Um . . . Robin?" Alan-a-Dale whispered. "You're forgetting the next part of our plan."

"OH YEAH," Robin Hood said. "THANK YOU, MY FAITHFUL MINSTREL. WE WOULD HAVE MET OUR DEMISE HAD IT NOT BEEN FOR YOUR STEEL TRAP OF A MEMORY. MOVING ON—*LOST BOYS, YOUR TIME HAS COME!*"

Suddenly, the Lost Boys from Neverland appeared on the rooftops of the Lincoln Center theaters and pelted the Wicked Witch with water balloons.

"Take *that*, you mean old hag!" Tootles said.

"Adults like you are the reason we don't want to grow up!" Curly said.

"Go back to the nightmare you came out of!" Nibs said.

"Leave our friends alone!" the Lost twins said.

Although Slightly had been a baby since the Lost Boys visited Morina's cottage, he still did his part and squirted the witch with his bottle. Soon the Wicked Witch was drenched, and she began to smoke and sizzle as the liquid melted her body. Just as it had happened with Captain Hook, instead of bodily fluids, the witch dissolved into *words*. All the prose L. Frank Baum used to describe the Wicked Witch in his books now dripped from the witch's body.

"You horrid little brats!" the Wicked Witch screamed in pain. *"You'll pay for this one day! You may have stopped me in the Otherworld, but I'll get my revenge in the Underworld!"*

The witch staggered across the Lincoln Center courtyard, leaving puddles of words as she went. She tripped and fell headfirst into the fountain and disintegrated completely. Friar Tuck knelt beside the fountain and said a prayer for the salvation of her soul.

Now that the Wicked Witch of the West was dead, her vicious spell over the Winkies was lifted. They dropped their weapons and pranced around the courtyard in celebration. Alan-a-Dale strummed a happy tune so that they had something to dance to.

"WHAT'S GOING ON?" Robin Hood asked. "WHY ARE THE WINKIES SKIPPING AROUND LIKE THEY'RE INTOXICATED?"

"Robin, they've been freed!" Beau Rogers called down to him. "The witch has been controlling them for years!"

"YOU MEAN, THE WITCH FORCED YOU TO WEAR THOSE OBNOXIOUS OUTFITS AND ANSWER TO THAT DEGRADING NAME?"

"No, we had those before the witch's spell," a Winkie said.

Robin was greatly disturbed to hear it. "MIGHT THERE BE *ANOTHER* WITCH INVOLVED?" he asked.

Suddenly, Blubo swooped down from the sky and landed on the edge of the fountain. He dived in and searched through the Wicked Witch's watery remains. The others were curious about what the monkey was doing and gathered around the fountain to watch him.

"I found it!" he announced.

Blubo resurfaced with the Wicked Witch's golden cap in his hands. He threw it on the ground and then smashed it with one of the Winkies' spears until it broke into hundreds of pieces.

"There!" Blubo said with a satisfied smile. "From this moment forward, no one will ever control the flying monkeys again!"

The Winkies cheered for the monkeys' newfound freedom. Although the Merry Men, the Lost Boys, and the archaeologists had no idea what Blubo was talking about, they joined the characters from Oz as they danced around Lincoln Center in celebration.

"SUCH A STRANGE PLACE, THIS *OZ*," Robin Hood declared. "IT'S NOT EVERY DAY YOU CONVERSE WITH WITCHES, MONKEYS, AND *WINKIES*. ACTUALLY, IT REMINDS ME OF A WEEKEND I HAD IN FRANCE."

The card soldiers and the Queen of Hearts followed the Tin Woodman from Midtown all the way to Washington Square Park in Lower Manhattan. The park was famous for the towering arch that stood at its north entrance. The Tin Woodman hurried through the arch, expecting to see the park filled with the Cyborgs from "Galaxy Queen," but the Cyborgs were late.

"Oh dear," the Tin Woodman said.

The card soldiers caught up with the Tin Woodman and formed a circle around him. They pointed the sharp ends of their staffs at the metal man, and he dropped his axe. The Queen of Hearts sauntered into the circle and strutted around the Tin Woodman, eyeing him like he was a delicious treat.

"Hold him down," she ordered with a devilish smile. *"I want to cut off his head myself!"*

The soldiers grabbed the Tin Woodman by the arms, kicked his legs out from underneath him, and forced him into a kneeling position. The Queen of Hearts picked up his axe and practiced swinging it.

"So *you're* the one they call the Queen of Hearts?" the Tin Woodman asked.

"That's correct," the queen said.

"But I don't understand," he said. "You invade other people's homes and claim them as your own. You cut off people's heads for sport. How can you be *the Queen of Hearts* when you act so *heartless*?"

"Is your head hollow?" the queen asked with a snort. "Every creature in existence has a heart—it's just a muscle that pumps blood through the rest of your body. What you're talking about is *compassion*—it's much rarer and a total waste of time, if you ask me."

The Tin Woodman's eyes darted back and forth as he tried to make sense of it all.

"So, what I've been searching for this whole time, *I've actually had inside me all along?*" he asked. His jaw dropped and his eyes opened wide as he made the greatest discovery of his life.

The Queen of Hearts shared a confused glance with her card soldiers—was the man she was about to decapitate asking *her* about life lessons?

"I'm told that that is a conclusion most people come to before the end of their life," she said. "Lucky for you, you've reached it just in time. Now hold your head steady—*this is going to hurt.*"

His realization made the Tin Woodman feel like he was seeing the world for the first time. He was so overwhelmed, tears filled his eyes—but he couldn't get emotional and rust. He needed to save himself from the Queen of Hearts so his new life could begin.

"Wait!" the Tin Woodman said. "If you're so fascinated by my head, you should see my *heart.*"

"Stupid man," the queen said. "You just said you didn't have one—now you want me to look at it?"

"I was mistaken," he said. "You may be the Queen of Hearts, but I guarantee you've never seen a heart like *mine* before."

The Tin Woodman had captured the queen's attention, and she raised a curious eyebrow.

"Very well, before I cut off your head, I'll have a look at your heart," she said. *"Turn him over!"*

The card soldiers pulled the Tin Woodman up and turned him on his back. The Queen of Hearts leaned over his metal torso and yanked open the small door in his chest. To her horror, the queen didn't find a heart at all, *but a tiny little woman standing inside him!*

"BOOOOO!" Trollbella screamed.

"AAAAAAHHHHHHHH!" the Queen of Hearts screamed.

The queen was so stunned, she dropped the Tin Woodman's axe and stumbled backward. The soldiers pinning the Tin Woodman quickly went to help the queen. Trollbella jumped to the ground, retrieved the axe, and tossed it to the Tin Woodman once he was on his feet. The Queen of Hearts roared with anger and pointed her finger at the unlikely duo.

"*SEIZE THEM AT ONCE!*" she yelled. "*AND OFF WITH BOTH THEIR HEEAAA—*"

Before the Queen of Hearts could finish her sentence, the Tin Woodman swung his axe with all his might and chopped the queen's head off. Again, just as with the other literary villains, the only thing that spewed out of her body was *words*. All the adjectives, adverbs, verbs, and nouns Lewis Carroll used to describe the unpleasant monarch sprayed out of the queen's neck. Eventually, the words dried up and the Queen of Hearts' dismembered body disappeared.

"*He's murdered our queen!*" a card soldier shouted.

"*He'll pay for this!*" shouted another.

The card soldiers charged toward the Tin Woodman and Trollbella, but just as they were about to be pierced by the soldiers' weapons, everyone in the park was suddenly distracted by a bright light in the sky. The Tin Woodman and Trollbella looked up and saw that the *BASK-8* had finally arrived!

The Cyborg Queen and Commander Newters observed the park from the window of the Command Bridge.

"I believe *this* is the park we've been looking for, Your Majesty," Commander Newters said. "Oh yes, this is definitely Washington Square Park, I can see it's filled with the boxy soldiers we agreed to defeat."

"This city has more *square parks* than all my planets combined," the Cyborg Queen said. "Anyhoo, I can see we're a little tardy. Send the Cyborgs to assist the metallic lumberjack and his vertically challenged friend."

"Yes, ma'am," Commander Newters said, and turned to the Cyborg soldiers. "You heard the queen—*to the park!*"

A wide door opened across the *Bask-8*'s belly, and thousands of Cyborgs glided into Washington Square Park. They descended using jetpacks, Hoverboards, and personal propellers. Before engaging in combat, the Cyborgs' first order of business was to transport the Tin Woodman and Trollbella to the top of the Washington Square Arch. Once they were safe, the Cyborgs wreaked havoc on the card soldiers.

The Wonderland natives were skilled fighters, but they were no match for the Cyborgs' laser guns, gamma bombs, and rocket launchers. It wasn't long before the cards surrendered and were taken aboard the *BASK-8* as the Cyborgs' prisoners.

As the battle ended, the Tin Woodman sat on the edge of the tall arch and let out a big sigh.

"What's wrong?" Trollbella asked.

"I've always been hollow, but for the first time in my life I feel truly *empty inside*," the Tin Woodman said. "I always thought a heart would fill the void, but now that I know I've had one all along, I'm not sure what to do with myself."

The Tin Woodman's dilemma was Trollbella's dream come true. She stared in wonder at the most beautiful sight she had ever seen: *an emotionally mature, vulnerable, and needy man*. The Troblin Queen had a seat beside the Tin Woodman and longingly gazed up at him, batting her eyes.

"You know, I fit perfectly inside your chest," she remarked. "Perhaps *I'm* the heart you've been searching for."

Trollbella put her tiny hand into his and rested her horns on his shoulder. In that moment the Tin Woodman was certain he had a heart, because the troll girl's touch made him blush.

Rat Mary and the witches flew through New York City as erratically as possible, but nothing threw off their determined followers. Lester, Jack, and Goldilocks soared after the witches as they dangerously zigzagged between buildings, looped around skyscrapers, and dived under bridges. Absolutely nothing was going to stop the daring parents from retrieving their son.

Lester was gaining more and more ground with each passing second. Soon they were in reaching distance of the bristles on the last witch's broom.

"I've got an idea," Jack told his wife and the gander. "We'll follow the witches to that cluster of buildings in the distance, but when we get there, we'll go around that green tower and cut them off before they reach the—"

Before Jack could finish unripping his plan, Goldilocks sprang into action with a plan of her own. She leaped off Lester's back and landed on the broomstick of the closest witch. Goldilocks fought the witch for control of the broom. Just as the witch was about to zap her with a magic spell, Goldilocks punched the witch in the face, and she landed in the East River.

Goldilocks gripped the broomstick tightly with both hands. She had never ridden on a witch's broom before, and it took her a moment to figure out how to work it. She was pleasantly surprised to learn that riding a magic broomstick was very similar to riding a horse. When she leaned forward, the broom zoomed ahead, and when she pulled up on the handle, the broom slowed down. Once she felt confident, she turned to Jack and Lester flying beside her and filled them in on her plan.

"I'm going to work my way to the front of the witches," she told them. "Then I'm going to hop aboard Rat Mary's broom and get Hero."

"Be careful, Goldie!" Jack said.

"Careful never got me anywhere," she said with a wink.

The courageous mother leaned forward, and the broomstick's speed gradually increased. As she flew past the witches, Goldilocks did whatever she could to knock them out of the sky. She slammed into them and shoved them off their brooms, she pulled the witches' hair so they'd fall backward into the city, and she kicked their brooms' handles and sent them spinning out of control. Finally, the only ones left in the flying procession were Goldilocks, Rat Mary, and Hero.

Goldilocks snuck up right behind Rat Mary's broom, then jumped off her own and landed beside the witch.

"Give me back my son!" she demanded.

"Why do breeders get so attached to their young?" Rat Mary screeched. *"You can just make another one, you know!"*

The witch twisted and looped through the air, she dipped and made sharp turns, she even flew upside down at one point—but nothing knocked Goldilocks off the broom. The vigorous movement only rocked Hero to sleep.

"Gosh, you're relentless!" Rat Mary said. *"Here! Just take the little rug rat! I'll find another one!"*

The witch sliced the strap of the BabyBjörn with her sharp fingernail. The contraption slid off the witch's body and fell toward the ground with Hero inside it. Goldilocks dived off Rat Mary's broomstick and caught her son in midair. The mother and child fell thousands of feet through the air. A few seconds before they would have hit the ground, Lester swooped under them and they landed safely in Jack's arms.

"Curses!" Rat Mary said. "I was hoping for a splat!"

Ironically, the witch wasn't watching where she was going and slammed headfirst into the Flatiron Building. The messy impact made one thing abundantly clear: Rat Mary's kid-snatching, broom-riding, potion-brewing days were over.

Jack and Goldilocks were overjoyed to finally have Hero back in their arms. The happy couple embraced their newborn son, and Lester carried the reunited family back toward Central Park to find their friends.

Chapter Twenty

TIMES SQUARE SQUARE-OFF

The spiraling light whirled out of Central Park and transported Alex and the lion statues to Times Square. They landed on the rooftop just below the Times Square Ball that drops every New Year's Eve. The world-famous intersection was completely empty, but all the flashing lights, the illuminated billboards, and the giant video screens had been left on during the evacuation.

Alex sat on the edge of the roof and sobbed over

the death of her friend. The curse made her emotions skyrocket, but she was consumed by much more than grief. Her head filled with thoughts of *guilt. It was her fault the witches had invaded the Otherworld. She was to blame for all the damage and fear they had caused. If it weren't for her, Rook would still be alive.*

As Alex tormented herself, she subconsciously caused vines and ivy to grow up the buildings around Times Square. Soon the entire square was covered in plants. Eventually Conner, his friends, and the Fairy Council stumbled into the square. Thanks to all the vegetation, they knew they were in the right place.

"I see her!" Conner announced. "She's up there under the New Year's Eve ball!"

The lion statues leaped off the roof and landed on the ground. The impact was so strong, Times Square rattled and the lions left paw prints in the pavement. Just as they had done at the library, the lions guarded the building and wouldn't let anyone get close.

"Alex, I know you're experiencing unimaginable pain right now, but it's very important you listen to us," Emerelda called up to the roof. "The curse you're under stems from a very powerful and very evil magic mirror. It's making you think things that aren't true, feel emotions that aren't real, and it's disturbing your point of view. As difficult as it is, you can't trust *anything* your body or mind is telling you. The magic only has one purpose: *to destroy everything its host holds dear.* If you let it deceive you, all will be lost."

"But it's all my fault!" Alex cried. "If I'd found my uncle Lloyd sooner, none of this would have happened! If I had stopped the witches in the fairy-tale world, they never would have come to the Otherworld! And if I had just forgiven Rook, he wouldn't have felt the need to prove himself and save me!"

"Alex, none of that is true, because *I'm* the one to blame," Emerelda confessed. "You knew the Masked Man was dangerous and you did everything you could to stop him. *I'm* the one who didn't believe you. *I'm* the one who demanded you call off the search. *I'm* the one who thought you were being irrational instead of recognizing the signs of a curse. And because of *my* mistakes, *I* wasn't there to help the kingdoms when the Literary Army attacked, *I* wasn't there to stop the witches from traveling to the Otherworld, and *I'm* the reason Rook is dead. I take full responsibility for everything that's happened, and now I need your help to fix it. So please, come down from there and we can fight the curse together!"

Emerelda seemed to ease Alex's suffering, but only slightly. Alex searched deep inside her soul and found the strength to block out all the terrible thoughts and feelings the curse inspired. She dried her tears and mustered the courage to join her friends and family below.

"Not so fast!"

Morina walked out from around a corner and stood between the lion statues. As soon as the witch's presence was known, Alex lost all self-control and the curse took over completely, returning her to Morina's command.

"Why can't you people just *stay* where I leave you?" Morina asked.

"Let my sister go, Morina!" Conner demanded.

"Sorry, but no can do," the witch said. "I've got big plans for your sister, but sadly, you'll just have to take my word for it—none of you will be alive by the time we're through."

"Haven't you caused enough damage?" Emerelda asked.

"Actually, I've just begun," the witch said. "Alex,

hold down your friends so we can finish what we started."

Alex nodded and waved her hand over Times Square. Vines shot out of the ground near the Fairy Council's feet and pinned them to the pavement. Long electric cables shot out of the giant video screens and wrapped around Conner, Bree, Red, and Froggy, then held them against billboards and banners above the streets. The lion statues leaped into the air and tackled Mother Goose and Merlin to the ground.

"Good girl," Morina said. "Now I want you to destroy everything and everyone in this miserable world, starting with New York City."

Alex nodded again and levitated into the sky high above Times Square. She summoned more vines to grow across the island, working their way through one neighborhood at a time. The plants wrapped around buildings, trees, cars, streetlamps, and mailboxes, crushing everything in their path like a tsunami of hungry anacondas.

"Since your plan didn't work, you're gonna take it out on the whole world—is that right?" Conner asked.

"In a nutshell, yes," Morina said with a sinister smile. However, the witch's smile vanished when she discovered Froggy pinned to a billboard above her. *"Charlie!"* she shouted. "How did you escape the magic mirror?"

"I performed a *good deed*," Froggy said. "That's a selfless act one commits for the benefit of someone else, in case you're wondering."

"Impossible!" she declared. "No one can leave a magic mirror once they're trapped inside it! That was the whole point of imprisoning you in one!"

"That's odd, because I can name *three* people who've been freed," Froggy said. "Perhaps if you were better informed, you might actually *accomplish* one of the atrocious plans you set forward."

Morina glared at the frog man. "There'll be no returning from where I send you next," she said. "That I *promise* you."

The witch raised an open hand toward Froggy and then clenched it into a tight fist. The gesture caused the cables around Froggy's body to squeeze and choke him. The sight of Morina torturing Froggy made Red's blood boil. When the witch wasn't looking, the young queen managed to free her left hand. She reached into her purse and retrieved the Swiss Army knife she'd bought at the airport. She quickly cut herself free and landed on the ground.

"Leave the frog alone, you goat!" she yelled.

The witch turned around and was very amused to find Red challenging her.

"Well, if this isn't the most pathetic thing I've ever seen," Morina said. "Do you actually think *you* can stop *me*?"

"Underestimate me all you want," Red said. "It's much easier than facing the truth, isn't it, Morina?"

"And what truth is that?" the witch asked.

"How sensationally *jealous* you are of me!" Red declared.

Morina howled with laughter. Conner and the others eyed one another nervously—they had no idea where Red was going with this.

"You think I'm *jealous*? Of *you*?" the witch asked.

"So far you've ruined my wedding, cursed one of my best friends, and trapped my fiancé in a magic mirror, and now you're strangling him in front of me," Red said. "If that isn't a personal vendetta, I don't know what is. Obviously *something* is fueling your obsession with ruining my life, and it doesn't reek of *jelly* on my side of the ballroom!"

"Please explain how someone like *me* could be jealous of someone like *you*," Morina said. "I've gutted canaries with higher intelligence."

"Like most aspects of my life, brains have nothing to do with it," Red said. "Face it, you're envious of my beauty!"

"Excuse me?" the witch asked.

"You heard me!" Red said. "I have flawless skin, beautiful eyes, fantastic hair, a naturally high metabolism—but I'm also *kind, considerate, giving,* and a *good friend*! I'm just as gorgeous on the inside as I am on the outside! And no matter how many potions you drink, no matter how many enchantments you make, there will always be a selfish, greedy, hateful, and *ugly* goat inside you!"

The queen's words hit the witch right where it hurt the most. Morina was so outraged, her eyes turned red and the blood in her veins became black. Red's friends and the Fairy Council closed their eyes, terrified to see how the witch would respond.

"You really are the biggest idiot in the universe," Morina said. "I consider *this* a favor to mankind."

The witch pointed with both hands at Red, and a bright violet light blasted from the tips of her fingers. Just as the deadly blast was about to hit the young queen, Red removed the hand mirror from her purse and used it to shield herself. Morina's magic bounced off the mirror and headed straight back to her. Morina was hit by her own magic and burst into millions of pieces.

"Who's the idiot now, *Morina*?" Red said.

When Conner and the others opened their eyes, they were shocked to see that Red was still standing and the witch was dead.

"Darling, that was incredible!" Froggy cheered.

"Red, you're a genius!" Conner shouted.

"How did you know the mirror would reflect her magic?" Bree asked.

"Glamorous Magazine," Red said with a shrug. "I read this wonderful article on the plane that said *'If a woman wants to be saved, she'll find her greatest savior in the mirror.'* I don't know who they were talking about, but they certainly saved me."

Her friends had never been so thankful for a misinterpretation. Red climbed a ladder and cut Froggy loose from the billboard with the Swiss Army knife. They helped each other to the ground, but before Froggy could help the others, Red stopped him.

"Charlie, I want to get married," she said.

"Well, so do I, darling—"

"No, you don't understand," she said. "I want to get married *right now*."

Froggy knew from the desperate look in her eyes that Red was dead serious.

"Sweetheart, are you sure *now* is a good time?" he said.

"I'm positive," Red said. "If the last month has taught me anything, it's how unpredictable life can be—especially when you're friends with the Bailey twins. This could very well be the last chance we'll ever get! Let's do it now, in the Square of Times, before another magical being can tear us apart!"

The idea made Froggy's heart fill with joy, but he wasn't convinced it was the right thing to do.

"Are you sure this is the wedding you want?" he asked. "I don't mean to be crude, but the whole street is covered in a witch's remains."

A large and self-assured smile grew on Red's face. "Charlie, I can't think of a better place to get married than on the ashes of your ex-girlfriend," she said. "Mother Goose, will you do the honors?"

Besides being pinned to the ground by a three-ton lion statue, Mother Goose couldn't think of a reason why she couldn't perform the ceremony.

"I suppose I'm available," she said.

"Wonderful!" Red squealed. "And for all intents and purposes, we'll say the Fairy Council are our witnesses, Conner is the best man, and Alex is my maid of honor. *Don't worry, Alex! This will only take a minute and we'll get right back to helping you!*"

Red and Froggy joined hands and stood in the middle of Times Square as Mother Goose officiated the impromptu wedding.

"Dearly beloved, we are gathered here today—against our will—to unexpectedly watch this frog and woman join in questionable matrimony. Do you, Charlie Charming, take Red Riding Hood as your lovably high-maintenance wife?"

"I do," Froggy declared.

"And do you, Red Riding Hood, take Charlie Charming as your adorably webfooted husband?"

"I do," Red said.

"Then it is with the power mistrusted in me that I now pronounce you husband and wife! You may kiss the frog!"

Red and Froggy shared their first kiss as a married couple, and their friends cheered.

"Beautiful ceremony, my dear," Merlin said.

"Believe it or not, this isn't the strangest wedding I've been to," Mother Goose said. "Now will someone get this stone feline off me?"

Fortunately, they didn't have to. Alex soared

across Manhattan as her magic consumed the island below her. The lion statues leaped off Mother Goose and Merlin and followed Alex, jumping from rooftop to rooftop across the city. Froggy and Red cut the cables around Conner and Bree and then sliced through the vines trapping the Fairy Council.

"What do we do now?" Bree asked.

"We need to get off this island and regroup with the others," Conner said. "Now that she's been ordered to destroy the Otherworld, Alex isn't going to stop until we break the curse."

"Any ideas how to break it?" Froggy asked.

"Just *one*," Conner said. "But I'm praying we find another way."

A BROTHER'S BURDEN

A wave of Alex's destructive vines chased after Conner, his friends, and the Fairy Council as they ran through the New York City streets. The fairies zapped the approaching plants with enchantments to keep them off their tail, but every time they destroyed one vine, a dozen grew in its place.

"It's like Manhattan is sinking into the Thornbush Pit!" Conner said.

"What's a Thornbush Pit?" Bree asked.

"It's a dangerous sinkhole in the fairy-tale world," Conner explained. "Alex and I had to go inside it to retrieve an item for the Wishing Spell. You know what's funny? After all this, *that* seems like a *good memory!*"

"Speak for yourself!" Froggy said.

Luckily, the group came to an intersection and crossed paths with Arthur, the Knights of the Round Table, and Cornelius. They, too, were on the run from the atrocious vines covering the city. The unicorn carried Rook's body on his back; the knights had covered him in candy wrappers from the witches' base.

"Did you find Alex?" Arthur asked.

"We did," Red said. "As you can see from the demonic plants covering the city, *it didn't go so well.*"

"A witch ordered Alex to destroy the world, starting with the city," Conner said. "We're trying to get off the island so we can come up with a plan to stop her!"

Eventually, they reached the Hudson River on the west side of Manhattan. Merlin transformed a pigeon into a small ferry and everyone quickly boarded it and sailed down the river toward Liberty Island. Conner was virtually speechless as he watched Alex's magic consume the city beside them. His sister had come a long way from the bookworm in Mrs. Peters's sixth-grade classroom.

The ferry docked on Liberty Island, and Conner reunited with his friends and characters from the Saint Andrew's Children's Hospital commissary. Charlotte and Bob were overjoyed to see that Conner and his friends were safe. They charged through the crowds on the island and gave him a huge hug.

All the pirates, superheroes, archaeologists, and Cyborgs appeared to be in great spirits given the circumstances, but their demeanors quickly changed when they noticed the body on Cornelius's back.

"What happened?" Bolt asked.

"Rook saved Alex's life," Conner informed them. "He stepped in front of a sniper's bullet before it hit her."

"My God," Bob said. "His poor father."

"Where is your sister now?" Charlotte asked.

"She's currently destroying the biggest city in the United States," Conner said. "You know, typical teenage stuff."

His mother let out a frustrated sigh. "Is there *nothing* we can do to stop the curse?"

"Nothing worth mentioning," Conner said.

Lester swooped toward Liberty Island with Jack, Goldilocks, and Hero on his back. Everyone was relieved to see that the parents had rescued their child from the witches, and Jack and Goldilocks were thankful that their friends had gotten out of the city in time.

"There you are!" Jack said. "We circled the park but couldn't find a place to land—the whole city is covered in vines!"

"Tell me about it," Conner said. "What happened to all the witches?"

"We took care of most of them, but a few might have escaped the city," Goldilocks said. "Any luck with Alex?"

Conner shook his head. "I wish I had better news."

"I do—*Froggy and I got married!*" Red announced. "Oh, and I also killed Morina with a hand mirror. I know an afternoon of *murder and matrimony* sounds awfully tacky, but it was quite lovely."

Froggy looked down at Jack and Goldilocks's newborn son, and a wide smile stretched across his face. "This must be Hero," he said.

"I keep forgetting you haven't met him yet," Goldilocks said. "Hero, this is your uncle Froggy."

She passed the infant into Froggy's arms. Froggy's eyes became extra glossy at the sight of his nephew. Hero stared up at Froggy like he was the most fascinating thing he had ever seen.

"He's beautiful," Froggy said.

"You should have seen what he looked like when he came out," Red whispered. "I didn't eat for days."

While the two were being introduced, Conner was shocked to see that the majority of the Literary Army was scattered across Liberty Island. The card soldiers from Wonderland and the pirates from Neverland sat on the ground in handcuffs. The Winkies guarded the prisoners, and although Conner couldn't put his finger on it, there was something very different about them—like the light had returned to their eyes. The flying monkeys were twitching, covered with static electricity, and lay across the grass virtually comatose—but Conner noticed a difference in them, too. He saw that Blubo was snuggled up in his parents' laps, happily picking the bugs off their bodies.

"Wait a second—did you guys defeat the *entire* Literary Army without us?" Conner asked with an excited smile.

"We sure did!" Peter Pan announced. "The *Dolly Llama*'s crew and I fought Captain Hook and his pirates on top of the Empire State Building! Auburn Sally sliced off his hand and the captain fell to his death!"

The Mad Moth roared like a Triceratops to remind Peter of its involvement, which startled everyone on Liberty Island.

"Oh, and the Blissworm hatched from its cocoon and saved Tinker Bell!" Peter added.

"*That's* the Blissworm?" Bree asked. "Boy, and I thought *my* imagination was warped."

"What else happened while we were in the park?" Conner asked.

"Bolt electrocuted the flying monkeys on the Chrysler Building!" Blaze bragged about his brother.

"The Merry Men and the Lost Boys defeated the Wicked Witch at Lincoln Center," Beau Rogers said. "And once she was dead, the Winkies and monkeys were free from her magic spell!"

"I'VE MADE MANY WOMEN MELT IN MY DAY, BUT SHE WAS THE FIRST ONE TO ACTUALLY *DISSOLVE*," Robin Hood said.

"The Tin Woodman beheaded the Queen of Hearts in Washington Square Park, and our Cyborgs captured her card soldiers," Commander Newters said.

Bree couldn't help noticing that Trollbella and the Tin Woodman were holding hands. "What's going on with *you* two?" she asked. "Are you guys like a *thing*?"

"If we *must* define our relationship in your uncivilized monster terms, then *yes*, we are a thing," Trollbella said. "I've spent my whole life longing after Butterboy, but it turns out what I really needed was a *Butter Tray*."

Conner was bursting with so much pride for all that his friends and characters had accomplished, he didn't have room to be disturbed by Trollbella and the Tin Woodman's new relationship.

"But who told you *how* to defeat the Literary Army?" he asked. "I mean, even I would have had to consult a librarian."

"Your mom did," Bolt said.

Conner was pleasantly surprised to hear it. *"Really?"*

"At first we didn't know what to do, either," Charlotte said. "Then I thought, *What would Alex and Conner do if they were in my shoes?* So I took a page from your book and *wrote a story* about meeting James M. Barrie, L. Frank Baum, and Lewis Carroll. I splashed the pages with a few drops of Portal

Potion, stepped into the beam of light, and asked the authors how to defeat their characters."

"And what did they say?"

"Sir James M. Barrie said Captain Hook's greatest weakness was *revenge* and that he'd never give up a chance to get even with Peter Pan for cutting off his hand. Mr. Baum said the Wicked Witch of the West was so evil she could be melted by water, so it's nice to know the movie depicted something correctly. Lastly, Mr. Carroll said the Queen of Hearts would never pass up an opportunity to chop off a unique head. I relayed all the information to Arthur and he put the plans into motion."

Over the years, Charlotte had given Conner plenty of reasons to be a proud son, but hearing how she'd acquired the information necessary to defeat an entire army definitely took the cake. However, before Conner could shower his mom with praise, he suddenly froze and went dead silent—her methods had given him an idea.

"Oh my gosh," he said. "I know how to break the curse! *I know how to save my sister!*"

Conner instantly had everyone's attention. Even Hero was interested in what he had come up with. But before Conner shared his plan, he ran to the edge of Liberty Island and looked across the river at the Manhattan skyline. Most of the island was covered in his sister's vines, but Alex herself was nowhere in sight.

"I need a better view of the city," Conner said. "Lester, could you give me a lift to Lady Liberty's torch?"

The giant gander leaned down so Conner could climb on his back. Bree's curiosity got the best of her and she hopped aboard Lester, too. They flew to the very top of the Statue of Liberty, and Lester dropped the teenagers off on Lady Liberty's torch.

"So?" Bree asked. "How are you going to break the curse?"

Conner shrugged. "Oh, I have no idea."

"Then what's your secret plan?" she asked.

"I'm going to ask someone who does have an idea," he said. "But first, I need to know *exactly* where Alex is—otherwise the plan isn't going to work."

They scanned the city like it was an ancient text. Finally, they spotted Alex drifting through the buildings of downtown Manhattan. She flew to the top of the Freedom Tower and watched her vines spreading through the streets below. The lion statues climbed the sides of the towering skyscraper and joined her.

"Great, she's landed!" Conner said. "If we can just get her away from those statues, I might have a shot at saving her!"

Suddenly, something moving in the Hudson River caught their attention. A small boat painted in camouflage colors was speeding up the river. The boat docked on Liberty Island, and they watched as General Wilson, a dozen Marines, and a very familiar old woman climbed onto the island.

"Cornelia?" Bree said in disbelief. "But what the heck is she doing here?"

Conner and Bree quickly climbed aboard Lester, and the gander transported them back to the ground. By the time they arrived, all the characters had gathered around Cornelia, the general, and his Marines.

"I'm here on urgent business, so everyone listen carefully," General Wilson said. "I don't know who you people are, where you're from, or why you're in my country, but you all need to return home immediately."

"Seriously, Gunther?" Cornelia berated him. "Do you really expect people to respect you when you address them like that? Not all of us are Marines, you know."

The general did his best to ignore her remarks,

but everyone could tell they were getting under his skin.

"In less than an hour, the United States military will be dropping a nuclear weapon on the city of New York," he announced. "Unless you want to be caught in its detonation range, you must leave this island at once."

"What?" Charlotte gasped.

"You can't nuke the city!" Conner yelled. "My sister's still over there!"

"I'm sorry for your loss, but the decision has been made," General Wilson said.

"This is *exactly* what I warned you about, Gunther!" Cornelia said. "Had you just listened to me when I first told you about the portals to other dimensions, none of this would be happening right now!"

The general's nostrils flared. "Cornelia, I invited you here to help me communicate with these people, not reprimand me in front of them!"

"You *invited* me here?" she asked. "Forty armed guards showed up at my house in the middle of the night, pulled me out of bed, and threw me into the back of a jeep! If that's your definition of an *invitation*, I'd hate to see how you *arrest* someone!"

"Cornelia, how do you and the general know each other?" Bree asked.

"We used to date," Cornelia explained. "I spent years trying to warn him about the portal between worlds, but no matter how much interdimensional evidence I gathered, he never took the Sisters Grimm seriously. And now here we are, minutes away from destroying the greatest city in the world!"

"This is not the time to say *I told you so*," the general barked.

"I don't need to say it," Cornelia snapped. "It's abundantly clear!"

"Okay, time out!" Conner shouted. "Obviously you two have issues that never got resolved, but can we go back to the part about *nuking New York City*? That can't be the only option!"

General Wilson pointed across the river to the vines demolishing the buildings throughout downtown. "We have to stop *that* from spreading to the rest of the world," he said. "Unless you've got a better idea, the army will be dropping a nuke in thirty-five minutes."

Conner glanced at his sister on top of the Freedom Tower. His plan to free Alex from the curse would be the most difficult mission of his life, but he would rather die trying to save her than do nothing and watch her perish.

"Actually, I *do* have a better idea," he said. "Who's got a pen?"

The Freedom Tower was the tallest building in Manhattan and provided Alex with a breathtaking view of the city as she destroyed it. At the very top of the building, wrapped around the base of the antenna, was the Communication Platform Ring. The three-level platform was filled with radio equipment, giant lights, wires, and hundreds of support beams. Alex and the lion statues walked around the platform as they watched the vines consume the Big Apple below them.

Suddenly, the Mad Moth whooshed out of the sky and knocked both lion statues to another rooftop nearby. The massive insect roared like a banshee and pounded the statues into smithereens. The Mad Moth gobbled up the small chunks of stone before they could rematerialize into the lions. A thunderous burp erupted from the alien's mouth, causing the windows of a neighboring building to shatter.

Unbeknownst to Alex, while she watched the Mad

Moth devour her stone guardians, Lester had snuck onto the roof behind her and dropped off eight passengers. Alex heard their footsteps as they spread out on the platform, but when she turned around, there was no one in sight. Alex briskly walked through the levels of the platform and searched for the intruders.

"I've spent the last thirty-eight hours wondering how to help you," Conner called out from his hiding spot. "I've thought of spells, potions, charms, enchantments—but none of them were powerful enough to break the curse. Then I remembered that when we were kids nothing helped you forget your troubles more than a good story. So I wrote you one—here it goes."

Conner stepped out from behind a support beam, and Alex hit her brother with a bright burst of light. It knocked him unconscious, and Conner collapsed on the platform. Seeing her brother injured, even by her own hand, broke the curse temporarily, and Alex returned to normal.

"Conner!" she yelled.

She hurried to her brother's side. When she arrived, she discovered that this wasn't actually her brother—it was *Arthur*! The young king had been transformed to *look* like Conner! Once Alex realized she had been tricked, the curse returned tenfold. The real Conner cleared his throat from wherever he was hiding and began his story.

"Once upon a time, there was a little girl. She was very smart and loved to learn more than anything else in the world. The little girl was the best student at her school and surpassed her classmates in every subject they studied. Unfortunately, the other students became jealous of the little girl and were intimidated by her. Instead of praising her intelligence, the children teased and bullied her for being so smart. They wouldn't play with her on the playground or eat lunch with her in the cafeteria, and the little girl became very lonely."

Alex saw her brother running across the third level of the platform. She zapped him with another burst of light and he collapsed. However, when she went to check on him, she found Jack lying on the floor instead.

"Whenever the little girl felt sad, she would read a new book from the library. The characters in the stories became her friends, inspiring the little girl to read as much as she could. The more she read, the smarter the little girl became. And the smarter she became, the more people resented her for it."

Conner appeared on the bottom level of the platform. He leaped over the railing and landed on the level above. Alex blasted her brother with a beam of light and discovered that he was actually Froggy. This time the curse didn't even break so she could check on him—it knew the game Conner was playing.

"By the time the little girl was a young woman, she was the leader of a faraway kingdom. The young woman's passion for knowledge made her a very wise ruler, and the mistreatment she experienced as a child made her sympathetic to her people's needs. Unfortunately, the young woman's superior leadership intimidated the adults in her life. They became envious of her abilities and made her life difficult whenever they could."

Conner popped up from behind a satellite dish. Alex struck her brother with another burst of light and Charlotte collapsed on the floor.

"Since there always seemed to be consequences for the young woman's *good qualities*, she gravely feared the consequences of a *bad quality*. So the young woman held herself to an unhealthy level of perfectionism and never allowed herself to make a mistake. It was hard enough being resented without reason—she couldn't imagine how difficult the world would be if she gave it a reason to hate her."

Alex saw Conner skipping across the platform above her. She hit him with a ray of light and Red rolled onto the roof.

"One day the adults in the young woman's life created a plan to exploit her abilities for themselves. They put a terrible curse on her that caused the young woman to feel and do awful things at their command. Even though she was being forced against her will, the young woman was such a perfectionist, she blamed *herself* for every terrible act she committed. She was so ashamed, she asked a loved one to take her life, believing it was the only way to end her suffering."

Conner suddenly peeked out from behind the Freedom Tower's antenna. Alex hit her brother with a powerful ray of light and he transformed into Cornelius.

"But it wasn't the young woman's fault for thinking this way. You see, no one ever told her it was okay to make mistakes. No one told her there was nothing wrong with needing help. No one told her it was normal to feel upset, or angry, or overwhelmed now and then. Everyone in her life took her perfectionism for granted and didn't realize how suffocating it was. And because no one gave the young woman permission to be *human*, she thought she was a failure for being one."

Alex spotted Conner doing a handstand on a radio antenna. She hit him with another blast of light and Emerelda tumbled to the floor.

"*You* are that young woman, Alex! People have made you feel bad for being *accomplished*, and now that you're cursed, it feels like it's the end of the world! You're so used to being in control, you think you've disappointed everyone by being vulnerable to something *you can't control*! But the only thing that would ever disappoint us is if *you gave up fighting*! So I won't let this curse be the end of you! I know you can save yourself from it if you just *cut yourself some slack*!"

Suddenly, her brother's binder of short stories slid between Alex's feet. The real Conner jumped out from hiding and wrapped his arms around her.

"*But if I can't convince you, I know someone who will!*"

Conner dropped the flask of Portal Potion and it shattered across the binder's pages. A beam of light shot up and the Bailey twins disappeared into the most important story Conner had ever written....

CHAPTER TWENTY-TWO

A SPECULATION STORY

The twins entered the bright and endless world of the Portal Potion. The story Conner had written was so short that it didn't take long for his handwriting to take shape and form the world he'd created. He'd written the story so quickly, there hadn't been time to include much detail. All that materialized in the empty space around them was a very familiar white door.

Alex's eyes stopped glowing, her hair stopped

floating above her head, and she looked around the story in a daze.

"I . . . I . . . I feel *normal*," she said. "Conner, you broke the curse! How did you make it go away?"

"Unfortunately, it's not over yet," Conner explained. "You're still cursed—it just can't affect you in this story. I wrote about a world where curses don't exist."

"It's nice to have a clear head again—even if it's only temporary," Alex said. "If we don't find a way to break the curse, I should just stay here. What kind of story is this?"

It was difficult for Conner to describe it. "It's sort of a speculation piece," he said. "I wrote a story about what our lives might be like if . . . *well*, if we'd never had a reason to move out of our old house."

His sister's eyes grew wide when she realized what he was implying.

"You mean . . ." she said, but couldn't finish her thought.

Conner sighed. "Maybe," he said. "Let's go inside and find out."

The twins went through the white door and stepped into the living room of their old house. At first glance the room was *exactly* the way they remembered it, but as they walked farther into the house, they noticed a few subtle changes. All the photos in the picture frames had been changed to current ones of their family. There were pictures of birthday parties, family vacations, holiday trips, and embarrassing school portraits. Even though the twins were present in each photo, Alex and Conner didn't remember *any* of the memories on display.

"It's like an alternate reality," Alex said. "Look, this school picture is me in the ninth grade—but I was already living in the fairy-tale world by then."

"Maybe we never discovered the Land of Stories," Conner said. "If we had stayed in this house, maybe Grandma wouldn't have had a *reason* to give us her storybook—if you know what I mean."

Alex absolutely knew what her brother meant and nodded. Suddenly, the sound of clanking pots and pans came from the next room—the twins weren't alone. They walked down the hall and peered into the kitchen, and both froze in the doorway when they laid eyes on the person making the noise.

"Daddy," Alex gasped.

It wasn't until she said the word that Alex realized how long it had been since she had last said it. The twins' father, John Bailey, was standing just a few feet away from them behind the kitchen counter. He wore an apron covered in flour and was in the middle of mixing ingredients in a large bowl. The twins noticed that their father was slightly older than their memory of him; his hair had started to gray around his temples and his crow's-feet were more pronounced than they used to be.

"Hi, guys!" their father said. "You're just in time. I know we promised your mom we'd try eating less sugar, but I left work with the *biggest* craving for chocolate chip cookies. I'm going to need help eating them before she gets home."

He looked at his children with a smile they hadn't seen in four years. Seeing their father again made Alex so happy, she cried harder than she had ever cried in her life. The tears of joy washed away all the specks of magic dust in her eyes, the warmth in her heart disintegrated all the magic dust in her lungs, and every trace of the witches' curse was erased from her body. Their father had barely said a word and had already done exactly what Conner had hoped he would. Even though it was only a story, Conner couldn't help becoming emotional himself. The person he had missed every day since he was eleven years old was standing right in front of him—how could he *not* be moved to tears?

John was very surprised to see the tears running down their faces. He wiped his hands on a washcloth and stepped out from behind the kitchen counter to take a closer look at them.

"Hey, what's wrong?" he asked. "Did something happen at school today?"

"No," Conner answered. "We just *really* missed you—that's all."

"It's so good to see you again." Alex sniffled.

The twins gave their father the biggest hug physically possible and cried some more into his shoulders. John eyed the twins suspiciously. Even in Conner's fictional world, John knew his children better than anyone.

"Are you *sure* everything's okay?" he asked. "I'd love to hear what's on your minds."

"Well, Alex had a rough day," Conner said. "Some girls at school were really cruel to her. They made her feel bad and do some stuff she regrets. And even though it wasn't her fault, she won't stop blaming herself for what happened."

"Oh, really?" John asked. "Well, if it wasn't your fault, why is it troubling you so much?"

Alex shrugged. "Even though I didn't intentionally hurt anyone, people still got hurt *because* of me. I didn't know I was capable of so much damage. It's changed how I look at myself."

John dried his daughter's tears with the edge of his apron.

"Well, the good news is it's never too late to rewrite your own story," he said. "If you feel like something is wrong, there's always a chance to make things right, no matter who's to blame. But you should never feel responsible for other people's choices. That's too big a burden for anyone to carry."

"I know," Alex said. "I just always want to be doing my best—I hate looking back and feeling like I could have done better."

"But, sweetheart, that's how we grow," John said with a laugh. "What makes you think you have to be so perfect?"

"I suppose it goes back to the stories you used to read us," Alex said. "You raised us to believe that if someone is kind, generous, and responsible, they'll have a *happily ever after.* So ever since I was a kid, I tried my hardest to be one of those people. I thought being perfect was the only way I could guarantee a happy ending.

"But now that I'm older, I realize life isn't a fairy tale. And no matter how much work you put into it, *happily ever after* doesn't exist."

Of all the things his daughter had said so far, this concerned John the most. He took Alex by the hands, sat her at the kitchen table, and had a seat beside her.

"Sweetheart, happily ever after *does* exist, it's just not what you think," he said. "*Happily ever after* isn't a solution to life's problems or a guarantee that life will be easy; it's *a promise* we make ourselves to always live our best lives, despite whatever circumstance comes our way. When we focus on joy in times of heartbreak, when we choose to laugh on the days it's hard to smile, and when we count our blessings over our losses—*that's* what a true *happily ever after* is all about. You don't get there by being perfect; on the contrary, it's our humanity that guides us. And that's what fairy tales have been trying to teach us all along."

"But what about death?" Conner asked. "How do you keep living a *happily ever after* when you lose someone you love?"

"Now *you're* troubled over something you can't control," John said. "The only power we have over death is how we choose to define it. Personally, when someone *dies*, I don't believe they cease to exist. The people we love the most will always be alive, thanks to the stories we tell and the memories we share. As long as we keep our loved ones in our hearts, their pulse will continue to beat through our own."

The twins knew their father was telling them the truth. If death was the end to a soul's existence, then how could he be sitting in front of them giving this advice? Conner barely had time to write the setting of the story—his father's words of wisdom weren't coming from *his* imagination.

"Well, I hope that was helpful," John said. "Are there any other questions I can answer for you?"

There were millions of questions Alex and Conner wanted to ask him. However, instead of taking the moment to ask him anything, the twins were both compelled to tell him something.

"I just want to say I love you, Daddy," Alex said. "With all my heart."

"Me too, Dad," Conner said. "And always will."

John was very amused by his teenagers' loving behavior, but the sentiments touched his heart nonetheless.

"I love you guys, too," he said. "And don't worry, I'll always be right here, whenever you need me."

A soft rumble came from another part of the house. The twins didn't recognize it at first but eventually remembered it was the sound of the garage door opening.

"I guess your mom got off work early," John said. "We are so busted! Quick, help me put away the cookie dough before she comes inside!"

Their father quickly got to his feet and ran back behind the kitchen counter. Strangely, the rumbling of the garage door never stopped. It became louder and louder, and soon the whole house was vibrating strongly. Object by object, the twins' former home turned back into the words in Conner's story.

"What's happening?" Alex asked.

"The story must be over," Conner said. "I've never seen it do this before, but I've never written something so short, either! We've got to get out of here!"

"I don't want to leave," Alex said.

"If we don't get out of here, we'll end with the story," Conner warned her. "It's a rule of the Portal Potion!"

Conner grabbed Alex's hand and pulled his sister out of her chair. Only after their father dematerialized into Conner's handwriting did Alex let him pull her away. The twins raced through the sitting room and out the front door and dived through the beam of light emitted by Conner's story. The twins landed back on the roof of the Freedom Tower, and the beam shining out of Conner's binder disappeared.

"Well, *that* was an emotional roller coaster," Conner said. "How do you feel?"

Alex was surprised by her answer. "Actually, I feel pretty good," she said. "I think a few moments with Dad was exactly what I needed. Thanks for coming to my rescue, Conner. You really are the best brother in the world."

"I know," Conner teased. "But you were worth the trouble."

The twins helped each other to their feet and walked to the edge of the roof. Now that the curse was broken, the magical vines had stopped destroying the city. Manhattan was covered in so many plants, the city looked like an enormous green grid.

"Wow," Alex said. "Did I really do *all this*?"

"Well, it certainly isn't my mess," Conner said.

"I barely remember any of it," she said. "I can't imagine how upset all the New Yorkers must be."

"Before you start writing apology notes, we should think of a way to clean it up," her brother said.

"Everyone in the world is going to know about the fairy-tale world after this."

Alex sighed. "Gosh, I wish there were a way to just put everyone to sleep and erase their memories," she said. "It'd sure help me deal with all the guilt."

"Well, why not?" Conner said. "It's kind of brilliant, actually."

"Do you really think it's possible?" Alex asked him.

For the first time in more than a week, Conner laughed. "Alex, you just destroyed New York City in your sleep," he said. "I think you're capable of doing *anything* you set your mind to."

CHAPTER TWENTY-THREE

A PRESIDENTIAL SURPRISE

In the residential suite at 1600 Pennsylvania Avenue, President Katherine Walker awoke in the middle of the night from a bizarre nightmare. She had dreamed that New York City was under attack by an army of fictional characters. The invasion became so extreme that she was forced to order the evacuation, and eventually the annihilation, of the greatest city in the world. The president sighed with relief when she realized it had only been a dream, but there was something incredibly unsettling about how *real* the dream felt.

President Walker decided to take a walk to calm her thoughts. She quietly climbed out of bed, careful not to wake the First Gentleman, and snuck out of the residential suite. The president wandered through the long halls of the White House in her slippers and bathrobe, but it was hard to take her mind off all the disturbing images she'd seen in the dream.

Also concerning was how *empty* 1600 Pennsylvania Avenue seemed. She was used to seeing the Secret Service and staff strolling through the halls at all hours of the night, but for reasons unknown to her, the White House was completely empty.

"Hello?" she called out. "Is someone there?"

All the president heard was the echo of her own voice. She searched the library, the State Dining Room, the Diplomatic Reception Room, and even the China Room, but she didn't find a soul. Finally, she heard people whispering and followed the sound all the way into the West Wing.

The voices appeared to be coming from inside the Oval Office, so the president gently cracked open the door and peeked inside. She saw a pretty young woman seated on the sofa and a curious young man inspecting the president's desk.

"Conner, what are you doing?" the young woman said.

"I'm looking for the red button," he said.

"What red button?"

"You know, *the president's red button*!" the young man said, like it was obvious. "The one they're always talking about in the movies that launches all the nuclear weapons."

"*Why?* Are you going to push it?" the young woman asked.

"Of course not, I just want to see—"

The young man froze when he spotted the president standing in the doorway. The young woman jumped to her feet and bowed awkwardly. The young man ran out from behind the desk and stood by her side.

"What are you doing in here?" the president demanded.

"Madam President, it is such an honor to meet you," the young woman said. "My name's Alex Bailey, and this is my brother, Conner."

"Pleased to meet you, ma'am," Conner said. "Our parents didn't vote for you, but it's still *super-cool*!"

The president eyed the twins up and down, especially Alex.

"Wait a moment, I recognize you," the president said. "You were the girl destroying New York City in my dream!"

"Actually, it wasn't a dream," Alex said. "But for the record, I was under a terrible curse and wasn't behaving like myself. But I've completely recovered, so you have nothing to fear. Normally, I'm quite a lovely, precocious, and well-mannered person. Actually, I've always thought you and I could be friends."

As friendly as the twins seemed, the president wasn't in the state of mind to *make friends*.

"Are you telling me that an army of fictional characters attacked New York City *in real life*?" she asked.

"You know, there's literally no easy way to put it, so I'm just going to say *yes*," Conner said. "But the army is gone, New York City is safe, and the whole world is asleep right now—so there's nothing to worry about."

According to the look on the president's face, she begged to differ.

"What do you mean, *the whole world is asleep*?"

she asked. "Will one of you please explain what's going on?"

"Madam President, you might want to have a seat first," Alex suggested. "There's a lot we need to fill you in on."

President Walker took Alex's advice and had a seat on the sofa across from them. Once she was seated, Alex and Conner sat down, too, and did their best to explain.

"As you probably know by now, *this* isn't the only world," Alex said. "There's another dimension very similar to this one. We refer to it as the Land of Stories because it's the home of all the fairy-tale characters we love; unfortunately, it's also home to all the characters we *don't*. Recently, a portal between the worlds opened, and the villains of the fairy-tale world emerged and tried to conquer this one."

"Once we defeated the army, Alex put the entire planet to sleep while we cleaned up all the damage they made," Conner said. "You were sleeping for a lot longer than you think."

"How long was I asleep?" the president asked.

"Two hundred years," Conner said. "Everyone you know and love is dead."

"*What?*"

Conner slapped his knee and burst into laughter. Alex shot him a dirty look.

"I'm just kidding, you've only been out for a week," he said. "Sorry, I've had a really serious month, so I'm getting my jokes out where I can. The good news is New York is completely back to normal—well, as normal as it was before."

"How did you rebuild an entire city in just a week?" President Walker asked.

"With the flames of an albino dragon," Alex said like it was obvious. "It's a magic fire that restores and heals everything it touches."

"It's also great for getting stains out of your clothes," Conner said.

"We covered Manhattan in the flames, and once the city was reassembled, we transferred all the sleeping New Yorkers back to their homes—that part took the longest," Alex said. "Then we erased the entire New York incident from everyone's memory. The whole world will wake up tomorrow morning and go back to their regular lives like none of it ever happened."

"If everything is taken care of, why bother telling me? Why not erase my memory as well?" the president asked.

"Because we need your help," Alex said. "Unfortunately, during the battle a few witches escaped. We thought the majority of them were dead, but when we rebuilt the city, their remains were gone. A secret society known as the Sisters Grimm has agreed to track down the witches. Here's a list of their names, contact information, and the government clearances they'll need in order to start."

Alex handed over a thick stack of papers, and the president gave the documents a quick scan.

"Who are the Book Huggers?" she asked.

"Oh, they're the Sisters Grimm's newest recruits," Conner said. "The Book Huggers asked us to use their alias instead of their real names. They said the government would frame them if we disclosed their identities—*you'd understand if you met them.*"

"There's one more thing," Alex said. "I did everything I could to close it, but the bridge between worlds is here to stay. However, I managed to move the bridge from the New York Public Library into the pages of *this book.*"

Alex handed the president a thick storybook with a magenta cover. The title was written in gold: *The Land of Stories: Volume Two.*

"You have to keep the book shut or the bridge will

reappear," she explained. "We figured it was probably best to leave it with the president of the United States instead of leaving it lying around our mom's house. You have to keep it somewhere safe and quiet so it doesn't end up in the wrong hands."

"Put it next to the flying saucer from Roswell," Conner said with a wink.

"Why are you trusting the United States with this?" President Walker asked. "I can keep this book as safe and quiet as I want, but if the next president has a different agenda, I won't be able to stop them."

"We can cross that bridge when we get to it," Alex said. "Due to a strange phenomenon, our worlds have collided, and I don't think something that significant happens by accident. So rather than fighting against it with more secrecy, maybe it's time we come together? Who knows, it might be what the worlds have been planning from the beginning."

"And why should I trust you?" the president said. "You say the curse is over, but how do I know the two of you aren't a danger to national security?"

Alex and Conner looked at each other, and both burst out laughing.

"Madam President, we are *absolutely* a danger to

national security," Conner said. "But luckily for you, we've got each other to check and balance."

"No matter how far we stumble from the path, we always guide each other back to it," Alex said. "So you can always count on us to do the right thing."

President Walker closed her eyes and rubbed her face. This meeting was providing a lot more information to digest than her usual appointments.

"I appreciate your coming here, but I'm going to need to discuss this with the Joint Chiefs of Staff before I can fully commit the United States to such a—"

When the president opened her eyes, the Bailey twins were gone. She looked around the Oval Office, but they had vanished into thin air. The president let out a deep sigh and glanced down at the magenta book in her hands. It was heavy in weight and in responsibility.

"And I thought *health care* would be my greatest hurdle," she said.

Chapter Twenty-Four

HAPPILY EVER AFTER, AFTER ALL

Once the Otherworld was finally put back in order, the twins and their friends returned to the Land of Stories to do the same. The flames of the albino dragon burned through the fairy-tale world until every brick the Literary Army had misplaced was restored. The kings and queens reclaimed their thrones, and their kingdoms entered a much-needed period of peace and prosperity.

Alex and the Fairy Council waited until all the other kingdoms were finished before turning their attention to the Fairy Kingdom. Once the gardens were replenished, the fairies hosted a service for Rook Robins. His grieving father watched proudly as a large statue was erected in his son's honor beside the statue of the late Fairy Godmother.

"There's nothing in the world I could do or say to ease your pain," Alex told Farmer Robins. "But I wanted to thank you. If you hadn't raised such an extraordinary son, I wouldn't be alive right now. I'll think about him and his sacrifice every day for the rest of my life."

"And I'll spend the rest of my life making peace with it," Farmer Robins said. "Rook was a stubborn boy, but he always followed his heart. And that's more than I can say about most people."

After the Fairy Palace was reassembled, Alex hosted a huge reception on the grand balcony to thank all the people who had helped her and Conner defeat the witches and the Literary Army. Characters from fairy tales, literature, and Conner's writing mingled while they enjoyed drinks and hors d'oeuvres. The pirates of Starboardia told the royal families tales from the Caribbean Sea, the Merry

Men flirted with the Fairy Council despite their blatant disinterest, and the Traveling Tradesman taught the Cyborg Queen how to arrange her galaxy so the planets would always be aligned in her favor.

Once everyone was settled in, Alex tapped the side of her glass to announce a toast. Seeing all the happy faces of her friends and family made her emotional before she had even said a word.

"Four years ago, a twelve-year-old bookworm and a sixth-grade class clown stumbled into this world by accident," Alex told the crowd. "They were both in desperate need of an escape—and boy, did they get one. Year after year, my brother and I have had one adventure of a lifetime after another. However, the more I immersed myself in this world, the more I learned a tough lesson: the *fairy-tale ending* I spent my whole life working toward didn't exist. But recently, someone very close to me redefined what a *happily ever after* actually was. As I look around the balcony, I think I finally understand what they meant.

"*Happily ever after* isn't a finish line, it isn't a paradise, and it isn't a phenomenon that makes all your dreams come true. *Happily ever after* is about finding happiness within yourself and holding on to it through any storm that comes your way. And nothing has helped me grasp that happiness more than having friends and family like you. Knowing I have so many people to love and support me is the most magical feeling in the world. Now I'm certain that *happily ever after* exists because *you* are the happy ending I've dreamed about since I was a little girl. So, to quote that bookworm when she departed this world for the first time, *'Thank you for always being there for me, you're the best friends I've ever had.'* And now, four years later, I still mean every word of it."

The conclusion of Alex's toast was met with passionate applause. She raised her glass to the people who gave her life joy and meaning, and they raised their glasses in return.

Soon the sun began its descent toward the horizon and the time had come for the Bailey twins to say good-bye to their friends from the worlds beyond the kingdoms. Conner laid out all his short stories and all the books of classic literature on the floor and the characters lined up behind the stories they belonged to.

"So long, my fellow explorers," Beau Rogers said. "Don't forget to write!"

"It's been an unforgettable voyage," Auburn Sally said. "I hope we cross paths again."

"Stay super!" Bolt said. "And don't be a stranger!"

"Good-bye, humans," said the Cyborg Queen. "Please don't bother us again."

"IT'S WITH THE HEAVIEST OF HEARTS THAT WE LEAVE ALL THESE ATTRACTIVE DAMSELS BEHIND," Robin Hood said. "FARE-WELL, FAIRIES, MAY THE MEMORY OF MY HANDSOME FACE KEEP YOU WARM AT NIGHT."

After saying good-bye, the Merry Men and all of Conner's characters stepped through the beams of light shining out from their stories and returned to their home worlds. However, the remaining characters from classic literature had a difficult time leaving.

"Hey, Tin! Are you going back to Oz?" Conner asked him.

"Actually, I've decided to stay and live with Troll-bella," the Tin Woodman said. "There's really nothing for me back in Oz now that I have a heart, and a cross-dimensional relationship sounds awfully tedious. Better to stay put where I feel the happiest."

"Do you hear that, Butterboy?" Trollbella asked him. "That's the sound of *commitment*. Take my Butter Tray's example and the Breemonster won't slip through your fingers as easily as I did."

Since Bree was standing right behind him, the Troblin Queen's comments made Conner blush so hard, he looked like a tomato. He turned around but could barely look Bree in the eye.

"*Soooo,*" Conner said with a nervous laugh. "That wasn't the segue I was hoping for, but have you ever considered—"

"Sorry, Conner, I can't be your girlfriend," Bree said.

All the color drained from Conner's face, and he did his best not to look disappointed.

"*That's-totally-fine-no-worries-I'm-super-okay-with-staying-friends,*" he said without pausing between words.

"It's not that I don't want to," Bree said. "I just know that as soon as I get home I'm going to be grounded for *months*. But once I'm free, I'd love to be your girlfriend."

All the blood quickly rushed back into Conner's face. "You *would*?" he asked. "Cool, well, I guess I'll see you back at home, then."

Bree kissed his cheek, then returned to the Otherworld through the *Land of Stories* treasury. Conner was so twitterpated, he practically floated across the balcony. He strolled right by his sister and didn't even notice that she was having a relationship conundrum of her own.

"I can't believe you're making me go back to Camelot," Arthur said. "Even after pulling the sword from the stone and founding the Knights of the Round Table?"

"You still have work to do, Arthur," Alex said. "You would never expect me to shortcut my legacy for you, so I won't allow you to shortcut yours for me. After you find the Holy Grail, your legend will be complete, and I'll have no reason to keep you there."

"Fine," the young king said. "I'll find the stinking Holy Grail—but only if it makes you happy. How long do you expect it'll take me?"

"Oh, it'll take you *years*," Alex teased. "Maybe even *decades*. You spend your whole life searching for it in the legend."

Arthur leaned close to Alex and kissed her passionately on the lips.

"I'll do it in two months," he said confidently.

Alex blushed. "I'm counting on it," she said.

Mother Goose rolled her eyes at both sets of love-struck teenagers.

"This place reeks of more adolescent pheromones than a middle school book club," she said. "Let's get back to Camelot before the Capulets and the Montagues show up—I'm late for a Pilates class with the Mists of Avalon."

The twins and their friends gave Mother Goose and Merlin good-bye hugs.

"Bye, M.G.," Conner said. "Thanks again for saving us in the—"

"Listen, C-Dawg, I need a favor," Mother Goose whispered while they were hugging. "Remember my vault in Monte Carlo? Well, I haven't paid the lease in over a year. They're going to throw my stuff out on the street if someone doesn't clean it out. In the back corner, behind Plato's scrolls, you'll find a brown paper bag. Keep whatever you want, *but flush the bag.* Can you do that for me?"

"Um . . . sure?" he said. "But what's in the—"

"You're a good man," she said, and patted him on the back.

Conner was equally intrigued and disturbed by the request—but that was how Mother Goose left most people she encountered. She, Merlin, and Arthur stepped through the beam of light and returned to the world of Camelot.

The only literary characters who hadn't returned to their story were the Lost Boys from Neverland.

They stared down at the book *Peter Pan* like it was a deep pool they didn't want to swim in.

"Tobias, what's wrong?" Red asked Tootles. "Don't you want to go home?"

"Miss Red, the Lost Boys and I have something we want to ask you," Tootles said as he nervously twiddled his thumbs. "We love living in Neverland, but now that Slightly is a baby and all, it's a lot harder taking care of ourselves. We know you were just *pretending* to be our mother when you visited, but would you ever consider being our mother *for real*?"

Red was very touched by their request and placed a hand over her heart. She turned to Froggy with large, pleading eyes.

"What do you think, Charlie?" she asked. "I'm never having children the natural way after watching Goldie give birth to Hero—*and Lord only knows what those children would look like.* So why don't we adopt the Lost Boys from Neverland? They're already housebroken, and they make a *delicious* coconut daiquiri."

The thought of being a father brought a huge smile to Froggy's face.

"Actually, I would *love* it if the boys came to live with us," he said.

"Did you hear that, boys?" Red said. "You're now officially part of the Hood-Charming family!"

The Lost Boys cheered, but Peter Pan wanted no part of it.

"Enjoy all your rules, chores, and bedtimes!" he said. "I'm going back to Neverland."

"But, Peter, how could you choose Neverland over being a Hood-Charming?" Curly asked him.

"Two words," Peter said. "*Tiger Lily*. See you later, boys!"

The Boy Who Wouldn't Grow Up flew through the beam of light and returned to his story with Tinker Bell at his side.

The impromptu adoption reminded Goldilocks of a matter she wanted to discuss with the young queen. "Red, could I have a word?" Goldilocks said. "There's something I've been meaning to ask you."

"The answer is *lather, rinse, repeat*," Red said. "Didn't we have this discussion already?"

Goldilocks sighed. "That's not what I was going to ask," she said. "Look, I know we don't always see eye-to-eye. We've had our share of disagreements, we often annoy each other to pieces, and we've each tried to kill the other at one point or another—but the truth, whether I want to admit it or not, is that you're my *best friend*, Red. Would you do me the honor of being Hero's godmother?"

Red gasped and happy tears filled her eyes. "Yes, of course I will!"

"Terrific," Goldilocks said. "Because I just asked Porridge and she turned me down."

Red was so moved by the request, it didn't even bother her that Goldilocks had asked a horse first. Froggy and Jack shared a laughed as they watched the exchange between their wives.

"So what's fatherhood like, anyway?" Froggy asked Jack. "Is it as wonderful as it seems?"

"Do you remember sailing through the clouds aboard the *Granny*?" Jack asked.

"How could I forget?" Froggy said, delighted to recall the fond memories. "The wind blowing across our faces, the birds soaring by our side, the sunrise peeking over the frosty mountains—it was a *breathtaking* experience."

"Right," Jack said. "Well, do you remember the part when we got shot out of the sky? Do you remember that feeling in the pit of your stomach as the ship plummeted toward the earth at hundreds of miles per hour toward a most certain death? *That's* what fatherhood is like."

Froggy gulped. "Lovely."

While their friends were busy adopting children and having heart-to-hearts about parenthood, Alex and Conner strolled to the far end of the grand balcony for a moment by themselves.

"That was a great toast you gave earlier," Conner said. "All that talk about *happily ever after* almost convinced me this was the end of our story."

"The *end* of our story?" Alex asked. "That's funny, because I was afraid this was only the beginning."

Conner laughed. "Yeah, you're probably right," he said. "I bet right now, as we speak, there's some big, brooding bad guy somewhere in the cosmos plotting our demise."

"One could only assume," Alex said. "I'm guessing the Evil Queen, the Enchantress, the Grande Armée, the Masked Man, the Literary Army, and the witches were just *warm-ups* compared to what's coming."

"Oh, they were *kid stuff*," Conner said. "We can't even fathom the level of difficulty we'll be up against next. In fact, we'd have nightmares for weeks if we had a glimpse of what's waiting for us in the future."

"And we'll most likely have to travel to galaxies far and wide to assemble what we need to stop them,"

Alex said. "Which will no doubt expose us to much more of Jack's and Goldilocks's fearlessness, Froggy's mindfulness, and Red's misguidedness."

"Sounds like fun," Conner said. "You know, whoever our next enemy is, I already feel awfully sorry for them."

"Me too," Alex said. "The poor thing doesn't stand a chance against us."

As Alex and Conner watched the sunset over the Fairy Kingdom, they each sighed with the greatest relief of their young lives. The twins weren't at ease because they expected the period of peace to last very long; on the contrary, they expected many new challenges in the days to come. However, for the first time, they didn't fear what they couldn't see.

No matter what obstacle came their way, Alex and Conner knew there was nothing they couldn't face together. And because of that, the Bailey twins and their friends lived *happily ever after* in the Land of Stories.

DO YOU BELIEVE IN MAGIC?

Charlotte "Charlie" Black sat at the top of the stairs eavesdropping on a conversation happening in the living room. In the months leading up to her parents' separation, Charlie had learned that the stairwell had superb acoustics. Unbeknownst to her arguing parents, Charlie had heard every detail about their approaching divorce settlement, their fight for full-time custody, and their plans for handling child support. It was a difficult subject to stomach at times, but Charlie had learned a lot about the state's legal system from her parents' arguments.

Charlie was an eleven-year-old whom people often described as *too smart for her own good*. She had short dark hair, big brown eyes, and beautiful olive skin. She always wore a big denim jacket with a short puffy skirt, bright leggings, and big boots. Charlie chewed on her favorite bottle-cap necklace as she listened to the discussion she wasn't supposed to hear.

However, tonight's entertainment had nothing to do with her parents or their pending divorce. Charlie was hanging on every word of a conversation between her mother and her uncle Matthew, and from the little she'd heard so far, they were talking about her beloved Grandpa Conner.

"I went to Dad's house around eight o'clock tonight to check on him," Matthew said. "When I arrived I found him in his study reading, just like normal, but when I took a closer look I saw he was reading one of his own books. I asked him what he was doing and he said *trying to remember*."

"But trying to remember *what*?" Charlie's mother asked. "Did he forget about something in his books?"

Matthew sighed. "It's *way* worse than that, Elizabeth," he said. "Remember the question he got asked on his birthday about Aunt Alex? Well, his answer wasn't a joke—*Dad genuinely forgot where she was.* But instead of asking one of us, he thought he could find the answer in *one of his stories.*"

"What? But that doesn't make sense."

"He convinced himself that the whereabouts of his eighty-year-old twin sister could be found in one of his children's books. He's been rereading the Fairytaletopia series, trying to find it."

"Oh my gosh," Elizabeth said. "I knew he was having trouble remembering things, but this isn't memory loss, this is classic dementia."

"Dad tried to tell me all his books were autobiographical—just like he always does with his readers," Matthew said. "All his stories about the fairy-tale world and his adventures in classic literature were fun when we were kids, but now they're really concerning. I think Dad has lost his grip on reality. Last month, he told Ayden and Grayson that magic was *real*—it took Henry and me a couple of days to convince them Grandpa was only teasing them."

"All right, I hear what you're saying," Elizabeth

said. "Dad needs help, that much is clear. But what are we going to do to help him?"

"Unfortunately, we don't have time to deal with this ourselves," Matthew said. "We've got kids, jobs, even *divorces* to worry about. So on my way here, I spoke with the manager of Sunset Crest—it's an assisted living community up the interstate. They've got people who are trained to handle this sort of thing. The manager said they can take him as early as Wednesday."

Charlie's mouth dropped open and her bottle-cap necklace fell from her mouth. She couldn't believe her uncle wanted to put her grandpa in an assisted living place. Her grandpa had always been wacky, that was why she loved him so much, but he was far from being a danger to himself.

"That's in two days, Matt," Elizabeth said. "We can't ship Dad off to some facility with such little notice. That's just cruel."

"It would be crueler if we did nothing," Matthew said. "Look, I love Dad more than anything—that's why I want to help him before it's too late. I know a judge downtown who'll give us power of attorney so we can make this as easy a transition as possible."

"I suppose if the roles were reversed, Dad would

do anything he could to protect us, and this is just returning that favor. But it's going to break poor Charlie's heart. She and Dad are so close. I hope she can handle not having him around."

Before her mother finished her sentence, Charlie already knew *exactly* how she was going to handle it. She quietly stepped out of her bedroom window, climbed down the branches of a tree, and hopped on her bike. She pedaled as fast as she could across town to Grandpa Conner's house so she could warn him about his children's terrible plans.

Her grandpa lived in a large brick house that sat on top of a hill and was surrounded by an iron gate. Charlie climbed over the gate and ran up the winding driveway to the front door. She rang the doorbell a dozen times and pounded on the door as if her life depended on it. A few moments later, Mr. Bailey answered the door in an awful fright.

"Charlie?" he asked. "What on earth are you doing out at this hour? Are you hurt?"

"I'm sorry for coming so late, but it's an emergency!" Charlie announced. "We need to talk right away."

Charlie stormed into the house and headed for her grandpa's study. She took a seat in the red armchair by the window, and he took the blue chair by the fireplace—their usual spots.

"Now tell me, what's so urgent?" Mr. Bailey asked.

"Mom and Uncle Matt are going to put you in a home," Charlie said. "They think you've gone crazy because you believe in magic and think your stories are real. They made plans to take you away on Wednesday and they know a judge who's going to give them power of attorney."

"Is that so?" Mr. Bailey asked with a blank expression.

"I heard the whole thing from the stairwell," Charlie said. "I'm not sure what *power of attorney* is, but if it's anything like the attorneys handling my parents' divorce, it can't be good."

Charlie was very surprised to see how calm Mr. Bailey was. Her grandpa just sat quietly in his chair and thought.

"Well?" Charlie asked. "What are you going to do? Are you going to run away to the circus? Are you going to flee to Mexico? You've got to do something before they take you, Grandpa—you're the only friend I have."

His granddaughter's concern warmed his heart.

"Don't worry, sweetheart, I'm not going to an assisted living facility on Wednesday," he reassured her. "As a matter of fact, I have plans to visit my sister this week, and they can't take a man they can't find."

"But Uncle Matt said you didn't know where your sister was," Charlie said.

Her grandpa nervously glanced from side to side like he was hiding something.

"Oh, well, I remember *now*," he explained. "You see, when you get older, things come and go like birds in a tree. When I finally remembered where my sister was, it also dawned on me that I had made plans to see her. So there you have it—a perfectly reasonable explanation."

Charlie wasn't buying it. She started to wonder if her uncle and mom were right to be concerned.

"Grandpa, do you *really* believe in magic?" she asked.

"Of course I do," he said. "Don't you?"

"Uncle Matt says I'm not supposed to," Charlie said. "He thinks it means someone's lost touch with reality."

Mr. Bailey let out a long, anguished sigh.

"Sweetheart, I love your uncle and your mother with all my heart, but they inherited their personalities from your grandmother's side of the family. Even when they were children, they were too practical for their own good. But don't *ever* let anyone tell you magic isn't real. A kid who doesn't believe in magic is like a painting without color."

"I want to believe," Charlie said. "But it's hard to take your word for it. I guess I'm waiting for some kind of proof."

"Ah, but that's the most mysterious part about magic," her grandpa said with a twinkle in his eye. "You never know when it's going to reveal itself to you. That's why it's so important to keep an open mind—you don't want to miss it when the time comes."

Even if her grandpa was crazy, Charlie still loved playing along.

Mr. Bailey glanced at his watch and jumped up from his chair. "Would you look at the time?" he said. "My sister will be here any minute to collect me and I haven't even had a chance to pack. You should head home before it gets too late."

"How long will you be gone, Grandpa?" Charlie asked.

"Long enough to teach your mom and uncle a lesson," he said. "But don't worry, I'll be back in time for your birthday. I have something very special I've been saving for the occasion. Now, off you go."

Mr. Bailey walked his granddaughter to the front door and hugged her good-bye. But Charlie wasn't ready to leave just yet. Instead of walking down the hill and getting back on her bike, she snuck into her grandpa's flowerbed and hid behind the bushes. She wanted to see if her great-aunt Alex was actually coming, or if her grandpa was as delusional as her mom and uncle thought.

Charlie had only seen her great-aunt once or twice in her entire life, so she wasn't sure she'd even recognize the woman. However, as the minutes dragged on, that proved to be less and less of a problem. No one drove up the driveway to collect her grandpa.

Suddenly, a bright flash shined out from her grandpa's house. Charlie peeked through the window to see what had caused it. It was hard to see past all her grandpa's furniture, but Charlie saw that a beautiful older woman had appeared in the living room. She had bright blue eyes and long white hair, and she wore a sparkling robe and headband made of silver flowers.

"Conner? Are you ready yet?" the woman called to him.

Charlie heard thumps as Mr. Bailey came down the stairs from the second floor.

"Sorry, I just remembered to pack!" he said.

"What do you mean, you *just remembered*?" the old woman asked. "We've had this trip planned for months. Are you taking the memory potion I left you?"

"I was until I forgot about it," Mr. Bailey said. "I found it in the fridge this evening and everything came back to me. You wouldn't believe how worried I was without it—I couldn't remember where you were and thought something terrible had happened to you when we were kids."

"You crazy old man," she said. "When I bring you back home, I'm going to leave a note in every room of your house to remind you to take it. Now come along, everyone is so excited to see you. Red's throwing an elaborate banquet for you, but fair warning, it's just an excuse to perform her one-woman rendition of *A Midsummer Night's Dream*. Oh, and word to the wise, Goldilocks broke another hip teaching her grandkids how to do back handsprings. You know how sensitive she gets about injuries, so don't call attention to it—*especially* if Jack and Froggy start joking about it."

"My lips are sealed," Mr. Bailey said. "I'm looking forward to seeing everyone, too. I'm not even there yet, but it already feels good to be back. Lead the way, Alex."

Another bright flash of light beamed out of the house. It was a few moments before Charlie could see again. By the time her eyes adjusted, her grandpa and great-aunt had *vanished*. Charlie knew they couldn't have just disappeared into thin air, so she climbed through an open window and searched the house.

"Grandpa? Aunt Alex?" she called. "Where'd you guys go?"

Suddenly, Charlie heard a mysterious vibration coming from above her. She followed the strange noise all the way up the stairs and into the attic. The attic was covered in dust and filled with boxes of her grandpa's old junk. Charlie searched the room for whatever was making the odd sound but didn't find anything out of the ordinary.

Just as she was about to give up and head home, Charlie spotted something out of the corner of her eye. In the middle of the dusty floor was a large emerald-green storybook she had never seen before. Charlie picked up the book, blew the dust off the cover, and read the golden title across the top.

"*The Land of Stories*?" she said. "Hmmm, that sounds familiar."

Although she was convinced her eyes were playing tricks on her, Charlie watched in amazement as the storybook's pages started to glow. . . .

The End

ACKNOWLEDGMENTS

I'd like to thank Rob Weisbach, Alla Plotkin, Alvina Ling, Heather Manzutto, Derek Kroeger, Rachel Karten, Lindsey Tillotson, Eugene Shevertalov, Marcus Colen, and my wonderful team at ICM.

The Land of Stories series would not have been possible without Megan Tingley, Melanie Chang, Andrew Smith, Nikki Garcia, Jessica Shoffel, Carol Scatorchio, Jackie Engel, Kristin Dulaney, Svetlana Keselman, Emilie Polster, Janelle DeLuise, Bethany Strout, Jen Graham, Sasha Illingworth, Virginia Lawther, and everyone at Little, Brown.

Thanks to Jerry Maybrook for surviving over a dozen audiobooks with me, and to the incredible Brandon Dorman for bringing my words to life.

Last but not least, thank you to Will Sherrod, Ashley Fink, and Pam Jackson, and of course my family. Your love and patience has made this adventure possible.